A DEATH WELL LIVED

A DEATH WELL LIVED

A NOVEL

Daniel Overdorf

CrossLink Publishing

CrossLink Publishing1601 Mt. Rushmore Rd, STE 3288, Rapid City, SD 57702

Ordering Information:Quantity sales. Special discounts are available on quantity purchases by corporations, associations, and others. For details, contact the "Special Sales Department" at the address above.

A Death Well Lived/Overdorf —1st ed.

ISBN 978-1-63357-188-4

Library of Congress Control Number: 2019944234

First edition: 10 9 8 7 6 5 4 3 2 1

This is a work of fiction. Names, characters, places, and incidents either are the products of the author's imagination or are used fictitiously. Any resemblance to actual persons, living or dead, businesses, companies, events, or locales is entirely coincidental.

To Peyton, Tyler, Claire, and Felicia.

May the story remain alive in you.

ACKNOWLEDGMENTS

My deepest gratitude to Cindy K. Sproles for the hours she invested helping me refine the manuscript and offering suggestions, encouragement, and instruction on the finer points of writing fiction.

To Jenny Holly, Cliff McCartney, Debbie Miller, Chad Moore, Ken Overdorf, Randy Overdorf, Rachel Ronk, John Veech, and Jason Warden for reading early versions of the story and providing such helpful feedback.

To Johnson University for sabbatical time away from my normal duties to research and write.

August, AD 29

"If you're going to hit him, *hit him!* Show yourself a man. A Roman."

Lucius stood back. Usually, he leaped into the fray, curses and fists flying. Anything to establish dominance. Exert power. But this time he watched, a wry smile spilling across his chin. "This spectator is out of control. He mocked you. Subdue him."

Punches sailed, most missing.

"He's inferior. And weak. You should have finished him by now."

The legionary glanced toward Lucius, his centurion, leaving his jaw open to an uppercut. He shook off the punch and countered with a blow to the gut. His opponent gasped and doubled over.

"End this!" Ordering a kill intoxicated Lucius.

The legionary pulled a dagger from his belt and raised it. Before he delivered the fatal stab, a pudgy, hairy hand grasped his wrist.

"That's enough," grumbled another centurion.

"Septimus. Greetings. I appreciate your compassion, but this soldier is beneath my command." Lucius turned to the soldier. "You will obey my order. Sink that dagger into your enemy."

The legionary attempted to raise his weapon again, but Septimus kept a firm grasp on his wrist. The soldier's opponent seized the opportunity to retreat, scrambling down the bleachers and continuing until he exited the stadium.

"They're all beneath my command." Septimus glared. "And so are you."

Lucius stepped toward Septimus, drawing near enough to smell his breath. He picked a piece of rotted food from Septimus's beard and flicked it to the side. His nose flared. "We're both centurions."

Septimus shook his head. "You know how this works. I command the first century of the cohort. You command the sixth. Five levels separate us." He crossed his arms. "You bow to me."

"I. Bow. To. No. One." Lucius's jaw clenched. He ground his teeth. He thought what he couldn't speak, lest he risk charges of insubordination. *You took what was mine. You don't deserve to command the first century. I do. And I will.*

"Lucius, you dare to undermine my command? You might find yourself impaled." The superior officer cocked his head. "Or, worse, you might find yourself unable to advance." He smiled. "You do want to advance through the ranks, don't you?"

Lucius kept his gaze locked on his superior. His fists clenched. He didn't blink.

Septimus held the stare for a moment, and then the corners of his mouth turned upward. His shoulders and ample belly shook. He laughed, threw a hand in the air, and descended the bleachers, chortling the whole way. "Someday you'll bow, my friend. Someday!"

Lucius seethed. He tromped down the bleachers and turned the opposite direction as Septimus. His boots scuffed the dirt. Septimus outranked him only because of his family's status in Rome—that, and Lucius's occasional inability to control his anger.

Wiry and athletic in frame, Lucius strode the length of Caesarea's hippodrome. The crimson plume that adorned his bronze helmet announced he was a centurion, which caused everyone within arm's reach to recoil. He relished the fear in their eyes.

To his left, an oblong, sandy track awaited chariot races. His gait matched those of the horses in the arena—purposeful but controlled, power waiting to be unleashed. The odor from the horses blended with that of the sweaty spectators packed into the stone bleachers. Lucius snarled. *Animals.* The rabble rushed through the gates before daybreak and fought for seats. Many were drunk.

The Great Sea thumped the shore to his right. Spray erupted from the rocks and mingled with dust that rose from the arena floor, forming thin layers of mud on Lucius's brawny forearms. He noticed but didn't care.

He reached the opposite side of the hippodrome and planted his feet next to another centurion. "Everything under control?"

The centurion glanced at Lucius and raised his brows. "Mostly, except that I have to watch your soldiers more closely than my own."

Lucius chuckled. "Ah, Decimus, my legionaries are doing fine. Just as I've trained them."

"That's the problem." Decimus grinned. "It seems they follow your philosophy. How do you say it? 'A few broken noses and bloodied ears are a small price to keep the peace.'"

"Sounds like wise leadership to me."

Their conversation was interrupted by the thud of a stone striking Decimus's helmet. He dropped to one knee and grasped his head.

Laughter and mockery erupted from the bleachers. "Take that, sir! The great centurion brought to his knees by a child. A girl tossing a pebble."

A stone the size of a fist lay beside Decimus. It left a dent on his helmet. Lucius extended his hand to help Decimus to his feet.

"I don't need your help," Decimus growled.

Lucius turned toward the crowd. "Who threw it?"

His demand was met with more taunts. "What are you going to do, flog us all?"

"That can be arranged." Lucius grabbed a man sitting on the closest bench and dragged him before the throng. "Tell me who threw the rock or accept the consequences yourself." The man's face turned pale. Lucius raised his fist and clenched the spectator's collar.

Decimus, having regained his bearings, rose to his feet and stepped in. "Not yet, Lucius. We have a long day ahead. Stay in control."

Lucius grunted, then flung the man against the bench. He hated to entertain the thought, but his encounter with Septimus may have pushed his temper too far.

Trumpets signaled the onset of the games. A roar flooded the arena. Everyone in the hippodrome turned toward the northeast corner.

Caesarean city officials, adorned in white robes, with garlands woven from olive branches hanging around their necks and resting on their brows, led the parade. The group of men could not have looked more different in features and stature, yet each had the same grin plastered on his face—like men who seldom received applause and relished this rare opportunity for attention.

A few paces behind the officials, priests from local temples pushed wooden carts that precariously held the gods who would bless the games and decide the victors. The priests paid little attention to the crowd, concerned instead with keeping the gods from tumbling to the dirt. Lucius chuckled at their clumsiness.

Athletes, freshly oiled and massaged, followed. Each wore a sleeveless white, blue, green, or red tunic that displayed his godlike physique. The spectators rose to their feet, whistled, and applauded.

Bookmakers in the bleachers took last minute wagers.

One man shoved his way through the crowd. "A denarius on blue in the second race!"

"Are you crazy? Blue is too scrawny." He lifted his hand and waved. "Over here. Two denarii on green. That's the winner."

Another pressed his way past. "Green has no chance. Out of my way, fool." He snarled. "Here, take my money. I'm betting on the strongest athlete in the arena, blue."

Trumpets blasted again, and Lucius turned toward the entrance. A troupe of soldiers and servants cleared people and debris from the path. The centurion crept closer in case they'd need his help.

Pontius Pilate sauntered through the middle of the troupe. "Out of my way. Move." The balding governor fell short in height compared to the soldiers and servants around him. He waved his hand, shooing the crowd. "I said, out of my way."

Jeers echoed from the rear of the crowd. "Where's that beautiful wife of yours? We'd rather see her prancing around the track."

Pilate stopped. He straightened the olive twigs resting on his brow and snickered under his breath.

Someone shouted, "I hear Tiberius is ready to toss you into the arena with the beasts. Think you can you handle a wild boar?"

Lucius tensed.

Another spectator raised his voice, "Take my horse, Governor. Show us what you can do. I'll gladly pay to see His Lord in the arena, or can you climb high enough to mount up?"

Pilate grabbed the arm of a soldier, his patience spent. His fingers tightened. "Find him." The solider took a step, but Pilate yanked him back. He shoved his finger into the soldier's face. "Make him take you to his horse."

"Yes sir."

Pilate's lip folded into a smirk. "Steal his horse. Then kill the man." He straightened the crimson mantle draping his left shoulder. The sun reflected off his bronze breastplate.

Lucius sighed. It would be a long day protecting such arrogance.

The procession snaked around the hippodrome, floating against the backdrop of the sea. For the remainder of his march, Pilate made only occasional waves to the crowd, exhibiting in posture and expression his disinterest in the whole affair. Lucius continued a few steps behind.

When the governor arrived at his box in the eastern bleachers, he took his place in the arena's only padded seat. He raised his hand. "Let the games begin." The crowd rose to their feet as the first of many competitors took their places.

Hours later, the sun descended toward the horizon and cast shadows across the stadium. The wine sold cheaper and flowed freer. Spectators, most having gambled away a month's wages, grew bored of watching chariots race in circles.

Decimus nodded toward the bleachers. "Weary crowds are dangerous crowds."

"Especially when they're both weary and drunk." Lucius scanned the hippodrome for his soldiers. A few remained attentive, but others leaned against walls, their eyelids heavy. "I'll wake our legionaries."

"No." Decimus grasped his friend's shoulder. "I'll go. I could use the walk."

Lucius grunted his appreciation to his comrade. He attempted to stay alert, but the breeze from the sea and the constant drone of cheering lulled him into drowsiness.

A shriek brought him back to attention. He searched the spectators until his gaze rested on a man six rows back with his hand in the air. He held a stone.

"Drop that rock!" Lucius leaped across the first few rows, snagged the man by the collar, and tossed him in a heap in front of the bleachers.

"State your name."

Silence.

"State your name!"

"To—"

"Louder!"

"Tobiah."

A dirty Jew. Most who attended the games were Roman, but the occasional Jew mixed into the crowd. They were a nuisance to Rome and an annoyance to Lucius.

Tobiah dropped the small, round object he'd been holding. A loaf of bread.

Lucius pretended not to notice it was bread. He was committed and wouldn't back down. The spectators nearby forgot the chariot race and focused on the centurion and the Jew, hoping for bloody entertainment. Lucius wouldn't disappoint.

Tobiah, one of the few spectators still sober, staggered to his knees. Before he could reach his feet, the heel of Lucius's boot landed on his chin, driving his jawbone out of socket. The centurion pressed his face into the dirt. Everyone within the first three rows heard the crack of the Jew's cheekbone. Lucius launched a kick to his ribs, another to his kidneys, and several to his legs.

He lifted Tobiah by the shoulders, threw him flat onto his back, and straddled him—the Jew pinned down under the centurion's knees.

Lucius's mind filled with images of Septimus's snarling face: "They're all beneath my command, and so are you. . . . You bow to me. . . . You do want to advance, don't you?"

Power. Dominance. I bow to no one.

A flurry of fists sent blood oozing from Tobiah's nose and mouth. He moaned, and his eyes rolled into his head. Lucius would've pummeled the Jew's body until dawn had Decimus not returned.

2

"I may've let this one go on too long." Decimus grabbed his comrade's shoulders. Lucius threw one last punch, but just missed. Decimus pulled him from atop the Jew. "Get off. He's had enough." Tobiah, mangled and motionless, looked like he might not wake up.

Decimus pointed to a nearby bench and gave his fellow centurion a push. "Sit down and get control of yourself." He spoke to Lucius as only a longtime friend could. Anyone else who attempted to step in would've invited a fresh flurry of fists, but Decimus had a way of calming him. Always had. Lucius mopped blood, Tobiah's blood, from his face and hands.

Spectators in nearby bleachers cheered. Soldiers circled, hungry for more bloodshed and hoping to take part. Decimus stared at the Jew and shook his head. Tobiah lay limp.

Decimus waved over a nearby legionary. "Take him away." He turned to the other soldiers standing around. "Empty the arena. Send all these people home."

Legionaries herded the crowd toward the exits. The people, exhausted and intoxicated, shuffled home as the sun disappeared behind the sea.

Decimus kicked dirt onto Lucius's leather boots. "Come on, soldier. Let's head back to camp."

Lucius rose from the bench and massaged his hand. His small finger protruded to the side. Decimus grabbed it. "Square your punch when you strike. Prevents this." He yanked the finger back into its socket. Lucius flinched but didn't speak.

"That was quite a beating." Decimus chuckled.

"He had it coming."

"Maybe." Decimus squeezed his friend's shoulder and looked him in the eye. "That loaf of bread would've inflicted some real damage."

Lucius conceded a wry smile. "So, you noticed?"

"Yes, but don't worry. I won't say anything." The two had kept quiet about various violent incidents over the years. They protected each other, and always would.

The comrades plodded side by side from the stadium, just as they had from the training field twenty years before and from battlefields numerous times since.

Decimus shook his head. Today's battle wouldn't earn Lucius additional adornment for his uniform. In fact, he could lose a medal or two.

He glanced at his friend. Lucius's shoulders relaxed. He no longer clenched his jaw. "Feeling better?"

Lucius shrugged.

He turned his attention to the landscape ahead. "Herod's handiwork always impresses, doesn't it?" A harbor sat just north of the hippodrome, its arms jutting into the sea as if reaching toward Rome. It boasted colossal statues of Augustus and Roma that reminded all who sailed beneath their shadows of Rome's dominance. "One afternoon last week, I counted three dozen ships docked. It could accommodate twice that many." Decimus stopped and pointed. "I hear Herod shipped in volcanic ash from Italy to make all those blocks. Some special kind of ash that hardens under water."

He talked, and Lucius listened. His comrade already knew about the harbor, but he hoped a conversation about familiar things might pull him from his mood. "Herod the Great, they called him. Wanted to bring the glories of Rome all the way to Caesarea. Not only the harbor, but the hippodrome, palace, and theater. It's amazing what a little imagination and a lot of engineering and sandstone can do for swampy coastland."

"And here we are, four decades later," Lucius mumbled, as though he'd heard the speech before. "Two centurions personifying what Herod envisioned. Roman dominance."

"With swagger." Decimus grinned.

They ambled northward. Stars dotted the sky. A half-moon shone brightly enough to keep them from stumbling on a stone or a vagrant. A breeze from the east carried the aromas of fires and grilled fish. The waves of the Great Sea provided rhythmic accompaniment.

Decimus cocked his head. "Quite a display from the governor back there, huh?"

"I guess. He didn't seem all that interested in the games."

"Oh, he was interested. It's just beneath him to look like he's interested. He had more money riding on those chariot races than anyone. Servants around the stables say he has ways of making sure the right chariots win."

"I don't know. Don't care, really." Lucius kicked a stone.

"Do you think he'll govern well?"

Lucius gave up his attempt at silence. "Who knows? These governors don't last long. He'll probably do something to make Tiberius angry, or his superiors in Syria. I hear he's brutal. Crucifies quicker than most. Sometimes nails bodies in different positions just for fun. Tiberius likes leaders like that." He flicked an insect from his arm. "Pilate must've done something right to become a governor. But not too right, since he's governor of Judea."

"What about the Jews?"

"You have no intention of shutting up, do you?"

Decimus ignored the remark. "How do you think Pilate will handle them?"

"Better than Valerius Gratus did, I hope." Lucius inspected the blood that had begun to dry on his knuckles, then picked at it with his fingernails. "Really, there's only one way to handle them."

They exchanged mischievous smiles.

Decimus decided to lighten the mood. He'd tortured Lucius long enough with serious conversation. "How's the family?"

"You know soldiers can't have families. Tiberius won't allow it."

Decimus chuckled.

"Nona keeps things together. I don't know how she does it."

"You don't deserve her. She's awfully patient." Decimus nudged his friend. "And those children. I don't know how a beast like you could produce such handsome offspring. They must get their charm from Nona." He paused. "You should see them more."

Lucius furrowed his brow. "I keep them fed. And clothed. I even hired somebody to teach Tullus to read."

"Maybe they need more from you."

Lucius didn't answer.

They reached the settlement that had arisen around the military camp. The community bustled with hucksters and tradesmen who made their living by supplying the thousands of soldiers who lived in the camp. During daylight, they provided grain, charcoal, and other staples. In the evening, wine and women.

The comrades ignored the vendors as they marched through the settlement. They brushed past the retired soldiers congregated around fires, grumbling and drinking into the night. Decimus nodded to one such vagrant.

Lucius stopped. "You go on ahead. I need to check on Nona."

"Give her my greetings."

The centurions parted ways.

———

Lucius veered from the main road that cut the settlement in half onto a narrower dirt path. He trudged past shops and brothels that crowded the pathway on each side, then reached the outer edge of the settlement where the hucksters bedded down at night. Mingled among the lean-tos stood the homes of children and their mothers kept by soldiers.

Lucius knocked three times on the timber doorframe of Nona's hut.

"Keep quiet." A hand appeared and pulled aside the canvas that covered the doorway. From inside the hut stepped a woman a full head shorter than Lucius. Her dark hair was pulled back, and her eyes stoked with fire. A jasper ring decorated her left hand, a gift from Lucius years before when he felt unusually loving and generous.

"Don't wake the children," Nona whispered. "They've had a long day. And tomorrow will be no different. What do you want?"

Lucius enjoyed visiting Nona. Her abrupt manner and common wisdom gave him a sense of security. She knew Lucius better than anyone, even Decimus. His uniform didn't intimidate her like it did others. And she liked him—loved him, really, though she'd never say it aloud. But he knew.

"Got anything to eat?"

Nona huffed and disappeared into the hut. She emerged moments later carrying a wooden bowl filled to the brim with barley porridge she'd boiled over the fire hours before.

Lucius took a bite. "It's cold."

"It's late." She stood with her arms crossed and watched as he ate in silence.

He handed her the empty bowl. "What'd the children do today?"

"Paulla helped me. This morning we walked to the harbor and bought a few fish from the early boats. Brought them back and cooked them and sold them. In the afternoon, we worked in the garden and brought in some vegetables. The squash, leeks, and radishes are doing well, but I'm disappointed in the lettuce." Nona put her hands on her hips. "Tullus built the fire when he got up this morning and then disappeared until nightfall. I worry about him. You need to talk to our son."

Lucius grunted. *Not this again.*

"He just wants to sit around with those old soldiers all day. They're half drunk, begging for bread. And everybody knows their war stories are made up—everybody except Tullus. I think he believes them. If they'd done the heroic things that they say, they wouldn't have ended up here."

Lucius knew if he continued the conversation, he'd end up committing to something he didn't want to do, like having a talk with his son. He reached into the leather pouch that hung from his belt. His fingers navigated bits of food and medical supplies until they found two silver coins. Her weekly stipend helped her survive and minimized the nagging.

She snagged the coins from his hand before he had a chance to offer them. "Be gone. I need to rest."

He chuckled and offered Nona a nod. He could sense her eyes on him as he disappeared into the sea of huts, tents, and vendors attempting to peddle their evening wares.

Lucius approached the gate to the military camp. A six-foot stone wall surrounded it, enclosing greater population and acreage than most cities. Towers protruded from each of the rounded corners.

A guard stood at attention. He saluted as the centurion neared. "Good evening, sir."

Lucius ignored him and hiked past offices and a dining hall.

The breeze had died down, leaving the air stale with the stench of five thousand soldiers who seldom bathed. Smoke drifted from the embers that remained from evening campfires.

Lucius would've rather spent the night with Nona. Some evenings, he did. It wasn't just the physical pleasure, though he certainly enjoyed that. He cared for her. Felt at ease with her, comfortable. Less angry, anxious, or on edge. And those children . . . nothing else in his life brought such joy. He wanted to make them proud, to provide more for them.

Because of what happened with the Jew in the hippodrome, however, he knew it was best not to stay with Nona tonight. He'd follow regulations and return to his quarters. No need to give Septimus an additional excuse to punish him.

If only he could find a way to punish Septimus. As a lower ranked officer, he couldn't reprimand his superior. So, no, not punishment, but plot. Scheme. Some ploy to undermine his authority, or an arranged circumstance to provoke Septimus to misbehave and draw the attention of those who outrank him. If Lucius planned carefully, he could boost his own standing in the process. Get what he was robbed of, a higher rank—Septimus's rank. Then his family would be proud, and he could give them whatever they wanted. Lucius's mind whirled with vague possibilities.

He arrived at his barracks and marched through a corridor that divided rows of small rooms, each holding several cots covered with woven mats. Lucius ducked his head into each room. Most of the men had retired for the evening. He yawned and looked forward to the same.

In the last room, a few soldiers gathered in the corner. A legionary threw dice against a wall. Another soldier scrambled to read the dice, squinting by the light of the moon that streamed through a window.

"What do they say?"

"A two and a five."

"So close! There's something wrong with those dice." He conceded a coin to another legionary.

"The dice seem perfectly fine to me." The winner snickered.

"This time, a four."

Lucius squeezed the leather pouch of coins on his hip and considered joining the fun, but decided otherwise. "You men need to get some rest. I do too. Be done."

His soldiers scrambled to put their dice and coins away. They respected him. Feared him. The same thing, in Lucius's mind.

He wandered into his room and fell on his cot. As a centurion, Lucius enjoyed a room to himself. It sat in the middle of the barracks so that he could keep an eye and an ear on his legionaries.

As soon as he closed his eyes, he drifted into sleep, without a thought toward Tobiah or the mess he'd left behind.

3

Deborah stepped out of her hut and scraped the last crumbs of bread from her plate. She tucked her chestnut hair behind her ears. Her elegant frame silhouetted against the dimming orange sky.

She waved to her friend. "Good evening, Esther."

"It's so pleasant out, isn't it?" Esther stood outside, also scraping dinner plates. "Have you heard from Tobiah?"

"Not yet. I expect him back any minute. He'll be exhausted, I'm sure, but full of stories from the games."

Esther smiled and disappeared into her hut.

The relish that Deborah prepared made the bread more palatable, but only slightly. Granted, her trouble eating had little to do with the bread or the relish. She didn't enjoy eating alone. She sighed. Fortunately, she didn't eat alone often. Usually, she and Tobiah spent the evenings enjoying dinner together, then mingling with friends in their village. They lived on the eastern side of Caesarea, close enough to the sea to watch the sun falling behind its waves.

That morning, after they ate, Tobiah massaged Deborah's feet and shoulders. She knew he wanted something, but played along, mostly because the massage eased her sore muscles. He was adorable. Like a little boy asking his mother for honey.

He finally spoke. "The games are in town today."

"Oh really?"

"That's what I hear."

She changed the subject to toy with him. "Did you see the boats that came into the harbor yesterday? They seem to get bigger and bigger. They can't be safe. All that timber on water. They look too heavy to stay afloat."

"Yeah, I guess." He continued kneading her shoulders. "The races are supposed to be especially exciting this year."

"What races?"

"The chariot races. At the games. At the hippodrome."

She turned and gave him a smile. "Then you should go." She worried, but she knew how he enjoyed the energy and the competition.

Hours after she bid him goodbye, Deborah stood watching the village children play. Their mothers would soon corral them and put them to bed. Until then, boys shoved and ran from each other, and girls held hands in a circle and danced. Deborah rested a hand on her swollen stomach and enjoyed the children's laughter. A ball rolled to her feet. She stooped, trying her best to keep her balance, picked up the ball and threw it back.

As the ball left her fingertips, the sound of her name met her ears. "Deborah!" The faint voice floated from the edge of the village. She couldn't see who called her name. She could, however, hear the urgency. Her heartbeat quickened.

One of the village men who attended the games with Tobiah stopped about fifty paces away. He cupped his hands around his mouth. "It's Tobiah. Come now!"

The wooden plate slipped from Deborah's fingertips, landed on a rock, and cracked.

———

A rooster crowed, and a trumpet blasted. Lucius rolled over, groaned, and rubbed his eyes. He rose to a sitting position, wincing from the pain. He glanced at his hands, bruised from fingertips to wrists, and still crusty with blood.

"Time to get up, you brute." Decimus stood in the doorway. "Septimus wants to see you."

"Already? He must get up an hour before the sun just thinking of ways to make my day miserable."

"Not an hour. Two. And it's all about you, my friend." Decimus threw a towel at Lucius. It landed on his shoulder. "Better clean up before you see him."

Lucius stumbled out of the barracks. What could Septimus want with him now? Barely a day went by when the bully didn't punish him for something. He stared at his bruised hands. *Must have something to do with the Jew.*

The centurion pulled the towel from his shoulder and draped it across the rim of a water barrel. The sun peaked above the horizon, and birds announced the new day. He could hear the settlement outside of the camp coming to life, its inhabitants rising to tend their gardens and prepare goods for the market. Nona surely scurried among them.

Lucius dipped the towel in water and began washing—first his face, his torso, and then his legs. Finally, he scrubbed Tobiah's blood from his hands and picked it from beneath his fingernails. Pain webbed through his fingers and forearms. Something was likely broken. Maybe a finger, possibly a wrist. *That's alright. It was worth it.* A smile crossed his lips as he remembered the Jew's wide eyes and trembling upper lip. The feeling never got old.

Lucius returned to his room, donned a fresh tunic, and adorned himself with a centurion's garb. His stomach growled its hunger, but food could wait. The tyrant wouldn't.

He hurried out of his barracks to the entrance of Septimus's chambers. A legionary stood guard at the doorway, his shoulders drooping, eyes glassy.

"Long night, soldier?"

The legionary snapped to attention. "No sir." He nodded toward the entrance to Septimus's office. "He's expecting you."

Lucius stepped through the doorway. Chipped tiles covered the floor, and worn rugs covered the tiles. Secondhand chairs provided seating for guests. Lucius rested his hand on the back of a chair; it creaked. He chose not to sit.

"The gods be with you, sir," he said.

"And with you." Septimus didn't look up. He sat behind an oak desk on a spindly chair that groaned beneath his weight. A stack of parchments lay in front of him, displaying diagrams, maps, and a few words. Septimus held one document in his hand and studied it. Lucius knew that Septimus couldn't read the words, and he probably didn't care about the maps and diagrams, but the superior officer kept his eyes fixed on the parchments anyway.

He cleared his throat. "You wanted to see me?"

"Yes, yes. Sit down."

Lucius remained standing.

"That was quite a display at the hippodrome yesterday." The ranking officer laid a parchment atop the stack on the table and looked up.

"The races? Yes, some impressive performances by the athletes and horses."

Septimus scoffed. "Not the races. You."

"Just doing my job, sir."

The officer drew a small knife from his belt and chiseled slivers from his leathery fingernails. "You really gave it to that one man." His gruff voice hesitated over each syllable. "I'd be surprised if he was still breathing by nightfall."

"Which man?"

"You know the one." Septimus tossed the knife onto the table and looked him in the eye. "The Jew. What did he do to deserve such a beating?"

"The spectators had grown increasingly violent." Lucius launched into the speech he'd prepared while washing. "By the end of the games, my men had broken up twenty or thirty fights." That was a lie, of course. The truth was that Lucius's men had started twenty or thirty fights. "Spectators were throwing things at the soldiers. Decimus had already been hit once. I saw the Jew

with a rock in his hand, ready to sling it. I had to stop him to protect my soldiers."

Septimus looked back at his fingernails. "I heard it was a stone
of a softer, more nutritious nature."

"It was a rock."

"Sure, sure. Whatever you say." The officer picked up the
same parchment he had laid on the desk and began studying it
again. "Be gone."

Lucius marched to the dining hall. He joined the soldiers beneath his command for a generous helping of bread dipped in
watered-down beer. Fuming from his meeting with Septimus, he
took his beer a little less diluted than normal.

He stood. "Finish your breakfast and your morning duties,
then suit up in full gear. Meet me in front of the barracks. Today
we march."

The legionaries groaned. Lucius glared. His soldiers would
bear the brunt of his frustration. They finished their bread,
gulped their remaining beer, and left in twos and threes.

An hour later, the century convened in front of their barracks.
Each soldier wore a bronze helmet, carried a curved shield and a
spear, and had a sword and dagger hanging from either hip.

Lucius looked them over. "Formation!"

The men hurried into columns.

"Military pace. March!"

In a perfect short-clipped step, the soldiers marched out of
the camp, through the settlement where Nona lived, and eastward, away from the sea and into the countryside. The sand on
which Caesarea was built gradually gave way to more fertile, red-
dish soil, which sprouted with groves of oranges, lemons, and
limes. Their citrus scent filled the air.

Lucius marched in front of his men to set the pace, occasionally weaving in and out of the columns to keep the soldiers in
step. Sweat beaded on his upper lip and ran down the back of his

neck. He inhaled deeply. The fresh air of the countryside rejuvenated him.

Once the camp and Caesarea disappeared behind them, the centurion adjusted the tempo. "Full pace!" His legionaries lengthened their strides, remaining in perfect rhythm. The century crossed the Plain of Sharon, then slithered northeast through the rolling hills of Samaria, like a school of sunfish gliding through the waves of the sea, every movement of every soldier in harmony with the others.

Lucius was in command. No superiors. No Septimus. Not even Decimus to nudge his conscience, or Nona to remind him of responsibilities. He raised his chin, threw his shoulders back, and marched with vigor. He needed to distance himself, even if just for a day.

The century continued at full pace for three hours until they reached the base of Mount Carmel.

"Halt!"

The soldiers, their tunics soaked with perspiration, stood at attention. Lucius meandered among the four columns. He occasionally rapped a legionary with his baton, sometimes to urge a soldier into proper posture, other times just to remind them he was there and had a baton.

"Fall out!"

The soldiers broke out of their columns and sat on the fertile soil. Some removed their boots to rub sore calves and feet, others laughed at those who did.

"You have thirty minutes. Rest, eat, drink. Do what you have to do."

The men untied supply bags that hung from their waists and pulled out bread, fruit, and nuts they had packed that morning. They gulped water from their canteens.

Lucius stood a few paces away and snacked from his own supplies.

A young legionary, the newest to the century, approached the centurion. "Has our performance today satisfied you, sir?" Lucius stared at him for a moment, then returned his gaze to the horizon. He took a bite from an apple. Undeterred, the wide-eyed soldier continued, "I find such hikes invigorating. The fresh air. Exercise. Comradery. This is why I love being a soldier."

Behind him, the more experienced soldiers snickered. Some centurions enjoyed casual relationships with their soldiers. They drank, laughed, and played dice with them. But not Lucius. He appreciated his legionaries, but in the same way he appreciated a sharpened dagger or a new pair of boots. They were tools, a means to accomplish what he wanted to accomplish. Nothing more.

He brushed past the young soldier. "Formation!"

The legionaries picked up their shields and spears and scrambled into their columns. They faced west, the direction from which they had marched. Mount Carmel stood behind them.

"Full pace!"

Lucius enjoyed the few hours of respite from his troubles in Caesarea, but the moment he saw the city approaching on the horizon, his angst returned. He left his equipment in his room and made the brief hike to the Great Sea. He sat on a rock. A few yards from his feet, waves lapped the shore. A half-dozen ships churned toward the harbor, hoping to dock by nightfall. Gulls cawed, dove, and skimmed the water, emerging with fish clamped between their beaks.

Every time he encountered a Jew, his life got more complicated. Why must they always cause problems? Their strange rituals, pagan beliefs. Rome forced everyone else to submit, to bow to the empire and to the gods, but they gave these Jews so many concessions. They didn't bow to the emperor. They could collect their own taxes and keep their own treasury. The rebels among them insisted they would one day overthrow Rome. It was an absurd notion, but every time Rome crucified another rebel, their resolve only deepened.

And Septimus. Lucius was certain the morning's conversation wasn't the last he'd hear about the incident at the hippodrome. His old rival had something brewing.

As Lucius watched the sun set, he wondered what its morning return would bring.

4

"Here, drink." Deborah pressed a cup to Tobiah's lips. The tea was brewed with a mixture of herbs and spices intended to deaden his pain. It may or may not actually work, but it's worth a try. Again.

Tobiah responded with a groan and a weak slurp from the cup. His moaning lessened through the night. She didn't know if that was a good sign or bad, but she chose to be optimistic.

As she kissed his cheek, two legionaries burst into her home. "You. Come with us."

Deborah gasped and backed into a corner. "I can't!" She pointed to Tobiah. "See my husband? Have some pity. You did this to him."

They ignored her pleas and grabbed her by the arms.

"Where are you taking me?" She struggled to free herself from their grasp. Her feet dragged in the dirt.

"Stop fighting and this will go easier for you."

"Esther, stay with him!"

Her dear friend had spent the night by her side, tending to Tobiah. "I'll take care of him." Esther hugged Deborah. "Just do what they say."

Soldiers ogled as Deborah was marched into the camp. "Which one of you beat my husband?" She pointed to legionaries as they passed. "Was it you? Or you?" In her mind, they all did.

One of the legionaries drew his hand back, as if to slap her, but didn't follow through. An idol threat, but enough to silence her.

The soldiers tossed her to the floor of a centurion's chambers. "Sir Septimus. The Jew's wife, as you requested."

Deborah crawled onto a chair and rubbed the back of her arm. Bruises already appeared in the shape of the soldiers' fingers. Septimus didn't raise his eyes or speak. She adjusted her head covering to hide her face. She glanced with embarrassment at her tunic, dusty from chores and bloodstained from trying to keep her husband alive. Shadows fell in circles below her puffy eyes.

The legionaries at her side stood at attention. Another soldier entered, wearing the uniform of a centurion. His stench took her breath.

The centurion fixed his gaze on Septimus. "You needed to see me, sir?"

Septimus nodded to the centurion, then stared at Deborah. "Jew, this is the soldier who killed your husband. His name is Lucius."

When he said "killed," Deborah could see Lucius tense. She did too, and wondered for a moment if something happened since she left Tobiah. Even if it had, though, Septimus couldn't have known yet. He was bluffing, but she didn't know why.

A smile curled the corners of Septimus's mouth, hidden slightly by his unkempt beard. "Lucius, this is the woman whose husband you killed. She wants to accuse you before the camp judge."

Deborah gasped. Accuse a centurion? She'd said no such thing. She clenched her teeth. Her heart raced, and her hands crept instinctively toward her abdomen. She ached for Tobiah. If he were here, he would know what to say. And what not to say.

Lucius stood frozen, his eyes fixed on Septimus. "When?"

"The judge will see you in three days."

From the moment he entered the room, Lucius hadn't looked at Deborah. She didn't look at him, either. He marched out.

Deborah glared at Septimus.

He cocked his head. "See you in three days."

She rose from her chair, took a few steps toward the door, and turned around. "He's not dead."

"I don't care."

Deborah hurried home, where Esther greeted her with a smile and a hug. Deborah melted into her friend's embrace and wept.

Esther brushed the hair from her eyes. "He's a strong man."

"I know."

"And you're a strong woman."

"That I don't know, but I'm surviving." She recounted her experience in Septimus's chambers.

Esther held her friend's hand and listened. "Do what they say and keep your head down. This will pass."

Tobiah had a stronger day and more restful night. Some color returned to his cheeks. Deborah tried to rest, but woke every time he made a noise—and he made a lot of noises. She changed his bandages and cleaned his wounds every few hours. The smell turned her stomach, but she ignored it and cleaned what oozed from them.

Esther returned at daybreak and sat a pot on the table. "This soup will help you keep your strength. If you can get Tobiah to eat any, all the better."

"You and Benjamin are such a blessing."

"You would do the same for us." Esther put her hands on Deborah's shoulders. "Benjamin will take care of the chores today. You just take care of your husband. I'll check with you again soon."

Deborah dipped soup into a bowl. Esther's soups were all she had been able to stomach since she became pregnant. Thankfully, her vomiting in the mornings eased a few days before Tobiah's beating. With their friends' help, she and Tobiah would survive this.

Two days later, an hour after sunrise, a knock at her door startled Deborah, though only for a moment. This time, she expected the soldiers. She didn't run or shriek. "Let's get this over with." She marched out of the hut, a legionary at each side.

When they arrived at the camp, they found the judge sitting at the head of a long, cedar table. Deborah had not seen the adornments hanging from his uniform. He must hold a higher rank than the soldiers who pass through the village.

The judge motioned Deborah toward the chair to his right. "Sit."

Lucius stood across from Deborah. Another centurion stood next to Lucius. Septimus sat at the foot of the table, opposite the judge.

"By the favor of Justitia, we gather to consider the charges brought against Centurion Lucius Valerius Galeo." The judge's deep voice settled her. The gray in his hair and the wrinkles that curled from the sides of his eyes gave him an authority that went beyond rank. "Who brings these charges?" The judge glanced toward her.

Deborah stared at the table and considered her options. She wanted the centurion punished, but she knew what happened to Jewish families who accused Romans, especially Roman soldiers of rank.

Septimus cleared his throat. "As you can see, sir, the Jewess is with child and is in mourning. She asked me to speak on her behalf." Deborah asked no such thing.

The judge rolled his eyes. "Continue."

"Four days ago at the games in the hippodrome, Centurion Lucius Valerius Galeo, unprovoked, grabbed this kind woman's husband and threw him from the benches. Though I made every attempt to stop the vicious display, this so-called soldier of Rome continued beating the Jew until he lost consciousness. Bones were broken, and blood covered the floor of the hippodrome. His act tarnished the great races that the esteemed Pontius Pilate brought to our beloved Caesarea."

"Is the Jew dead?"

"Yes."

Deborah wanted to scream, *No! He's not dead. He is recovering. Slowly. Every day is better than the last. He will walk again and work again. He will care for me and our child.* But she kept quiet.

The judge turned to Lucius. "I see you brought someone with you."

"Yes sir. This is Decimus Cornelia Metellus, my fellow centurion and witness to the events of that day."

"And what did you see, Decimus?"

"My comrade was provoked. Earlier that afternoon, the Jew threw a rock and hit my head. You can see this dent on my helmet." He held out his helmet for the judge to see. "It knocked me to the ground. Other than some dizziness and a headache the next morning, I was uninjured. Later, though, during the last race, Lucius saw the Jew raise his arm again, with another rock in his hand. By stopping the Jew, Lucius protected me or whichever legionary the Jew planned to attack next."

Lies! Deborah thought it; Septimus said it.

The judge tilted his head. "Decimus, your perspective differs from that of your superior officer. Are you contradicting his word? Are you proposing that Septimus would give me false testimony?"

Decimus clenched his jaw. "Of course not, sir." He paused. "When I was hit the first time, Septimus was at the southern end of the hippodrome, too far away to see. So, when he saw Lucius beating the Jew, he thought it was unprovoked. He didn't know that Lucius was protecting me."

Septimus shifted in his seat. Deborah saw a glint of confusion in the blink of his eyes. She knew both soldiers were lying, but she didn't know why. Nor did she care. She didn't want to be there.

"Do you have anything to say, Miss?"

Deborah shook her head. She just wanted this parody of a trial to end so she could return to her hurting husband. He needed her.

"Anything else, soldiers?"

They shook their heads.

"Lucius Valerius Galeo, by the favor of Justitia, I declare you innocent."

Lucius smirked. "Good try, Septimus, but you lose." He stomped from the room.

"You'll not disrespect me!" Septimus stormed after him.

The judge turned to Deborah. "My scouts told me your husband is alive. I knew Septimus was lying." He cleared his throat. "You and your husband, and your friends in the village, stay out of trouble. Don't cause any problems. We want peace here. Understood?"

"We will cause you no more problems, sir." She stood. "Can I leave now?"

"Yes."

Deborah ran for the door and back home.

———————

"*Who* is sending you *where*?"

Three weeks had passed since the camp judge declared Lucius innocent. Now he stood before Nona. He dreaded this conversation, but the time to leave drew near, and he had to tell her.

"Pontius Pilate is sending me to Jerusalem." He didn't try to soften the blow. Sensitivity never came naturally for him.

Nona stared at the onion she sliced for a stew. The knife, rusty and dull, took chunks more than slices. "How long will you be gone?"

"I don't know. He's sending our cohort to Antonia, the fortress Herod built that's connected to the Jewish temple. The soldiers there now aren't handling the Jews very well. Pilate wants us to get them under control."

Lucius sipped water. He peeked at Nona over the rim of the cup. She finished slicing the onion and tossed pieces into a pot hanging from a tripod over the fire. Knife still in hand, her eyes locked on his, the anger in her stare flamed more fiercely than the campfire. She gestured with the knife and opened her mouth as if to speak. Instead, she remained quiet and hung her head. She reached to the pile of onions, took another, and began slicing it.

"When do you leave?"

"Tomorrow."

"And when did you find out?"

"Two weeks ago."

"And you're just now . . . ," Nona's voice quieted.

Tullus emerged from the hut carrying three plates. The fourteen-year-old walked with the brisk confidence of a centurion's son. Nothing scared him, even things that should. His wavy hair grew wavier as the day wore on. In recent weeks, Lucius noticed stubble budding from his chin and upper lip.

Paulla, four years younger, followed. She carried a pitcher of water in one hand and three cups, stacked, in the other. Her complexion was darker than her brother's, and her cheek still felt soft when Lucius kissed it.

"Father!" Paulla hurried around the fire and wrapped her arms around his waist. Her brother tried to hide his excitement, but his wide smile betrayed him.

Nona took another onion.

"Did you use your sword today?" Tullus asked. "Or your javelin? Or maybe you just needed your fists again. All my friends are talking about what happened at the games."

Paulla, her arms still around her father's waist, frowned at her brother. Lucius frowned, too. He didn't realize they knew.

"Don't be surprised." Nona smirked. "We all heard about what happened at the games. You know how word spreads around here. That Jew didn't deserve such a beating."

Lucius rolled his eyes.

Nona turned her attention back to the children. "Your father has some news."

Paulla leaned back. "What is it?"

Lucius pulled away from his daughter and stepped toward the fire. He held his hands over the flames. He needed to gather his thoughts and choose his words carefully.

"The governor reassigned my cohort."

"What does that mean?" Paulla asked.

Her brother jumped in, eyes wild and words tumbling from his lips. "Is he sending you to war? Where are you going? Who will you conquer? Do you have your sword sharpened and your shield polished? They're going to regret the day they faced Lucius Valerius Galeo!"

Lucius picked up a stick and poked the fire. "No, not to a war. To Jerusalem."

"Jerusalem?" The boy furrowed his brow. "Why is he sending you to Jerusalem?"

Lucius expected this response from his son. Of all the glorious posts where Pilate might send him, Jerusalem was at the bottom of the list. "Apparently, some of the Jews there have gotten out of control. Pilate thinks my cohort can do a better job than the soldiers stationed there now."

Paulla stepped around the fire and stood next to her mother.

"Will you be alright there, Father?"

"I'll be fine. The Jews are just a nuisance, like annoying gnats that can't really hurt you, but need a good slap from time to time." Lucius threw the stick into the fire and watched as it took hold of a nearby flame. Soon it glowed. "I leave in the morning. I've left your mother enough money to last until I can visit. I'll have somebody check on you every few days."

Paulla ran into the hut.

Tullus stood, arms at his sides. He glanced at his mother, then his father. "Don't stay gone too long." He took two steps toward the hut, then turned around. "And spill some blood."

After Tullus disappeared into the hut, Nona tossed the final onion slices into the boiling water.

"They'll be fine." Lucius nudged an ember with his boot. "And you will too."

"Maybe." Nona paused. "No, not maybe. We will be fine. We can survive without you." She stepped toward him and lifted his chin. "But someday I want to do more than just survive."

5

"Move! Clear the path." The soldiers' barking woke Tullus. At first, his subconscious incorporated the sounds into his dream. He charged across the British countryside alongside Julius Caesar. He was brave. Brutal. His enemies cowered. Then the commotion in the real world lured him out of his grogginess. He opened his eyes. Still a boy living in his mother's hut.

He peeked out the doorway but couldn't see anything. The sounds came from the road that led to town. He tiptoed outside, trying not to disturb his sister. His mother had already risen to begin early morning chores.

Tullus snuck down the dirt path, muddy from the heavy dew. Last evening's campfires smoldered on either side. He crept past lean-tos where his neighbors lived, and weaved through shops, their owners setting out merchandise for the day. When he reached the road, he crouched behind a shopkeeper's table and peered over its edge.

"What are you doing here, boy? Be gone." The shopkeeper shooed Tullus with his broom. "Hide someplace else."

"But sir—" Before Tullus could continue, a company of soldiers rounded the curve and drew near. The shopkeeper joined Tullus behind the table.

"Out of the way!" The soldiers scowled at anyone who looked their direction. One grasped the table where Tullus hid, sneered, and flipped it. Grapes and cucumbers spilled across the ground. "These are unacceptable. Go back to your garden and find something better."

Tullus scurried to hide behind another stall. The shopkeeper, his hands and voice shaking, scrambled to pick up his dirty produce. "Yes sir. Please forgive me. It won't happen again."

The soldiers marched in an oval, two deep. At their center, a short man pulled the reins of a white steed. His bronze breastplate, crimson sash, and cold expression left no doubt who was in charge. "Get this rabble away from me."

Pontius Pilate. Tullus recognized him from a parade he watched a few months before. He'd never forget that scowl. He tried to imitate it when no one was looking.

The soldiers and Pilate swept through the settlement and into the camp, leaving a wake of toppled merchandise and exasperated merchants.

Tullus emerged from his hiding place and stood in the middle of the street, staring at the gate where the soldiers entered the camp. Three retired soldiers appeared and stood next to him. Tullus nodded his greetings. He'd spent many hours listening to Gaius, Quintus, and Hostus tell war stories. They treated him warmly, often indulging his curiosity into the night, then sending him home early enough to avoid his mother's punishment.

"Impressive display, wasn't it?" Gaius leaned on a walking stick.

"Quite," Tullus responded. "What's Pilate doing here?"

"I hear he's sending a cohort to Jerusalem."

Tullus remembered the conversation with his father the night before.

Hostus, missing an ear and an eye, cocked his head. "It's awfully strange for the governor to get his boots dirty in the camp." He talked louder than most. "Must be important business in Jerusalem for him to come all the way out here to see the soldiers off."

Tullus puffed out his chest. "I hear he's fed up with the Jews there. He's sending a new group who can keep them in their place. He probably came this morning to lecture the soldiers about what to do when they get there."

Quintus spoke up. "Somebody told me he's going to Jerusalem with them. Maybe he has something planned for the Jews that he wants to oversee personally." He turned his gaze toward the camp. "That Pilate, he means business."

Tullus smiled.

The dirt beneath their feet began to vibrate. The three retirees scrambled to the side. Tullus remained in the middle of the street. The gate opened and hundreds of soldiers poured out, marching straight toward him in quick rhythm and full gear. Tullus stood petrified until Hostus cupped his hands around his mouth. "Better get out of the way, boy! They'll plow you under like a turnip."

Tullus took a few steps backward, eyeing the approaching Roman soldiers. Their armor gleamed in the morning sun. Their gazes fixed on the road and the mission ahead. Tullus knelt beside the road.

Six soldiers on horseback led the way, followed by a flag bearer who held a pole twice as tall as a man. A square, crimson flag fluttered from the top of the pole, adorned with a bull stitched in gold. Eight columns of legionaries followed. An entire century!

On their heels, a second century, then a third.

As the legionaries marched past, Tullus rose to his feet, mesmerized by the display before him. His eyes grew glassy. "One day." His chest swelled. "One day." He stretched his right arm in front of his body in the Roman salute, his fingers together and palm facing down. The retired soldiers behind him snickered, but Tullus ignored them.

Pontius Pilate, on horseback, followed. Guards surrounded him, ready to protect their leader.

Decimus led the next century. He sometimes accompanied Lucius to Nona's hut. He'd slip special gifts into the children's hands, perhaps a hair ribbon for Paulla and a piece of honey and nut candy for Tullus. At his last visit, he gave Tullus a dull, used knife like soldiers carry, and promised, "Soon I'll bring you an old sword."

The final century of the cohort approached, led by Lucius Valerius Galeo. Tullus, still standing with his arm outstretched, beamed. "Father!" Lucius couldn't hear above the pounding of boots against the dirt. "Father!" He yelled the second time for the benefit of those standing near him. Even if his father heard, he wouldn't look over.

Lucius kept in rhythm with his soldiers, moving amid the columns, his baton ready to rap across the bare thigh of any soldier who fell out of step.

Just as Lucius passed Tullus, the centurion shouted, "Full pace!" At his command, the soldiers extended their strides and accelerated. They passed through the settlement and headed southeast toward Jerusalem, toward the risen sun.

Finally, a line of servants trudged behind, leading mules burdened with tents and other supplies.

Tullus returned to the middle of the road and kept his arm outstretched in salute until the procession disappeared over the crest of the hill. When the cohort was out of sight, he turned and ambled to where his retired friends gathered, sitting on chairs they'd salvaged from the trash heap and kept by the road for their daily debriefings. He tried to wipe the tear from his cheek before they saw it.

"That Pilate is a wicked man." Quintus leaned back in his chair. "One of the most violent I've seen."

Gaius nodded. "Isn't it great? We need a governor that people fear. It's good to see everybody shake and scurry when he goes by." He pointed at Quintus with his walking stick. "If we don't respect him, or the emperor, or the others in charge, the whole system crumbles."

Tullus tilted his head. "I don't understand why he has to hurt the shopkeepers. There was nothing wrong with those vegetables his soldiers sent flying. Does he have to be that mean?"

"Yes!" The old soldiers replied in unison.

"I guess so." Tullus remained quiet for a moment then changed the subject. "Tell me what it's like to fight in a war." He'd asked the question many times before. The old soldiers always responded with the same grins and stories.

Hostus took the lead. "I marched with Sejanus against the Parthians. Must've been a quarter century ago. Those Parthians wanted that land, but we weren't going to let them have it. I ran across that field like a gazelle. Oh, we started in formation, but when their javelins flew and our men fell, the formation fell apart and I took them on." He stood and acted out the battle, bobbing and weaving as much as an old man could. "Arrows and spears fell around me. With a single launch of my javelin, I speared three at once!"

Tullus's eyes grew wide and his heart raced. He never tired of the story. He imagined himself on that battlefield.

"And then I pulled out my sword. Swishing it left, swinging it right. I must've taken out thirty or forty." Tullus remembered the number being twenty-five.

Gaius scoffed. "You never—"

"Sure I did. Where do you think I lost this eye? It's probably still rolling around on that field somewhere, winking at whoever comes by."

Quintus laughed so hard he almost fell backward in his chair. Tullus cleared his throat and laughed along.

"You didn't lose your eye on that battlefield." Gaius snickered. "You lost your eye when that girl over in Cana got fed up with you and—"

"No, no, no. That's just a rumor. What I'm telling you here and now is fact."

The stories would continue for hours, but Tullus knew his mother would be looking for him. "I have to go now. Can I come see you again tomorrow?"

"You can come see us anytime, young soldier." Gaius rested his hand on Tullus's shoulder. "That will be you out there marching someday. I hope I'm around long enough to see it."

Tullus blushed. He bid goodbye to his friends then stepped back into the street. He stared into the distance, toward the horizon where his father and the cohort of legionaries disappeared.

"Be kind," his mother often said. "Respect people. Stand up for yourself when you need to. Be a man." She would take hold of his shoulders and look him in the eye. "But be a man who has consideration for other people. Who cares about them."

Those he respects most, though, don't fit that description. They're proud. Hateful. Others fear them. They stand ready to tear down their enemies with words or fists. Or both. The people he admires most are people like his father.

6

"**H**alt!" Lucius faced his soldiers. "Fall out." After six hours of marching, he needed the break as much as they did. The rudimentary road that snaked southeast from Caesarea brought them into the plains of Samaria, a safe place to rest. He pulled a leather pouch from his belt and took a swig of water. The sun stood straight overhead.

Decimus also gave his soldiers a break, and stood next to Lucius. "Any sign of rebels?"

"Not that I've seen." While he marched, Lucius searched the horizon and roadsides for Jewish rebels. They were thirsty for Roman blood and often hid behind rocks or just beyond the crests of hills. "An attack is unlikely today. Not as many hiding places along this route. Tomorrow, though, the terrain will be more rugged. And word will have spread about our procession. We'll have to keep our eyes open."

Servants mingled among the soldiers, passing out bread and fruit.

"How far will we march today?"

Decimus grinned. "You'll have to ask the one in charge."

Lucius raised his brow, then grimaced when he heard the familiar voice.

"Yarkon River. That's where we'll stop for the night."

"Septimus, so gracious of you to join us."

The superior officer ignored the pleasantry and spit out a pomegranate seed. "That is, if you have the strength."

"I think I can make it."

Decimus put an arm around Lucius's shoulder and the other around Septimus. "See, isn't it more pleasant when we all get along?" He laughed as his fellow centurions slid from beneath his embrace.

Septimus glared at Decimus. "How are your men holding up?"

"As strong as ever. Those marches to Mount Carmel prepared us well."

Septimus grunted and returned to his cohort.

Lucius felt his skin crawl as he watched Septimus walk away. He'd suspected Septimus might punish him for beating the Jew, but not that he'd accuse him of murder. Septimus wasn't the smartest soldier in the camp, but he could be the shrewdest. Had the judge convicted Lucius, he'd have been discharged from the cohort, and Septimus would've boosted his standing before Pilate.

Decimus interrupted his thoughts. "You look like you're ready to punch somebody."

"You can guess who."

"He's inept, but harmless. Gives us somebody to laugh at." Decimus took a drink from his canteen. "Why do you have such a problem with him?"

Lucius stared at Septimus, now a hundred paces away. "Pilate gave him command of the first century because his family has money and supports Tiberius. The position should have been mine. He's a poor leader. I could do better." He shifted his glare to Decimus. "And he's not just inept; he's a fool. A disgrace to Rome." His heartbeat quickened and his face reddened.

"You're exaggerating."

"I'm not. There must be a way to show his true idiocy to Pilate." Lucius thought for a moment, then whispered, "If we got a couple other centurions to help, we could go before Pilate and accuse Septimus of something. Something big. Pilate is so eager to make a name for himself that he might believe us without investing carefully."

Decimus shook his head. "This is ludicrous. If we're discovered, we're crucified. Why are you saying this?" He put his hands on his hips. "What is it that you want, Lucius?"

Lucius clenched his teeth. Balled his fists. A vein popped out on his neck. "I want power."

"Power?"

"I want people to salute me. To bow to me. To cower before me."

"You're a centurion in the most dominant army in history. People already salute you, and cower. What more could you want? Who do you want power over?"

"Those who don't deserve respect."

"Like Septimus."

"And those who are weak."

"Like the Jew at the games."

"I want them to hide when they see me coming. To breathe a sigh of relief when they see me going. To never forget me."

Decimus put his hands on Lucius's shoulders and stared at him. "You're making yourself and everyone around you miserable."

Lucius swept Decimus's arms away and stomped back to his century. *Some friend. Imagine him questioning me. What right does he have?* He picked up a stick that lay on the ground and broke it. Then he broke it again and tossed it aside. *Miserable. I hope they do feel miserable.*

"Formation!" Lucius's soldiers scrambled into columns, then joined the rest of the cohort to continue the journey.

The cohort reached the Yarkon River two hours before sunset. Septimus raised both arms. "We'll stay here for the night." His voice projected with such power that the last column of soldiers heard as though they stood by his side. "Set up camp."

Lucius rolled his eyes and grumbled to his century, "You can get a drink first. Then you know what to do." The legionaries hurried to the river. They dropped to their knees, cupped their hands, and raised cool water to their mouths. Lucius kneeled alongside them. River water never tasted so good as after a long march.

The soldiers hurried into action. Lucius's century dug a ditch three feet deep and four feet wide to form a perimeter. He inspected their work. "Straight lines and sharp corners." They piled the dirt next to the ditch to form an embankment, and planted stakes at the top for further protection.

Lucius stood with his arms crossed. He gave an approving nod to his soldiers, then scanned the rest of the camp construction. Servants untied supplies from the backs of mules. Decimus supervised a group who assembled tents inside the perimeter in precise rows and columns. At the center, they erected a tent for Pilate, twice the size of the others and decorated as fitting for the governor.

The legionaries in Lucius's century completed the ditch and wall. "What next, sir?"

"Half of you, patrol the perimeter. The other half, go to the river and fill buckets with water for cooking and drinking."

As the soldiers completed their tasks, they trickled toward the corner of the camp where the food was prepared. Cooks scooped wheat porridge flavored with honey into the men's bowls.

Lucius finished his meal, then strolled among the legionaries. "Eat up. You'll need the energy tomorrow." They devoured the porridge and washed it back with river water.

The entire cohort retired to their tents to rest for the next day's march. They didn't build campfires, lest they reveal their location to potential enemies.

Centurions had the luxury of tents to themselves. Servants positioned Lucius's cot in the middle of his tent. He scooted it to the back, as far from the doorway as possible, to give himself more time to respond to an attack. He removed most of his armor, leaving only his tunic and a vest of iron rings. He laid his sword on the floor, within reach, then lay on his back on the cot.

He folded his hands across his chest. He breathed deeply and relaxed.

Lucius drifted into sleep and his surroundings melted a dream. He mounted a gallant white steed, like the one Pilate rode. Instead of hooves, the heads of Pilate, Tiberius, Septimus, and Decimus dangled from its legs. Lucius galloped through Rome, then Caesarea, and then Jerusalem, as if the three cities adjoined.

He held a sickle in his left hand and used it to sweep bodies from the ground, tossing them onto the sharp end of a giant javelin.

The bodies impaled on the javelin were Jewish men, women, and children, all faceless but two. Tobiah and Deborah. Every so often, Tobiah and Deborah reappeared, each time wearing the same expression. Tobiah's face twisted into bloody anguish, and a tear rolled from his eye until it fell from his cheek and crashed to the ground like a wave from the Great Sea during a midnight storm. Deborah's face remained frozen, her brows furrowed, eyes fixed on her husband. Her mouth formed a perfect oval as if she wanted to scream but couldn't.

When the javelin was almost full of bodies, skewered and pressed against each other, Lucius flung three final people onto it. These three hadn't yet appeared in the dream. They wore the dress of Romans rather than Jews. He caught a glimpse of their faces. Nona, Tullus, and Paulla.

Lucius woke. His heart raced. Sweat puddled beneath his neck. The scent of morning flowed through his nostrils, and a trumpet blast pierced his ears. He shook his head, attempting to disentangle the dream from his cobwebbed mind.

Servants and legionaries disassembled tents, refilled trenches, and ate their morning meal. Septimus's voice boomed across the camp, "Assemble before the governor!"

Lucius pointed his century toward the assembly, and rapped the slower soldiers with his baton. "Move. Quicker." He remained at the edge of the rectangular formation. His soldiers stood at attention, bronze helmets adorning their heads, shields in their left hands, and javelins in their right. Outside of the rectangle, servants briskly secured tents and other supplies to the backs of mules.

Pontius Pilate sat atop his horse, which strutted back and forth in front of the soldiers. "Today we continue our march to Jerusalem." His voice, usually of a higher pitch than most men, deepened when he wanted to impress or intimidate.

Lucius smirked. *We already know we're going to Jerusalem, pompous fool.* He glanced around to make sure the words had been only in his mind. *And who is this "we" that will march? That horse will do all the work for you.* Lucius gritted his teeth.

"By the power of Jupiter," Pilate continued, "we will arrive tomorrow after sunset. Jewish people have traveled great distances and gathered in the city. In a few days they celebrate Yom Kippur. They believe their god looks favorably on them when they sacrifice bulls and goats." The soldiers hissed. Pilate raised his fist in the air. "We will erect images of the emperor and of the true gods, showing them whose favor they should seek. And if some blood needs shed in the process, so be it. The gods be with you!" The soldiers erupted in a cheer.

Pilate's words surprised Lucius. Previous governors hadn't placed such images in Jerusalem, not so much to respect the Jews but to keep them quiet. They followed strict laws against worshipping any gods other than their own.

Lucius leaned forward and caught Decimus's eye. He was certain Decimus shared his thought. *This could be fun.*

The cohort marched through the next two days and arrived at Jerusalem an hour after sunset. They skirted the northern edge of the city, headed toward its northeast corner. The few people who remained in the streets scattered as the soldiers passed.

Lucius stood to the side and took a drink from his canteen. He had visited Jerusalem once, years before, but forgot how the Jewish temple dominated the city. Its massive walls reached into the night sky. South and west of the temple, towers dotted the skyline and pools reflected the light of the moon.

Lucius rejoined his century. Moments later, they arrived at Antonia. The fortress butted against the northwest corner of the Jewish temple. The two structures shared a wall. From Antonia's four corners rose towers, each one hundred feet tall. He could see soldiers stationed in the towers, some monitoring the nighttime activities in the temple below, while others scanned the horizons around the city.

"Continue! Don't slow down." Lucius's soldiers hadn't visited the city, and they gawked at the scene before them.

He led his century up a series of steps into Antonia's entrance, then through the fortress corridors that emptied into a courtyard at its center. Other centuries stood in formation before Pilate. Lucius led his soldiers into place to complete the formation. The inner walls of Antonia rose high above them.

Pilate raised his arm, and the soldiers grew silent. "Look around. Sixty-five years ago, Herod the Great constructed this masterpiece in honor of Marc Antony. Its glory provides an oasis to the stench of the Jews and the city that surrounds it. No fortress has ever been built with such magnificence, or ever will be."

Lucius chuckled. Sure, Antonia was superb, but hardly unique across the Roman Empire.

"Behind these stone walls sit barracks, reception halls, and training courts. Every accommodation and convenience a soldier could hope for. One fortunate cohort has the honor of living in this luxury. Beginning today, you are that cohort."

Lucius doubted any soldier felt honored to be assigned to Jerusalem, even if they lived in Antonia, but they cheered anyway.

"Tonight, I will stay here with you."

Pilate would stay in Antonia, as he sometimes did when visiting Jerusalem. But "with" the other soldiers was a stretch. Their quarters and his barely compared.

"You will find one room in Antonia particularly interesting." Pilate raised his brow. "You may not visit it, but you should know it's here."

Lucius cocked his head.

"Herod the Great knew how to deal with the Jews who infect this land. He had enough Jewish blood in his veins to understand the people and their customs, but he was loyal to Rome. Here in Antonia, he constructed a stone vault to store the Jewish high priest's vestments. Three times a year, for the Jews' most significant feasts, we deliver the vestments to their high priest. In just a few days, we will take the vestments to their priest for Yom Kippur.

"In respect for the vestments stored here, we have kept Antonia free of images of our great emperor, Tiberius, those who ruled before him, and other gods who have shown their favor to Rome." Pilate paused. "Tonight this changes!"

The men cheered with such vigor that the stone walls around them seemed to shake.

"Servants, bring the symbols." Servants entered the court carrying tall poles that held crimson banners adorned with golden images of bulls and eagles. The servants waved the poles back and forth, creating ripples in the banners. They formed a semicircle around Pilate.

"And now, the busts." A second group of servants marched into the courtyard, each carrying a bust of gold, silver, or bronze above his head. The busts depicted Tiberius Caesar and the gods Jupiter, Mars, and Venus.

The servants completed a circle around Pilate. The governor stared straight ahead, his lips pursed and jaw clenched. The soldiers grew silent, fell to their knees, and bowed in worship of the symbols.

"Adorn the towers!" Pilate commanded.

The soldiers renewed their cheers. Though Lucius was far from the ranking officer in the room, he led the chant. "All hail Tiberius Caesar! All hail Jupiter! All hail Mars! All hail Venus!" Hundreds of soldiers joined. A pleased expression crept across Pilate's face. Septimus caught Lucius's eye, crossed his arms, and growled.

7

At first light, Lucius climbed the stairs of the tower that rose from the southwest corner of Antonia.

"The gods be with you, sir." The soldier on guard saluted.

"And with you."

Lucius gazed across the city. From his perch, he could see miles to the west, the direction from which the cohort entered the city the night before. "Tell me what I'm looking at, soldier."

"To the west is Jerusalem's upper city, where the wealthy live. You can see the palace built by Herod the Great."

"Impressive."

"To the south, on the other side of the temple, is the lower city, where the poor try to scrape together a living. And there to the east," the soldier pointed, "the Kidron Valley and the Mount of Olives."

Lucius shielded his eyes from the sun rising over the mount. "I'll have to learn my way around the city."

"Yes sir."

The centurion lowered his gaze to a Jewish man who scurried on the street below. He secured baskets of fruit on a wagon. The rest of the city slowly came to life around him. He peered toward Antonia. His eyes settled on banners hanging from Antonia's towers and busts sitting atop the walls—the Roman gods that Pilate's servants erected the night before.

The Jew's eyes grew wide and he dropped a basket of figs. He shook his head. "No. It can't be. Surely not. They would never. No!"

Lucius grinned.

By midday, Jews marched through the streets, banged on the doors of Antonia, and chanted in the temple courts. "Remove the symbols. They defile the high priest's vestments. They desecrate the temple!"

Lucius and his comrade, Decimus, stood in one of Antonia's towers, watching the demonstrators and the soldiers who patrolled the edges of the crowd.

"A few banners, a few busts. I'm surprised they're upset." Decimus chuckled.

"I know. Who would've imagined such a response?"

The Jews' chants continued from below. "Remove the symbols. We demand an audience with Pilate!"

"Do you think Pilate will respond?" Lucius asked.

"I know he won't. He's not here."

Lucius raised a brow.

"He slipped out in the middle of the night. He's well on his way back to Caesarea."

Lucius laughed. "Erect Roman gods on Antonia next to the Jewish temple, then leave town before the Jews see them. Maybe it's cowardly, maybe it's courageous. Either way, he's crafty."

Decimus smiled. "Much to admire about our governor." He sighed. "Our legionaries have everything under control. Have you eaten?"

The comrades descended the towers. Another flight of stairs took them to the soldiers' dining room.

An hour later, just after Lucius returned to his quarters, Septimus banged on his door. "Gather your men and go to Caesarea. The Jews are on their way, a whole mob of them, and Pilate will need additional protection. I give this honor to your century." Lucius knew the decision was less to honor his century and more to irritate him.

"Yes sir," Lucius mumbled.

"What was that, soldier? Speak up when you address a superior officer."

"Yes sir!"

Septimus closed the door. Lucius threw a boot at it. Apparently the Jews were more determined than Pilate anticipated. The governor would arrive in Caesarea several hours before the Jewish mob, and the soldiers stationed in Caesarea stood ready to protect him. No need to panic.

He poked his head out the door and beckoned the first legionary who walked by. "Spread the word that our century leaves for Caesarea in three hours." As the messenger passed from room to room, a wave of groans followed him. Lucius felt the same. They'd barely unpacked their gear in Antonia. Now they'll turn around and go right back. Another three days of marching. Another seventy miles.

Tobiah rose to tackle the daily pursuit of survival. He ached from head to foot, but he moved. A month had passed since a centurion beat him almost to his death. His injuries prevented him from traveling to Jerusalem for Yom Kippur with Benjamin and others from the village.

He swung his legs from his cot and rested his feet on the floor. His right leg struggled, but made the trip successfully. He retrieved a walking stick from the floor.

When he and Deborah moved to Caesarea from Galilee, five years before, they left their families behind. Tobiah's conversation with his father echoed in his memory.

"Why must you go, dear son?"

Though he'd explained before, he repeated his rationale. "I want the best for Deborah. We'll have more opportunities in Caesarea. A lot of trade goes in and out of the harbor, and there are more people to sell to. The Romans have made it a center for culture, art, and education."

His father nodded, looking at the floor instead of his son.

"The Romans aren't all bad, Father."

"Maybe not. But be careful, Tobiah. Protect your precious new wife." He paused. "And remember Yahweh."

Distant cousins who lived in Caesarea helped construct their one-story stone house. The Romans called the village the Jewish quarter. It sat just inland from the hippodrome and harbor.

Tobiah leaned heavily on his cane as he shuffled out of the house and into the courtyard he shared with a few neighbors. With his free hand, he grasped the rope handles of two wooden buckets. The first bucket sloshed with water, the second held a canvas bag filled with grain.

Tobiah seated himself on a small stool next to two goats he kept tied to a post. He removed the canvas bag of grain from one of the buckets, wincing as pain shot through his ribs. He sat it before the goats. Their heads nudged one another as they ate.

Tobiah rubbed his hands together to warm them. He washed the first goat's udders with water, then coaxed milk from its udders into a bucket. He repeated the process with the second goat, left the grain and water for them to finish, then leaned on the walking stick to stand. He carried a bucket half filled with milk and hobbled back to his home.

As he reentered his house, he heard a voice from the other side of the courtyard.

"Shalom, Tobiah."

"Benjamin, is that you?"

"Yes, it's me. A good morning to you." Benjamin emerged from his doorway.

"I thought you were in Jerusalem."

"I was. But duty called me back."

Tobiah furrowed his brow.

"I arrived late last night. All the men from our village came back. A few hundred brothers from Jerusalem joined us."

Tobiah thought he heard noises the night before, but dismissed them, assuming frightening dreams had invaded his sleep again. "What's happening?"

"Four days ago Pilate rode into Jerusalem, along with a cohort of the Roman guard that he transferred from here to Antonia. They arrived secretly, at night. Before the sun rose the next morning, they had desecrated the temple and the high priest's vestments by placing their pagan symbols around Antonia's towers. Pilate, the coward, left to come back to Caesarea before anyone knew what had happened."

Tobiah clenched his jaw.

"At midday we will gather in the hippodrome. We'll stay there until the governor agrees to remove the symbols from Antonia."

Benjamin leaned in. "We must take this stand, Tobiah. Pilate continues to push his boundaries. He's threatened us and ignored the agreements we have with Rome. He tells his soldiers to bully us if we get in their way. This can't continue. He can't silence us, and he won't ignore us."

"I'll go with you." Tobiah spoke the words before he considered them. He wanted to support his brothers, but any time he neared the hippodrome his heart raced and his hands became clammy.

"No, Tobiah. I admire your resolve, but you're not able."

Tobiah took a deep breath. "This is too important, Benjamin. I need to go."

"Your injuries are still mending, my friend. Let them heal. And, this could get dangerous. If you go to the hippodrome, and something happens to you again, Deborah will never forgive us. Neither will Esther." Benjamin's tone softened, and a slight smile crossed his face. "And we don't want to live the rest of our days with unhappy wives."

Tobiah's eyes dropped and settled on the bucket in his hand. He swirled the milk around. "Then what can I do?"

"Pray to Yahweh. Ask him to give us strength and to break the governor's will."

For four days, Tobiah heeded his friend's advice and his wife's subsequent warnings. He stayed away. When the protestors synced their chants, their voices carried far enough for him to hear. "Remove the symbols. Protect the vestments. Purify the temple!"

That evening, Benjamin returned to the village for supplies. "Our numbers are growing each day," he told Tobiah. "Our brothers from throughout Judea are joining us."

"Any sign of Pilate?"

"None. His soldiers patrol day and night, but he hasn't left his palace." The governor's palace sat immediately south of the hippodrome. "Keep praying, Tobiah. Yahweh will not abandon us."

By the fifth day, Tobiah could hold back no longer. He rose early and lifted himself from his cot, careful not to wake Deborah. He maneuvered to the corner of the room where Deborah prepared and stored food. He reached to the shelf for a loaf of bread. His ribs protested. He rummaged through a basket of fruit and found figs, dates, and pomegranates. He laid the food on a piece of square fabric, drew in the corners, tied them together, then tied the sack to the top of his walking stick.

He turned to leave, but stopped when Deborah rolled over. Their eyes met from across the room. Hers filled with tears, his with resolve.

"I'm sorry to wake you."

She stared.

"I must go."

She knew where.

"I must."

"Why do you say 'must,' Tobiah? Who compels you? Who stands at the door with a sword or a whip?" Her voice fell to a whisper. "You don't have to go."

He considered various responses, but none felt adequate. Nothing he could say would convince her that he needed to join his brothers.

Deborah caressed her stomach. She quietly sang.

When the princes in Israel take the lead,
when the people willingly offer themselves—
praise the Lord!

Hear this, you kings! Listen, you rulers!
I, even I, will sing to the Lord.
I will praise the Lord, the God of Israel, in song.

God chose new leaders
when war came to the city gates,
but not a shield or spear was seen
among forty thousand in Israel.
My heart is with Israel's princes,
with the willing volunteers among the people.
Praise the Lord!

Tobiah shuffled out the door. He knew Deborah feared for him, but she was still proud of him. She couldn't say it, but she could sing it. He understood. He loved his wife. And he loved their child who grew in her womb. For these reasons and a host of others, he must go.

8

Tobiah shuffled toward the hippodrome, his body leaning on his cane, his leg dragging behind him. This awkward posture caused his ribs to scream with every step. First they ached, then burned, and by the time the stadium came into view, it felt as though every rib was a double-edged sword slicing his insides. Still, he continued.

Before his injuries, Tobiah could hike from the Jewish village to the hippodrome in half an hour and barely break a sweat. Today, the journey took two hours of painstaking, slow progress.

When he hobbled through the arena's north entryway, he stopped, gaping at the scene before him. He nodded to a Jew who stood nearby. "Where did everybody come from?"

"All over Judea. Some even from Galilee."

"How many?"

"Three thousand. Maybe four. More come every day. And the crowd grows more agitated by the hour." The man looked Tobiah over. "I'm not sure this is the best place for you."

"Not the first time I've heard that today."

He tottered toward the west side of the stadium, which bordered the sea. Gulls squawked, dove into the waves, and emerged with mouthfuls of nourishment. Two dozen ships, their sails rising toward the sky, caught the late-morning breeze and slithered through the waves toward the harbor.

A less majestic scene unfolded inside the hippodrome. Men huddled in groups around smoldering fires, which charred the precious stadium floor. The resulting smoke merged into a haze, a gray dome hanging above the stadium.

Younger Jews sat on the ground, encircling elders who sat in rickety chairs. Ash and grime clung to their forearms and tunics.

"Tell us about Judah Maccabee, Samuel," a young man asked an elder.

Tobiah stopped to listen.

Samuel stroked his white beard. "One hundred ninety years ago, Antiochus Epiphanes was determined to turn us into Greeks." His voice was husky and hoarse. "He wanted us to talk like Greeks, dress like Greeks, eat like the Greeks. And worship their gods. Antiochus even demanded that we worship him." He rose from his chair and poked the fire with a stick. "Yahweh's patience ran out, and he poured his power into the son of a priest, Judah Maccabee. Judah took to the mountains. He gathered his army and swept across the land God gave Abraham, spilling pagan, Greek blood everywhere he went."

Those encircling Samuel grunted their approval.

"In Jerusalem," the old man's voice quickened, "Antiochus defiled our temple, forbade circumcision, and burned our scrolls. He sacrificed a pig on our altar." He turned his head and spat on the ground. But he wasn't finished. A veteran storyteller, he knew how to build momentum. "He dedicated our temple to Zeus."

Listeners roared their disapproval.

"Judah Maccabee galloped into the holy city, his band of rebels marching behind."

Roars of disapproval turned to cheers of jubilation.

"By the mighty right arm of Yahweh, Judah Maccabee wielded sword and spear and invaded every corner of the holy city, slicing and bludgeoning those devils until they lay dead in the street or limped their way into the horizon. He restored our city. He purified our temple. He conquered the evil ones."

Tobiah knew what would come next. The man standing next to him cried out, "Remove the symbols. Protect the vestments. Purify the temple!" Others nearby joined in, but the chant died out before it swept across the stadium. After five days of demonstrations, emotions erupted with exuberance but didn't last long.

Tobiah kept walking. He passed dozens of huddles and heard the same stories endlessly repeated. Every few minutes, the chant would begin in a different part of the stadium, "Remove the symbols!"

After he waded through most of the arena, he saw Benjamin thirty paces away. Tobiah hurried as much as his injuries allowed, weaving through the throngs, then embraced his friend.

"Tobiah, it's great to see you." Benjamin's elation faded into concern. "How did you get here? You should be at home."

"I couldn't stay away, Benjamin. Conscience and duty. I have to stand with my brothers."

"Conscience and duty sound noble, dear friend, but they won't heal your leg and ribs." Benjamin stepped back and inspected his comrade. Tobiah tried to look strong, but his crooked, scrawny body depended on a cane. Before the attack, Tobiah stood proud, a healthy Jew with a strong back who could work from sunup to sundown, but not today. Sweat trickled down both sides of his face, leaving trails of grime across his pale skin. "You need to rest. Stay here and talk with our brothers. I'll find some fruit and cool water for you. Before nightfall I'll walk you back to the village. You don't want to stay here overnight."

Tobiah neither agreed nor disagreed; instead, he changed the subject. "What's going to happen here? What will come of all this?"

"I wish I knew. We hope Pilate will send a message to Jerusalem to remove the symbols from Antonia, but so far he hasn't shown his face. Other than sending the soldiers to keep us under control, he's ignored us." Benjamin paused and looked around at the masses packed into the hippodrome. "But he can't ignore us forever."

"He might try. He's stubborn."

"Maybe. But so are we. Four hundred years of slavery in Egypt, forty years wandering the desert. Five days in a stadium are nothing. We can outlast any Roman aristocrat."

Tobiah chuckled. "You'll stay again tonight?"

"Yes."

"Then so will I."

By the fourth day of demonstrations, Lucius's diminishing patience yielded to disinterest. On the fifth day, his disinterest gave way to irritation. And by the sixth day, his irritation conceded to exasperation. And violence. He hadn't weaseled his way to the rank of centurion to spend his days doing crowd control.

"Cursed Septimus, sending me here." He spoke to no one in particular. He sat in the highest row in the bleachers, affording him a view of the entire hippodrome. "Someday I'll give the orders and you'll obey. Someday soon."

Lucius's soldiers joined legionaries stationed in Caesarea to keep the demonstrations under control. A thousand patrolled the hippodrome during the day, five hundred at night. Lucius returned to the military camp each night to rest and to garner the will to return the next day.

He sighed, his mind wandering to Nona and the children. When he visited them last evening, Tullus asked, "Father, can I join you at the hippodrome?"

Nona glared at Lucius. He shook his head. "No, son. It's too dangerous."

"I like dangerous."

"Your mother doesn't. Nor do I. It's best for you to stay here." He put his hand on his son's shoulder. "I need you here to protect your mother and sister."

"I'll do my best, Father."

He smiled as he recalled Tullus's zeal.

He returned his attention to the present. So far, the demonstrators had remained relatively peaceful. At some point, that would change. It would have to. Some demonstrations began large and boisterous, then weakened as the days continued. These pesky Jews did the opposite. They gained in number and resolve each passing hour. Soon, either they would turn violent or Pilate would order the soldiers to.

Lucius descended the bleachers and swaggered through the heart of the stadium. He cast a menacing glare toward an elder telling a story of a past Jewish rebellion. The more these stories filled the air, the greater the likelihood of an uprising.

The sun, now glaring straight above, reflected from his armor, bouncing gleams of mirrored light all around. He positioned his sword such that it mirrored the sun's beams directly into the eyes of the elder telling the story. This game was one of several that helped him pass the time and annoy the Jews.

"Go bathe." Lucius kicked a younger man from his path, a peasant covered in ash and grime. The stench of the Jews filled the stadium and mingled with the odor of fish and fire. An occasional gust swept in from the sea, cleansed the stale air, and gave his nostrils brief respite. Then the odor crept back through the stadium.

He stood silently, the dull roar of a thousand conversations filling his ears. He scanned the edges of the hippodrome. Soldiers posted around the perimeter stood at attention, eyes fixed on the crowds. Each grasped a spear with one hand and rested the other hand on his sword. Additional legionaries meandered through the mass of demonstrators. Any Jew could look any direction and see multiple Roman soldiers watching over him.

A Roman servant approached. "Sir, a message from the governor."

"What is it?"

The messenger whispered in his ear. "The governor wishes to address the crowd. Clear a path from his palace to his box in the east bleachers. Once he takes his place, have the soldiers surround the demonstrators. Encircle them so that no Jew can flee. Have your swords ready and be prepared to follow orders."

The servant scampered back through the crowd to Pilate's palace, a majestic vision of white marble surrounded by columns and gardens.

Lucius signaled a few nearby soldiers. He drew them close and passed along the instructions he'd received. He dismissed the soldiers, took a deep breath, and grinned.

At that moment, he felt as though someone was watching. He turned and locked eyes with a pale-skinned Jew leaning on a cane, a few paces away. The Jew studied the centurion. The man seemed familiar to Lucius, but only vaguely. He served for a long time in Caesarea and crossed paths with many Jews. This one was like all the rest. Still, the inquisitive look in the Jew's eyes unsettled him. He nodded toward the man, then disappeared into the crowd.

Minutes later, trumpets blared from the palace. Pilate marched through a corridor created by the soldiers.

When the Jewish masses heard the trumpets and caught a glimpse of Pontius Pilate, they erupted into a cheer, one united voice that swelled and poured out of the stadium and across the countryside. Lucius cocked his head and raised his brow. They had never cheered for Pilate before. Then he heard a few Jews shout above the cheers.

"Finally he emerges from his palace."

"He heard us."

"Our cries reached his ears."

"Remove the symbols. Protect the vestments. Purify the temple!"

Lucius tried to hide his grin. *These fools actually think Pilate cares about their concerns.* From the corner of his eye he could see soldiers drifting toward the edges of the crowd. He rested his hand on his sword and joined them. The centurion moved deftly, careful not to raise suspicion. The Jews were caught up in their chants and oblivious to the soldiers' movements.

9

"**C**lear the path for the governor," the lead guard grumbled. "Step back. Quit staring. Show respect." He shoved any Jew who came too close.

Lucius stood at attention on the edge of the crowd next to the hippodrome's bleachers, muscles tensed and eyes scanning the throng for danger.

Pilate, surrounded by his personal guard, navigated through the demonstrators and climbed to his box in the east bleachers. He pursed his lips and raised both arms into the air. The sun reflected from his bronze breastplate, and the breeze lifted his crimson cloak into a flutter behind him. When the last murmurs stilled, he lowered his hands and raised his voice.

"I hear your cries." The Jews erupted into cheers, then silenced so Pilate could continue. "I understand your objections to the symbols placed at Antonia." Smiles appeared on the Jews' faces. "But I don't care." The smiles disappeared. Some gasped. Pilate continued. "The symbols are sacred to Rome. We erect them wherever we go for the pleasure and protection of our gods, and to honor our emperor Tiberius Caesar. Jerusalem is no exception."

The Jews grew still, eyes wide. The governor motioned to the soldiers who had circled the demonstrators. "Guards, stand ready." Lucius rested his hand on his sword. The Jews looked around, soldiers had hemmed them in. They huddled together. "Jews, disperse. Go back to your farms, back to your synagogues. I'm tired of your noise and your stench."

No one moved.

"Go home!"

The Jews looked at each other.

"Guards, raise your swords."

Lucius pulled his sword from its leather sheath, as did a thousand other soldiers. The sound and shimmer caused even the bravest Jew to cower.

"You Jews," Pilate growled. "You hold to your traditions and your myths while all the world passes you by. You think you can sway me by your chants? I will sway you by my swords. Scatter. Go home. Now. Or feel the blade on your necks."

Lucius stood with steel eyes, both fists wrapped around the handle of his sword. Sweat trickled between the raised veins on his forearms. Today, this moment, Rome will finally force the Jews into submission. He bent at his knees and hips, his weight centered on the balls of his feet, ready to pounce.

Seconds felt like minutes.

An old Jew who stood just a few paces from Lucius dropped to the ground. His tattered robe, once white but now caked in ash and dirt, fell in a wrinkled mess atop his bony body. He rolled onto his back and pushed his chin into the air, exposing his neck. "I would rather your blade slice my neck than your symbols desecrate my temple." His shrill, shaking voice rose from the stadium with supernatural volume.

One by one, in eerie silence, thousands of Jews fell to the ground and thrust their chins into the air.

Lucius remained in ready position. He adjusted his grip on his sword. His eyes roved from Jew to Jew. His ears perked waiting for orders.

Pilate glared.

Lucius widened his gaze. These Jews were ridiculous. Didn't they see the soldiers? Didn't they know of Rome's brutality, and of Pilate's lack of patience? Had they never felt the sting of a sharpened sword? What gave them such . . . courage?

That last word, courage, burst into Lucius's mind before he realized it was a compliment. Wherever the term came from, it was accurate. *Courage. Ludicrous, sure. Nonsensical, without question. But courageous.*

Pilate watched from his box. He hadn't spoken or moved since the old Jew cried out in defiance. He scanned left and right, soaking in the scene in front of him.

Finally, he beckoned his messenger and whispered into his ear. With no acknowledgement to the crowd, the governor climbed down from his perch in the bleachers and marched through the pathway created by his guard.

The Jews and soldiers watched Pilate disappear into his palace, then all eyes turned to the messenger in Pilate's box. The messenger stiffened his body and focused his eyes above the crowd. "By order of our infinitely gracious governor, Pontius Pilate, the Roman symbols that today hang from the towers of Antonia in Jerusalem . . . will be removed by sundown tomorrow."

The messenger hurried from the bleachers and followed Pilate. The Jews rose back to their feet. Their mouths gaped. They stared at the spot where Pilate had stood.

Lucius re-sheathed his sword. The proclamation shocked him as much as it shocked the Jews. Why would Pilate relent and give the Jews victory? Perhaps he feared the ramifications of a slaughter in front of his palace. Or, maybe it was an issue of timing, and Pilate had something more devious planned. Either way, Lucius sensed this wasn't the end of the conflict between Pilate and the Jews. "Soldiers, stand down," his voice boomed.

The Jews, still tentative, glanced around. The elder who first defied Pilate and offered his neck to the sword stood with both arms raised. "Hear, O Israel: The Lord our God, the Lord is one."

The demonstrators cheered. Another elder began to sing. All joined in.

May God arise, may his enemies be scattered;
May his foes flee before him.

As smoke is blown away by the wind,
May you blow them away;
As wax melts before the fire,
May the wicked perish before God.

But may the righteous be glad and rejoice before God;
May they be happy and joyful.

Sing to God, sing praise to his name,
Extol him who rides on the clouds—his name is the Lord—
And rejoice before him.

As the Jews sang and danced, Lucius signaled the soldiers nearest him to exit the stadium. These soldiers passed the message to others, and soon all the legionaries filtered out of the hippodrome. The Jews barely noticed their exit.

As Lucius left the stadium, he noticed a young man several paces ahead attempting to mingle with the soldiers and engage them in conversation. A Roman boy with a familiar gait and wavy, dark hair. Tullus.

———————

That evening, as the sun melted into the western horizon, Lucius sat next to a fire outside of Nona's hut. His children and their mother warmed themselves by the fire.

"Got any bread?" Lucius asked.

Nona pointed to a basket near the fire. "Just a couple more loaves. We could use some, too."

Lucius pulled a loaf from the basket and tore it into pieces. He kept the largest for himself and passed the rest around.

"Anything else to eat?"

"No, that's all I prepared for the day. Make it last."

A murmur of conversation hung over the settlement, seeping into the air from the families and friends who circled the fires that dotted the streets. Occasionally, the cackle of a lady rose above the murmur, as she attempted to lure a suitor into a business transaction. The humid air gathered the smoke into an umbrella above the settlement, giving the sense that the conversations and cackles fell from the clouds.

"Do you have to leave again, Father?" Paulla linked her arm inside his and rested her head on his shoulder.

"I have no choice." When Lucius recognized the gruffness of his response, he brushed the hair from his daughter's eyes and kissed her forehead. "Hopefully the governor won't keep me there forever."

"He'll do whatever he pleases," Nona said, "with no concern for how it affects soldiers and their families."

"Soldiers can't have families." Lucius reminded her of Tiberius's policy with his usual poor timing and lack of consideration. He took a gulp of water from a mug that sat at his feet.

Nona stood and snatched the basket that sat between them, but not before he snagged the last loaf. "Let's leave the men to talk, Paulla." Nona glared at Lucius until he understood what he was supposed to discuss with his son. Paulla squeezed her father's arm, then followed her mother into the hut.

Lucius picked up a stick from the ground, a stick as long as his arm and sturdy enough to poke the fire. He nudged one burning log so that it leaned against another. He cleared his throat and eyed his son.

"I saw you today, Tullus."

The boy raised his gaze to his father's, the dancing flames still separating them. "Where? I was here most of the day."

"At the hippodrome."

Tullus's cheeks flushed.

"That was no place for a boy."

"I'm not a boy. I can do everything a man can do. Some things better than most men."

Lucius stifled a chuckle. "Like what?"

His son picked up a stick and drew spirals and squares in the dirt. He sat with his knees together and drew to the side. "I can chop wood and build a fire. I can throw a spear. I can fight."

"Fight?"

"Just ask my friends. They all know not to cross me."

"You've fought them?"

"Well, sort of. I was racing one of my friends, and he cheated. He took off before he was supposed to and got four steps ahead. I'm the fastest boy around, so I caught up to him, and I wrestled him to the ground. I pinned him to the dirt." He snarled his nose. "Then I hit him. Right in the nose. Just once, but that's all it took. Nobody will ever cheat against me again. Nobody."

Lucius couldn't help but smile. The boy was his, alright. His mind traced back to the first time he felt the crack of someone's nose. He made a fist with his hand, then released it.

"Maybe you're right. Your mother doesn't want to believe it, but you're becoming a man." He poked the fire again, creating a swell of sparks that rose and disappeared into the night. "Even so, the hippodrome today was too dangerous for a man of your age."

"It wasn't dangerous enough."

Lucius didn't have to ask what Tullus meant. Pilate's decision to back down surprised him and every other soldier in the arena.

"Why do you think he did it?" Tullus asked.

"What did you want to happen?"

"Well, I didn't hike all the way down there to see a bunch of Jews get their way. The governor should've lopped off at least some of their heads. That would've sent the rest of them scattering like a school of minnows. Execute a few old men and he'd never have a problem with those Jews again."

"I'm not so sure." Lucius tossed his stick into the fire and sat down.

"What do you mean?"

"If we'd have swung our swords, drawn blood, even executed some of them . . . well, I wonder how the rest would've responded. Instead of scaring them off, if we killed some of their elders, it might've sparked a battle that would fill the whole arena with blood. Some of it Roman. And it wouldn't stop there. More Jews would march to Caesarea, including bands of rebels, who aren't well trained but are well armed and passionate. More soldiers would have to respond. There's no telling how long it would go on."

"You mean you didn't want Pilate to unleash your swords?"

"Of course I wanted him to. Those Jews are an embarrassment to Rome. They won't worship our gods. They won't bow to our Caesars. They've manipulated Rome into making exceptions to all kinds of laws. Those symbols in Jerusalem are just one example among too many."

Tullus bit his lip and waited for his father to continue.

Lucius glanced around to make sure nobody else could hear the conversation, then whispered, "I've just never seen anything like them. It's like they actually believe what they say about their god. And they're willing to die for what they believe. Those elders laid their necks bare today, inviting us to send their heads rolling. They would rather accept the sword than allow a few flags to wave near their temple."

"Well if I'd been the governor . . . " Tullus didn't have to finish the sentence. Lucius knew what he meant. And it sent his heart simultaneously swelling with pride and cowering with fear.

Lucius tossed a leather pouch filled with coins across the fire to his son. Tullus snagged it from the air with the grace of a boy—a man—well on his way to dodging javelins and dancing with swords.

"Tell your mother I'll send more money. And I'll visit when I can."

10

October, AD 29

Lucius stood in a tower at Antonia. He nodded to a guard, then scanned the temple courts bustling below. "Why all the activity?" A few weeks into his posting in Jerusalem, he was still learning how the city operated.

"Mostly just their daily routine." The guard pointed to men carrying buckets of water and coaxing animals. "Those are the Levites. They help the priests and keep things moving. And the ones in fancier clothes are the priests. They chant prayers, sacrifice animals, and lead ceremonies." The soldier raised his eyebrows every time he spoke. His Syrian accent both amused and annoyed Lucius.

"Your name?"

"Avitus."

"And you've been here a while?"

"Yes sir. Stationed in Jerusalem for three years now." Avitus seemed to enjoy sharing information. And Lucius had a lot to learn.

"Is it always this busy?"

"Always busy, but not always this much. It's almost time for their Feast of Tabernacles. The priests and Levites have a lot to prepare. Jews are arriving from all over, pitching their tents around the city."

Lucius had noticed the tents dotting the hillsides and fields outside of the city walls. They increased daily. "What are they celebrating?"

"I asked once. They're celebrating a time in their history when they lived in tents for forty years in the wilderness. They'll feast and dance and celebrate for eight days. And they'll sacrifice animals in the temple."

The two soldiers stood silently for a moment. "That incessant bleating of sheep is enough to drive a person mad." Lucius rubbed his ears. "Not to mention the haggling with the animal sellers. Do they ever tire?"

"Sadly, no." Avitus smiled.

The Jewish temple impressed Lucius. Walls and pillars fashioned from white marble. Curtains of deep blue separated courts from other courts. Vine and grape clusters, formed from gold and as tall as men, decorated doorways. Bronze, silver, and other precious metals gleamed in the afternoon sun. "Did they build the temple themselves?"

"Hardly," Avitus replied. "It was Herod the Great, a generation ago. There was a temple here already, that the Jews did build themselves. But from what I hear, it was shabby. Herod wanted this new one to remind the Jews of the temple built by their great king, Solomon, a thousand years ago."

Lucius had visited impressive Roman temples, including some larger than this one, but the shrine in Jerusalem to the god of Israel brandished a unique glory. It held its own among the temples across the empire. "Why did he build it?"

"Wanted to improve relations with the Jews."

"An expensive gesture to appease peasants."

"Well, he also wanted to impress Rome. He tried to create legacy as a great builder with all these grand construction projects." Avitus rested his hands on the edge of the wall.

"He built some impressive things in Caesarea, too."

"I've heard. The harbor, right?"

"And a hippodrome, palace, and theater, all right next to each other. They're on the shore of the Great Sea, which provides a scenic backdrop." Lucius missed the sea breeze that refreshed Caesarea. The air in Jerusalem was stale and dusty. "Why does it always smell salty here?"

"The nearest water is the Dead Sea. It's about a day's walk, southeast. It's so salty nothing can live in it. Or around it. Most everything between here and the sea is scraggly and dusty. Wilderness."

Lucius lifted a canteen to his lips. He could get used to Jerusalem if he had to. Endure it. But he hoped he wouldn't stay that long.

"I'd better look around," Avitus said. "There's more to patrol than just the temple." He strode to the north side of the guard tower.

Lucius remained on the south side of the tower, watching the activity in the temple below. He took a deep breath and felt at peace. The Jews were under control, at least at the moment. After Pilate backed down in the hippodrome, he worried the Jews might feel emboldened and rebel. But they were focused on their upcoming festival and hadn't caused any more problems.

He hadn't seen Septimus today. By design. He'd learned the centurion's routine and managed to avoid him most days. When Lucius lay in bed at night, his imagination scrolled through various schemes to undermine his superior. But not this afternoon. No need to scheme today. He closed his eyes and felt the sun on his face.

"Sir, you might want to come over here." Avitus interrupted his moment of calm.

Unhurried, Lucius returned his canteen to his belt and paced to the northwest corner of the fortress. "What is it, soldier?" Lucius could see nothing out of the ordinary.

"There, that rabbi in the street." Avitus pointed to a teacher who wore a simple white robe with a blue sash, common for a Jewish peasant. His dark hair brushed his shoulders, and his tanned, olive skin evidenced days spent outside. The rabbi's muscular forearms betrayed a past that included physical labor. A few people followed him. "We're supposed to keep an eye on him."

"Why? What do you know about him?"

"Not much, really. He's from Nazareth. Not a cultured background. He spends most of his time up in Galilee, but comes south every now and then. He was a carpenter before he began teaching." Avitus leaned on the top of the wall and looked down. "Some say he does miracles. Turned pitchers of water into wine at a wedding feast, healed some who were blind or had leprosy. Cast demons out of people. Not sure what's true. You know those Jews and their stories."

"Why are people following him?"

"Curiosity, maybe. They say his teaching is different from other rabbis. He isn't demanding like most Jewish teachers, or harsh. Except he can be harsh when he talks to the other teachers. But most of the time, people say he has compassion in his voice. And grace in his touch."

"What do the temple officials think about him?"

"They don't like him. I think they're jealous, mostly. And they feel threatened. They don't like it when their people start listening to somebody else." Avitus sighed. He kept his eyes fastened on the teacher, but his interest appeared to be waning.

Lucius fixed his gaze on the rabbi. "What's his name?"

"Jesus."

The rabbi walked toward a pool just north of the temple. He moved slowly through the crowd, stopping often to talk to people. His smile never left his face.

"Why are so many people crowded around that pool? I see them there every day."

"It's called Bethesda. It's a reservoir. Water is piped in from springs in the north to provide for the temple and the city. Some parts are deeper than a man can swim and keep his breath. In the shallower areas they clean sheep before taking them to the temple for sacrifices." Avitus craned his neck and pointed to the right. "You can't see it from here, but a gate over there goes into the temple. They call it the Sheep Gate. That's where they bring in the sheep they cleaned."

Lucius looked the direction Avitus pointed, then back at the pool. "But why all the people at Bethesda?"

"Some think the water is magical. That it can heal people. A few times a day, bubbles appear on its surface. People believe it's an angel stirring the water, but it's probably just air bubbles and water rising from the springs beneath it. The Jewish officials think these rumors of healings are absurd, and they don't like any talk of magic, but they just look the other way. They have other things to worry about."

The two soldiers stood in silence, watching Jesus.

"Thanks for your help, Avitus. I have a lot to learn." He glanced at the legionary. "I'm going down for a closer look. I won't forget your help, and I may call on you again. You seem to know the city well."

"Yes sir. I'm glad to help."

Lucius arrived at Bethesda a few steps behind Jesus. He stayed on the edge of the crowd hoping to stay inconspicuous, but a Roman centurion in a Jewish crowd seldom remained unnoticed. People kept a wary eye on Lucius and moved to get out of his way. He walked through the crowd as though a bubble surrounded him.

He leaned against a column that supported a colonnade, which separated two large, rectangular pools. He crossed his arms. Bethesda reeked of unwashed bodies and sheep. The centurion covered his nose and mouth with a scarf.

"Jesus, just touch my cloak. I'm sick. Heal me." People pressed close to the rabbi. "Teach us. We want to hear more."

Jesus's gaze rested on a paralytic lying on a mat. His atrophied body lay in a tangled mess, as if someone dropped him in that spot without bothering to straighten his arms or legs. The rags he wore barely covered his body. People in the crowd avoided him. No one looked the paralytic in the eye. Except Jesus.

The rabbi waded through the crowd and sat next to the paralytic. He rested his hand on his shoulder.

Those who had crowded closely to Jesus stepped back. A lady whispered, "Rabbis don't touch such people!"

Her companion responded with a sniff. "He's not like other rabbis."

Lucius maneuvered through the throng until he could hear Jesus speak.

"God's peace to you, my friend." The rabbi had a Galilean drawl.

The paralytic turned his head toward Jesus, grimacing at the pain of the movement.

"Life has been difficult for you."

The paralytic scanned the faces of people who had gathered—those who saw him every day but ignored him. He looked back at Jesus. Words leaked from the side of his greasy mouth. "Thirty-eight years since I've taken a step."

Jesus squeezed his shoulder.

"Some days, when he remembers, my friend brings me here. Hopes the magic will work and the water will heal me."

"Do you want to be well?" Jesus asked softly.

An odd question, thought Lucius, *with an obvious answer.* Of course, the paralytic would want to be well. The pain, the shame. The looks and comments he must receive. But the man didn't respond right away. He stared into the dirt.

He finally responded, but not with a yes or no. "Sir, I have no one to help me get into the pool when the water is stirred. I try to drag my body toward the water, but I have no strength in my arms or legs. Others get to the water before me."

Jesus lifted the man's chin. "Friend, rise. Pick up your mat. Walk."

A woman in the crowd gasped.

The paralytic steeled his eyes on Jesus. His jaw clenched. He looked at his feet. Gray, mangled, and withered. Lucius's eyes widened as, slowly, the gray color in the man's feet lightened. A fleshly tone crept from the end of his toes, to the bridges of his feet, and then to his heels and ankles. Twisted bones gradually straightened. His mangled legs uncurled, and muscles appeared in his torso, arms, and fingers.

Lucius stared, his body frozen.

The now former paralytic rose to a seated position. Gingerly, but gaining confidence with every movement, he planted one foot on the ground, then the other. Wobbling like a newborn deer, the man stood for the first time in thirty-eight years.

Someone applauded. Others joined. The healed man picked up his straw mat. He rolled it up then raised it in the air. "Hallelujah!"

Lucius scowled, pushed his way through the crowd, and marched to Antonia. He made his way back to the guard tower. He leaned gingerly on the edge of the wall. He watched as the rabbi walked through the crowd. Then Jesus raised his head and looked toward the tower. His eyes met with Lucius's. The centurion took a step back.

He skipped the evening meal and retreated to his quarters. His room was less than extravagant. Stone walls, no windows, and flimsy furnishings. It was private, and he needed to think.

Was the healing a trick? An illusion? He'd heard of illusionists in Rome. Occasionally one came to Caesarea, but their tricks seldom stood up to scrutiny. Anyone with a trace of intelligence could see through the deception.

Or, maybe it wasn't an illusion, but an act of the gods. Certainly Jupiter could perform such a feat, or Apollo, the god of healing. Many Romans believed the gods performed miracles, but he'd always been a skeptic. He prayed to the gods and spoke of them, but more as ritual and allegiance to Rome than a belief in their actual existence.

Jesus didn't pray to the gods or credit them for the healing. And surely the gods, if they were real, wouldn't perform a miracle through a Jewish rabbi who denied their existence. This rabbi, if he's legitimate, has access to some kind of power unlike anything the world has seen.

11

Deborah stirred garlic into an olive oil dipping sauce. "Are the lamps filled?"

"Yes," Esther replied, "though we need to buy more oil at the market next week. And Benjamin topped off the water jugs."

"The bread looks perfect." Deborah placed several loaves into a basket and covered them with a cloth. She filled a bowl with dates, figs, and almonds.

Three sharp trumpet blasts, coming from the synagogue, pierced the night air. "Sabbath begins." Deborah smiled at her friend. The rhythms of life in Caesarea's Jewish village gave her a sense of security, of normalcy, which she'd needed the last several weeks. Tobiah's beating and the trial at the Roman camp affected her more than she allowed Tobiah to see. She cried on Esther's shoulder more than once.

"It all smells delicious." Tobiah limped into the house and hugged Deborah. He seldom needed the cane anymore.

Benjamin followed. He sniffed the air. "Goat, cheese, onions, and squash. You ladies have prepared quite the feast." He and Tobiah wore their newest, cleanest tunics.

"And honey treats for later," Esther said.

Deborah lifted cloths from the dishes that sat on the table. She poured wine into four cups. It wasn't the best wine available, but the best they could afford, saved for Sabbath. Esther lit two candles and sat them in the middle of the table, the flames cast a glow across their faces.

Tobiah raised his hands and prayed. "Blessed are you, Lord our God, king of the universe, who has sanctified us with your law and commanded us to kindle the light of the holy Sabbath. We ask that you bless our families and our homes, protect us and give us strength to reflect your light and bless your world."

Following the leisurely feast, the two couples joined other families in the courtyard in the center of their homes. By the light of lanterns, one of the elders read from the Torah, families sang hymns, and women recited prayers.

Deborah smiled as she watched the village children gather in a circle around Tobiah. "David placed one of those smooth stones in his sling, then whipped the sling around and around." His gestures were animated, and his voice danced. "Finally, he let that stone fly and planted it in the center of Goliath's forehead. Like a giant cedar, Goliath fell, and the whole countryside shook."

"Tell us more! Please, another story." The children laughed when Tobiah was funny, and their faces grew solemn when he described the sacrifices of their people and the goodness of God.

Deborah caressed her swollen belly, relishing this moment of quiet joy and thanksgiving. She loved Tobiah—she had since she was a girl. She loved him even more now, as their child grew in her womb. She was committed to him and the life they had together in Yahweh. Not just committed, but enthralled with their shared future. These feelings only intensified when she almost lost him at the hands of the brutish centurion.

That evening, after the festivities died down, Deborah and Tobiah held one another as they lay in bed.

"What would I have done if you weren't here anymore?"

"My family would have taken care of you."

Men are so practical. "It's not just that. You're more to me than a provider. You are a provider, and I appreciate that. But you're my husband. I can't imagine waking every morning without you here."

"But I am here. And I will be here."

Deborah brushed hair from Tobiah's eyes. "How did you get along today?"

"Pretty well. My ribs are mostly healed. They still hurt a little if I twist or turn in a certain way, but otherwise I don't notice them anymore. My leg is getting stronger. I feel like I have more energy as each day goes by."

Even if he did still hurt, he wouldn't admit it.

"More importantly," Tobiah continued, "how are you feeling?"

Deborah appreciated Tobiah's concern. Men didn't typically talk about women's pregnancies, even with their wives. They preferred blissful ignorance. But Tobiah was more curious than most and asked a lot of questions when the two were alone. Deborah didn't mind. It pleased her to share as much of this experience with him as she could.

"I get tired more quickly than I used to," she said. "Today, when Esther and I prepared for Sabbath, she had to tell me to sit down a couple times. I needed to catch my breath."

She smiled. "I think I felt the baby move yesterday."

"Really?" Tobiah's eyes grew wide. "You felt it move? What did it feel like? Did it hurt?"

"No, it didn't hurt, really. It just felt . . . odd. Like a big butterfly fluttering around in my belly."

They remained silent for a few moments. Deborah's mind filled with images of their son or daughter. She envisioned preparing their child's favorite dishes for Sabbath, seeing their little one take steps, speak words, pray to God, and gather with the other children to hear Tobiah tell stories of the patriarchs.

Her husband lay by her side poking his stomach. Deborah raised herself on an elbow and watched him. "Are you imagining what it would feel like to have a butterfly in there?" Tobiah smiled sheepishly. Deborah chuckled.

"What do you think life will be like for our child?" Deborah asked.

Tobiah took a deep breath. "I don't know. Honestly, I worry. Rome just grows more powerful and more violent. They used to leave us alone and let us worship as we believe. But what happened to me at the games seems to happen more and more." Tobiah rested his hands behind his head. "When Pilate hung the symbols at Antonia, I felt like I needed to stand with my brothers in the hippodrome. When I got there, I could sense an anger boiling during the protest that frightened me. There has always been talk of revolt, and some rebels have reared up from time to time, but it's escalating." He stared at the ceiling. "I hear that more groups, and larger groups, are forming in Galilee. They're arming themselves and making plans."

Tobiah rolled onto his side and faced his wife. "Yahweh promised to preserve us and to restore us. I pray he sends his anointed one soon." He sighed. "Please Lord, come soon."

A banging on his door woke Lucius with a start. He was too groggy to respond right away, his mind hazy with memories of a paralytic standing and a rabbi waving off the cheers of a crowd.

The knocking came again. He didn't have to ask who it was. Septimus so enjoyed waking him. "What do you want?"

"Activity is picking up in the city." His superior officer's voice bellowed enough to wake the entire cohort. "More pilgrims came in last night for the festival. Take a couple legionaries and look things over. See if any problems have come up that we need to address."

"You must be joking."

"What's that, soldier?"

"Yes sir."

Lucius laced his boots and smoothed his uniform, which he hadn't intended to sleep in. He trudged to the dining hall. Unlike the banquet room where Pilate hosted feasts, the soldiers' dining hall boasted no oriental rugs or Greek art, and it offered little joy in its daily fare. The morning meal consisted of barley porridge and stale loaves of bread left from last night. Lukewarm, watered-down beer helped wash it down.

Lucius downed his portion then looked around for a couple of soldiers to commandeer for patrol. The Syrian walked by. "Avitus, you're coming with me."

"Where?" The soldier raised his brows.

"For a walk around the city."

Lucius hadn't talked with Decimus much lately, and he'd enjoy his friend's companionship. He scanned the dining hall until his eyes came to rest on his old comrade. When he caught Decimus's attention, Lucius waved him over. Decimus sighed, stuffed his last bit of bread into his mouth, then ambled across the dining hall.

"Where to?" Decimus asked.

"The city."

"Who's this?"

"Avitus. You'll love his accent."

The Syrian furrowed his brow.

"Get your armor. I don't anticipate trouble, but we should take precautions."

They reconvened outside of Lucius's room, marched through the labyrinth of hallways in Antonia, and emerged from its double-arched front entrance. They stood on the landing at the top of the stairway. Lucius looked as much like a veteran athlete as a soldier. Decimus exhibited a sturdy frame and a few more gray hairs than his comrade. Avitus's soft skin, rosy cheeks, and skinny frame contrasted his burlier and more experienced superiors.

Lucius glanced toward the temple. In the outer court, a group of Jews had encircled two men. One was Jesus, again wearing a white robe with a blue sash. Lucius didn't recognize the man with whom Jesus talked.

"Looks like a disturbance in the temple," Lucius said. "We'd better start there."

"As long as we stay in the outer court," Avitus said. "I stepped into their inner court once. You wouldn't believe the uproar."

The soldiers marched south for a few paces and entered the west side of the temple through a small gate. After a quick scan of the crowd, Lucius's eyes fell on Jesus. He led the other soldiers through the crowd of Jews until they stood near enough to hear the conversation.

"Why were they angry with you?" the rabbi asked.

"They said I broke the law of Moses by carrying my mat on the Sabbath."

Now Lucius recognized the second man. It was the paralytic. Today he was dressed normal and appeared healthy. An astounding transformation. Or was it? Maybe it was an illusion after all. Perhaps he hadn't been a paralytic to start with. With careful use of the shadows from the colonnades, a little gray clay, and even amateur acting ability, people could be fooled.

"In their zeal for the law, they forget that the Sabbath was made for man, not man for the Sabbath," Jesus responded.

Lucius didn't understand the rabbi's response, but it calmed the man.

"Did they say anything else?" Jesus asked.

"They asked me who you are."

"How did you answer?"

"I told them I didn't know. You disappeared into the crowd before I had a chance to thank you, much less to ask your name."

The rabbi grinned, obviously enjoying the conversation. "My name is Jesus. I was a carpenter from Nazareth before I began traveling through the towns and villages to proclaim the coming kingdom of God. You will find out who I am in due time."

"What am I supposed to do now?"

"Live righteously. Love the Lord your God with all your heart, soul, mind, and strength. And love your neighbor as yourself. Turn from your sin, lest you face something of greater consequence than paralysis."

With that, the rabbi waded through the crowd. As he brushed past Lucius, he looked the centurion in the eye and smiled. He slipped from the temple otherwise unnoticed. The rabbi had a way with quiet exits. A dozen men who looked Galilean followed Jesus.

"Not much of a disturbance," Decimus said. "What's going on, Lucius? Why do you care about somebody carrying a mat on the Jewish Sabbath?"

Lucius mumbled something unintelligible, then marched off. Decimus caught up. Avitus struggled to keep in step with the two centurions.

Twice now the rabbi had looked Lucius in the eye. These looks haunted him. It was as though Jesus knew him. But Lucius didn't want to be known. Especially by a Jew. Granted, this one seemed different, but Lucius couldn't figure out why. He'd crossed paths with a few rabbis in Caesarea, but none with the following and influence that Jesus had. It wasn't just that he had a following, though. Something else gnawed at Lucius. Something in the eye of the rabbi.

Lucius emerged from the south side of the temple. He adjusted his helmet to shield his eyes from the afternoon sun, then descended a grand stone staircase that spilled onto the street below. Decimus and Avitus followed. Small limestone houses, weathered into a yellow-brown tint, lined the narrow, unpaved streets of Jerusalem's lower city. Potters, weavers, tailors, and carpenters worked in open-air shops squeezed between the houses.

His ears filled with sounds of merchants bartering and hooves clattering, as peasants led donkeys and carts up and down the market street. "The finest tunics in all Jerusalem. In all Judea. The best prices, today only." A Jew exchanged a coin for a discolored tunic. "Yes sir, you have a deal. You'll be the envy of all Jerusalem."

Decimus snagged a cluster of grapes from a table. "But sir," the shopkeeper said, "these are my livelihood. My family's existence." Decimus glared at the shopkeeper then winked at the other two soldiers. He tossed a grape into his mouth. Avitus followed his superior's example and snagged a loaf of bread from another table.

"Fresh fish. Caught from the Great Sea just this morning." The merchant held out his basket to the soldiers. Lucius chuckled. Even the fittest soldiers took three days to travel from the Great Sea to Jerusalem. Those dried, withered fish were at least five days old.

"The city is busier today than usual," Avitus said. "The festival brings Jews from all around Judea and Galilee. Some come from even further away." He walked behind the two centurions. They

wandered the lower city's streets, a web of pathways with no rec-
ognizable pattern. Conversation remained scarce, aside from a
few grunts, fingers pointed at frightened shopkeepers and customers, and subsequent chuckles.

Decimus spoke up. "Heard anything from Nona, Lucius?"

"Nothing."

"Are you sure?"

"Yes, I'm sure. I haven't heard a thing since I left her in
Caesarea."

"That's interesting." Decimus smiled. "Because there she is."

Lucius turned the direction Decimus pointed. Nona stood a
few feet away, with the children by her side. Each had a canvas
sack, almost overflowing, resting at their feet. Nona gave a silver
coin to a shopkeeper, who handed her three small loaves and a
dried fish. She gave a loaf to each of her children and kept one for
herself. She tore the fish into three pieces. The mother and her
children ravaged the food.

Lucius stood spellbound.

Tullus was the first to see him. "Father!" The boy sat his food
on top of his canvas sack and ran. His sister followed.

Lucius, still speechless, allowed his children to hug him. He
stared at Nona. Neither blinked or expressed any emotion on
their faces.

"Who are they?" Avitus whispered.

"These are Lucius's children," Decimus responded, "and
standing over there is their mother. They live in Caesarea. At
least that's where they used to live. I don't know why they're in
Jerusalem."

"Lucius doesn't seem to know why they're here, either."

The children let go of their father. Lucius moved tentatively
toward Nona. When he stood directly in front of her, he raised
his brows.

She answered his unspoken question: "If you come to
Jerusalem, we come to Jerusalem."

"But . . . you can't." Still shocked to see her, Lucius couldn't form any more words.

"Why? What keeps us in Caesarea? We have no family there. We can try to scratch out a living in that settlement, but without you nearby to take care of us, we'll starve or come near to it." She paused, giving Lucius a chance to respond.

Various thoughts raced through his mind, but nothing clear enough to articulate. It seemed she had rehearsed this speech, likely while dragging the children across the seventy miles that separated Caesarea and Jerusalem.

"You can't just leave us there and forget about us. Who knows how long Pilate will keep you in Jerusalem?"

Lucius turned toward Decimus, who took the hint and stepped toward the pair. "Welcome to Jerusalem." He smiled and hugged Nona. "And how was your journey?"

"Long." Nona's eyes remained fixed on Lucius.

"How did you endure such a trip, especially with Tullus and Paulla traveling with you?"

"We managed." Nona finally glanced at Decimus.

Lucius appreciated the break from her glare and took a deep breath. He stepped back and stood next to Avitus, leaving Decimus to talk with Nona.

Her countenance softened, shoulders relaxed. "We traveled for seven days. Some nights we found inns. Other nights kind families gave us beds and warm meals. The gods protected us. We arrived in Jerusalem yesterday."

"Where are you staying in Jerusalem?"

"We found an inn south of the city. Everything in Jerusalem is full because of an upcoming festival." Nona lowered her voice. "I only have enough money for one more night. And we have nothing left for food."

Decimus reached into a pouch attached to his belt, placed a few coins in Nona's hands, and squeezed his palms around hers.

"This will help. We will find you again soon." He added in a whisper, "It may take him a few days to process this."

"Let's go," Lucius barked. "We're on patrol." He had to get out of this situation.

Decimus tussled Tullus's hair and gave his sister a squeeze on the shoulder. The three men marched away, the clatter of their armor warning bystanders to clear a path.

Decimus waved to Avitus. "You take the lead." After what he just witnessed, he needed some conversation with Lucius. The three soldiers weaved through the streets until they arrived at a rickety, wooden flight of stairs.

"These steps have been here for generations." Avitus's face was still pale. Apparently, he didn't care for uncomfortable conversations. "They connect the lower city to the upper city. You're going to see a big difference when we get to the upper city. It's where the wealthier Jews and most of the city's Romans live."

Decimus stopped at the top of the stairs. The legionary was right. In the lower city, commoners lived and worked in cramped quarters amid mazes of dusty, noisy streets. The upper city sprawled before them in elegance. Palaces boasted gardens, courtyards, and pools. The wide streets followed an orderly pattern.

Avitus pointed toward a mansion fashioned of white stone, surrounded by columns and courtyards. "That's the palace of the Jewish high priest. Caiaphas, the current high priest, doesn't actually live there. He lives a little further north. But their ruling council, called the Sanhedrin, still meets there."

The trio turned north on the spacious, stone-paved avenue. They arrived at a theater that resembled the one in Caesarea. The open-air, three-story, semi-circle structure was decorated with Roman arches and columns.

"Herod the Great built it," said Avitus. "They have Greek and Roman plays there. The wealthy Romans love the plays. They come in their fanciest clothes, and their servants dote all over them. I think they come to be seen as much as to see the plays." Avitus tilted his head. "A few Jews come, too. Only the rich ones who like to spend time with Romans. The Jews who live in the lower city don't have much good to say about their brothers who attend the plays."

Decimus could tell that Lucius wasn't paying attention. "That was odd," he said.

"What was odd?" Avitus asked.

Decimus ignored Avitus and turned toward Lucius. "It was odd that Nona would drag those two children of hers—of yours— all the way from Caesarea. Wonder why she would do that?"

Lucius remained motionless, staring at the theater.

"Any idea why she'd come to Jerusalem?" Decimus was determined to discuss how Lucius had behaved when he saw Nona.

"No idea," Lucius mumbled. He squinted in the afternoon sun as his gaze roved over the theater's columns and arches.

"And what was almost as surprising as Nona and the kids making the trip was your reaction to seeing them."

Lucius dropped his gaze to the ground. "I just wasn't expecting her."

"Obviously," Decimus said with a sarcasm Lucius wouldn't have permitted from anyone else.

"I don't like surprises." Lucius crossed his arms. "Of course, I want Nona to be OK. And I wish I could see my children more. It was painful to leave them behind when we transferred to Jerusalem."

"Then there was no reason to respond so coldly. You should've been celebrating when you saw them." Decimus put his hand on his friend's shoulder. "How long have we known each other, Lucius?"

"Too long."

Avitus's voice raised. "If we keep walking, we'll see more of the upper city."

Decimus had no intention of continuing the walk, at least not yet. He faced Lucius. Lucius raised his eyes, turned them briefly toward Decimus, then returned his gaze to the theater.

"She could tell, you know," Decimus said.

"She could tell what?"

"That you don't want her here."

"It's not that I don't want her here. It's just that—"

"It's just that what?"

"I don't know what to say, Decimus. Maybe I'm worried about Nona. And about Tullus and Paulla. I know how things work in Caesarea. And so do they. We know where to go and where not to go. We know people in the city, and the city knows us." Lucius sighed. "But that's not the case in Jerusalem. I don't even know my way around the streets yet." He looked his friend in the eye. "And these Jews don't want us here. They don't just despise Roman soldiers, they despise Romans. At least some of them do. Maybe I'm just worried."

He wasn't going to let Lucius off so easily. "Sounds noble, but I don't buy it."

Lucius glared at him.

Avitus cleared his throat and stepped backward. His face reddened, and his voice squeaked. "We can still make it to the market while some of the goods are out. The market in the upper city is much nicer than the one in the lower city."

The centurions ignored Avitus.

Decimus continued, "Well, I don't buy it completely. You might be worried, but that wasn't just worry that I saw back there. What was it?"

"I have no other explanation." Lucius turned his back to the theater and gazed south toward the mountains that stood to either side of a valley. "Maybe I don't feel like taking care of them in Jerusalem."

Decimus knew Lucius too well. He pounced. "That's it, isn't it? You don't want to have to worry about them. You don't want the responsibility. You selfish . . . I can't believe that woman has anything left in her heart for you."

Lucius didn't answer for a few seconds. Then he changed the subject. "You see that valley?" Decimus looked south, where Lucius pointed. "It's called the Kidron Valley. When it rains, water washes from those mountains into the valley, and all the way to the Dead Sea. I feel like a twig caught in up that torrent and getting dumped into the sea. A twig in the Dead Sea. That's what I feel like right now."

This response caught Decimus off guard. He'd seen a lot from Lucius over the years. Selfishness, aggression, pride—these had always erupted from Lucius's heart and mouth with ease. But guilt? This was a new emotion for his comrade. Concern? Compassion? Caring for anything other than himself? Maybe his friend was growing. Just maybe.

13

Lucius threw his shoulders back and marched past Jerusalem's theater. "We continue."

Decimus and Avitus scurried to catch up. By the time the two reached their comrade, he'd settled into a more leisurely stroll, headed west along the wide thoroughfare in Jerusalem's upper city. On each side of the street, white marble mansions rose toward the sky, adorned with immaculate pools and gardens, tended by assiduous servants.

"And here, sirs, is the upper city market." Avitus waved his hand as though the market were his to reveal. "You can buy more luxurious products here than in the lower city. Oils, perfumes, jewelry. Silk from the east." By this time of day, the booths had been picked through, and the shopkeepers stashed their wares into baskets to take home for the evening.

A woman in a flowing robe stood at the edge of the market, a veil covering her face. "Refresh yourself with wine, from the best grapes in all Israel." She pointed the soldiers toward an earthen jar at her feet. "Rest from your travels, enjoy red wine as splendid as Rome's."

Lucius tossed her a coin. She retrieved a cup from her satchel, dipped a ladle into the jar, and poured crimson wine into the cup. She did the same for Decimus and Avitus.

"Tell us what we see before us." Lucius took a swig of wine, swished it in his mouth, and spit it on the ground.

"Over there is the Garden Gate." Avitus pointed north. Just inside the gate, animal vendors kept donkeys, sheep, and camels tied to posts. The dusty afternoon breeze carried their bleats and odors across the market. "And south of the Garden Gate,

Herod's Palace." The palace fortress dominated the western side of Jerusalem almost as much as the temple dominated the eastern side. "Herod the Great built it, like he built most of the impressive structures around the city. He stayed there when he came to Jerusalem."

Lucius scanned Herod's palace, which sat on a platform the height of four men. Guard towers climbed from the palace toward the sky. Marble porticos and bronze statues adorned the grounds, along with groves of palm and olive trees and gardens of tulips, poppies, and daisies.

"The palace and its towers were constructed with massive blocks of white marble, each block thirty feet long, fifteen feet tall, and five feet deep." Avitus enjoyed rattling off numbers and information. "Herod demanded that the blocks be hewn, polished, and joined so the walls looked like they were a single stone. Inside are banquet halls, lodging, and baths for hundreds of guests and soldiers."

"Who lives there now?" Lucius asked.

"No one all the time, other than some soldiers and servants." Avitus took a drink. "Dignitaries lodge here when they pass through the city. Pilate sometimes stays at the palace instead of Antonia."

Lucius stood next to his fellow soldiers, appreciating the extravagance of the palace. As he admired it, his appreciation evolved into envy. "And tonight we'll sleep on cots in damp rooms of grey stone."

"And Nona?" Decimus responded.

Lucius's conscious panged. She might not even have a cot. Certainly not a room to herself. He hoped she and the children were safe.

His stomach growled. "The wine is refreshing." Lucius took the final gulp from his cup. "But not filling. I need something to eat."

"I know just the place." Avitus started across the market and spoke over his shoulder. "There are a few inns around the edges of the market that serve food. I'll take you to my favorite." He stopped in front of an inn that sat on the north side of the marketplace and butted against the city wall, a few paces from the Garden Gate.

Before they entered, Avitus faced the two centurions. "This inn is operated by a Jewish couple. There are a few things to keep in mind. Don't tease them about their laws or their god. Switch from wine to water before your vision gets blurry. And be kind to the wife. His name is Ephraim and hers is Miriam." Lucius thought the legionary was done and stepped toward the door, but Avitus continued. "They aren't able to have children, but they've poured themselves into managing this inn. Miriam wishes they could quit renting rooms and just serve food, but Ephraim thinks they still need the income, at least until he sells the land they own just north of the city."

Lucius eyed Decimus and smiled. Avitus's face turned red. "I come by any time I'm on patrol. They're friendly. And their roasted lamb is the best in town!"

Ephraim's inn didn't have the luster of most homes in the upper city. It appeared to have been constructed at least a couple generations before, its limestone blocks dulled by decades of wind and dust.

Avitus ducked his head to enter the wooden doorway. The two centurions followed and found themselves in a room of humble comfort. Worn drapes decorated plaster walls, and timbers stretched across the ceiling. The floor was inlaid stone. The setting sun cast an orange glow throughout the room. Candles were already lit, anticipating dusk.

A slender Jewish man sashayed into the room. His dark hair had gray at the edges and flopped to the side. "Avitus, my friend, it's been too long!" The Jewish man kissed Avitus on each cheek. Lucius felt uncomfortable already.

"Ephraim, I couldn't stay away from your roasted lamb any longer," Avitus said.

"I saved some for you today. I knew you would come."

"You have the intuition of a prophet, kind sir."

Ephraim turned his attention to Lucius and Decimus, his eyes resting on the crimson plumes that adorned their helmets. His voice lost its eagerness. "So, my friend, you bring centurions with you today. Either you are in trouble or I am."

"Neither," said Avitus. "These officers are new to Jerusalem, and I am showing them around. No tour would be complete without a stop at the city's best inn."

"You are too kind to me, sir. Too kind."

Lucius raised his brow. He'd never seen a Roman soldier treat a Jew with such kindness. As a friend. He glanced at Decimus. They'd need to talk with the young legionary later that evening.

"Please, please recline at the table. I will bring wine and bread." Ephraim left the room.

Avitus motioned his superiors toward the table. He offered a reassuring smile. The two centurions, clutching the swords at their sides, made their way across the room. They reclined next to the walnut table and rested their elbows on tattered orange cushions.

A short, plump, red-faced woman pranced into the room with baskets of bread in each hand. "Avitus, we have missed you. You're too skinny. You've not been eating. You will eat well tonight." She laid both baskets in front of the young legionary.

"And for my comrades, Miriam?"

"You can share, but not too much." She tossed the response over her shoulder and marched out of the room, leaving as quickly as she'd entered.

The centurions reached in front of Avitus and grabbed loaves before he had a chance to.

Ephraim sauntered back into the room, gracefully avoiding a collision with his wife. He carried a tray that held olive oil, saucers, cups, and pitchers of wine and water

"The bread is too dry. Too dry!" Ephraim's voice pitched high and projected the exuberance of an actor in the theater. "I told Miriam to bake more at midday. This morning's bread is not worthy of such distinguished guests. You need oil." With a flurry of skinny elbows and waving arms, the Jew sat a saucer before each soldier and filled them with olive oil. Next, in one sweep, he placed wooden cups before each of them and filled the cups with red wine. "Enjoy. I will return with your lamb."

Lucius and Decimus had yet to utter a word since they entered the inn. They munched the salty bread and gulped the crimson wine as if they wanted to finish before anyone saw them. Avitus dined unrushed, chewing slowly and savoring small sips between bites.

A servant entered the room. The boy wore a frayed tunic that had once been white. He carried a bucket and a towel. "Welcome to the inn, sirs." The servant removed Lucius's sandals, poured water onto his feet, then scrubbed them with the towel until they were clean. He pulled out a small bottle of oil and poured on a few drops. The fragrance of flowers filled the room. The boy massaged the oil into the centurion's feet. He then washed the others in the same manner.

Lucius finally felt relaxed. He took a deep breath, then a slow sip of wine.

Avitus tore a piece of bread from a loaf and dipped it in olive oil. He glanced at Lucius. "Where do you come from?"

"Caesarea."

"I know that. I mean, before you were stationed in Caesarea. Where is home?"

"Why does it matter?"

"It doesn't. I just wondered."

Decimus nudged Lucius. He didn't say the words, but Lucius knew what the nudge implied. *Quit being rude and answer the boy's question.*

Lucius, remembering Avitus's warning, filled his cup half with wine and half with water. "I spent my boyhood north of Rome. We could walk to the city in a couple hours. My family farmed."

"Of all the occupations by which gain is secured, none is better than agriculture—none more profitable, none more delightful, none more becoming to a free man," Avitus said.

"You've read Cicero?" Decimus asked.

"Who hasn't?" Avitus replied.

Both men looked at Lucius.

Lucius rolled his eyes, then continued. "We dabbled with a few things, but mostly we kept a vineyard, olive orchards, and grew grain." He chewed and swallowed a piece of bread. "When I was a boy, I worked in the fields with the servants. As I got older, I went with my father to the markets in Rome. We loaded a cart with whatever we were producing at the time, hitched the cart to a mule, and headed south. During harvest season we made the trip three or four times a week. We would leave well before the sun rose, arrive at the market just as the city awoke, then sell all we could until afternoon. We'd return home that evening."

Lucius shifted his body and leaned on his other elbow. "Eventually my father let me make the trip by myself, with just a slave or two to help. He was never satisfied with how much I sold. He always said he could've done better." He frowned. "I haven't thought about my father in a while. I prefer not to, I guess."

"It's difficult to be raised by a man who can't be pleased," Decimus said. "Who thinks you're not good enough."

Lucius remembered the excitement on Tullus's face when they saw each other that afternoon. *Perhaps I'm doing better than my father did.* Then he remembered the confusion on his son's face when he abruptly left. *Perhaps I'm not.*

"Was it a big farm?" Avitus asked.

Lucius cleared his throat. "Yes. Well, not early on. When I was small, we only had about forty acres. Then we expanded. Father began buying land from area peasants. Their farms were too small to make a living, so father snatched a few acres here, a few more there, until we had well over five hundred. He was a shrewd businessman."

"What happened to the peasants?"

"Some ended up as slaves, for us or for other farmers who were wise enough to expand." Lucius scratched his chin. "As for most of them, though, I don't know. Father never seemed to care. So I didn't either."

Avitus sipped his wine. He dipped another piece of bread into olive oil and devoured it. "So why did you become a soldier? Wouldn't you have been better off farming?"

"Why so many questions?" Lucius usually avoided these kinds of conversations. "Why do you care?"

"Just curious."

It was a pleasant evening. The wine was tasty, and the lamb would arrive soon. Lucius decided to continue indulging the inquisitive Syrian. "You're right. I would've made more money farming, especially if I continued working for my father and if he helped me build a farm of my own. But I don't know if he would've helped me."

Lucius swirled the wine in his cup and watched bubbles form on its surface. "As I got older, and he got older, he became harsher. And I got brash. One day he took a swing at me. His fist landed on my jaw. It wasn't the first time, but I decided it would be the last. I swung back and sent the old man to the ground with one punch." He looked Avitus in the eye. "I walked back to our house, packed some supplies, said goodbye to Mother, and marched to Rome. I never went back."

Decimus flashed a wry smile. "The bravest of men and the sturdiest of soldiers come from farms." He took another sip and gazed at Lucius over the brim of his cup. "At least that's what I hear."

"When I got to Rome," Lucius ignored Decimus, "I headed straight for a military camp. Told them I wanted to enlist. They evaluated me, I took the oath, they trained me, and here I am: in a musty inn in nowhere Jerusalem about to be served a mediocre dinner from a rotten Jew and answering annoying questions from a thickheaded Syrian."

Avitus dropped his head. Decimus slammed his elbow into Lucius's arm. "Must you?"

Lucius grinned.

Ephraim and Miriam swept back into the room. He carried platters spilling over with meat and vegetables. "Roasted lamb basted in garlic and lemon. On the side, onions and cucumbers in a vinegar sauce. Enjoy!"

"And another basket of bread," Miriam said. "I can bring more if you need it." She refilled the soldiers' cups from a pitcher that looked to hold more water than wine.

Lucius tore into his dinner with both hands. The conversation ceased, but Lucius's mind continued. Decimus hadn't even heard some of that story. He hadn't talked about his father in years. He wasn't even sure if his parents were still alive.

He always swore that if he had children, he would do better. But he swore a lot of things.

14

Nona wrapped her fingers around the coins Decimus placed in her hand. "Thank you," she whispered. She wiped a tear from the corner of her eye as she watched the three soldiers disappear into the crowd.

She hadn't intended to surprise Lucius. She knew her arrival in Jerusalem would shock him. She'd hoped to find work and a permanent place to stay first, then she would track him down at Antonia and break the news. The fluke meeting on the street complicated things.

She kept one of Decimus's coins in her hand and hid the others in her canvas bag. "Children, finish your food." They sat and munched on stale bread and dried fish.

"When will we see Father again?" Paulla asked.

"Soon. He had to go on patrol today, but we'll see him again before long."

Paulla appeared satisfied with the response. Her brother, engrossed with his food, showed no interest in the conversation.

Nona approached a nearby vendor and handed him a coin. "Honey and almond treats, please." The only money she had remaining was what Decimus gave her, but she knew he'd check in again, making sure they were cared for. And Lucius would come around soon enough.

She placed the treats in her children's hands. "I've put you through a lot these last few days. I appreciate how patient you've been. You deserve something sweet."

"Thank you, Mother!" Tullus devoured his candy. His sister ate half, savoring each bite, then wrapped the other half in a cloth and slid it in her satchel for later.

"Come along. We need to get back to the inn before dark. It's not safe out here once the sun goes down. And I don't know how long the innkeeper will keep a bed open for us."

Nona threw her canvas sack across her shoulder. Her children did the same. "Here, hold my hands. These streets aren't friendly." The three zigzagged through the crowded lower city, toward its southeast corner.

"This section is called Ophel. It's the oldest and grimiest part of the city." A kind shopkeeper who feared for the family had oriented Nona to the layout of the lower city. If she shared this information to her children, perhaps she could distract them from its dangers and odors. "All of Jerusalem's trash and sewage is brought here. After it collects, they take it through the Dung Gate, then burn it in the Valley of Hinnom outside the city walls."

Tullus perked his ears. "Trash and fire? I like this city more every day."

"Just be careful where you step." They weaved through piles of garbage and diseased people, passed through the gate, and emerged on the northern edge of the Valley of Hinnom.

"Oh, the smell." Paulla crinkled her nose.

"Hurry. This path will take us around the valley." Nona held a cloth over her face. "Cover your noses, children. Try not to breathe deeply." Paulla lifted the top of her tunic to her face and clamped her nose.

The three continued south until they arrived at a rugged lodging house with walls of gray stone and a thatched roof. Mules, donkeys, and goats were tied to posts outside.

A man sat at the gate, which was nothing more than an opening in the stone fence that surrounded the property.

He looked up at Nona and mumbled, "One bed left."

"Thanks." She gave him a coin.

Each of the lodge's four walls contained an open doorway, allowing a breeze to circulate and cleanse, at least marginally, the stale air inside. Nona led the children into the building and through rows of cots. "Stay close. Don't touch anything, and don't look at anyone." The other guests gawked at the nervous Romans as they passed. She prayed to the gods that no one would touch them.

They found the one vacant bed in the back corner. Paulla almost sat. "No, no. Not yet." Nona pulled two rags from her satchel and handed one to Tullus. "Help me, son. It hasn't been cleaned in months." They wiped down the bed as best as they could. She pulled a threadbare blanket from her bag and spread it across the bed. "You two lie beside each other on the bed. You need to rest tonight." The previous night, the noises of the animals and of the other guests—some of the sounds unfamiliar to the children, and embarrassing to Nona—had prevented the three from sleeping well. She hoped that tonight their exhaustion would eclipse the noise and discomfort so they could rest.

Paulla obeyed and lay on the bed. Her brother didn't. "But where will you sleep, Mother? You need rest more than I do. I don't want you on the floor like last night."

"I'll be fine, Tullus. Now just do as I say and lie down."

Tullus sat on the side of the bed. He put his hands on his knees, then looked at his sister, who had already stretched out beside him. He turned back to his mother. "No, you will sleep on the bed tonight."

"Tullus—"

"I insist."

She'd heard the tone and seen the narrowed eyes before. Not from Tullus, but from his father. She knew better than to argue. And, she admitted to herself, Tullus's gesture made her proud. Her son was growing into a man. A man, she thought with a twinge of hope, who showed concern for someone other than himself.

Tullus stood. Nona lay on the bed and draped her arm around her daughter. "Rest well, my sweet girl." She could feel Paulla's body grow limp as she surrendered to sleep. Tullus lay on the floor, pushed his feet beneath the bed, and left his upper torso protruding into the pathway between the cots. He used his satchel as a pillow, and he, like his sister, soon drifted into slumber.

Despite her weariness, Nona stared at the wall. She felt Paulla breathing next to her, and heard her son snoring beneath her. Her mind raced. She loved Lucius, but he was just so irritating—and not just in small ways. No, this was a big deal. These were his children. She was his wife. Despite what Rome or its laws said. No governor or edict could cheapen the relationship and commitment they had shared for almost two decades.

But he could be so selfish. Boyish. Didn't he care about them? Of course he did; she knew that. But his response to seeing them in Jerusalem had been the wrong one.

Nona closed her eyes, and the words melted into pictures: the hospitable family that kept them and fed them warm bread and goat's milk during the journey from Caesarea. Her first glimpse of the temple, gleaming like a jewel in the sunlight. Innkeeper after innkeeper in the city turning her away, "No room!" Decimus's friendly smile and reassuring voice. Lucius's scowl. Tullus's face lighting up when she handed him the honey almond treat.

The images grew blurry, and Nona finally yielded to sleep.

On their way out the door, Lucius slid a few silver coins into Ephraim's hand. "This should cover all three meals." He enjoyed the food but was ready to leave. The longer they stayed, the more questions Avitus asked.

The Jew bowed in gratitude. "I hope you gentlemen will return. You have to try my hummus and my beef stew."

"You have been most kind, Ephraim," Decimus said. "We will return. We look forward to trying your other dishes. Please thank Miriam for her hospitality."

Lucius still felt awkward about interacting socially with a Jew. "Yes, thank you," he mumbled.

They stepped out from the warm inn to the cool evening air. The sun had plunged beyond the western horizon, and the moon, brighter than normal, provided sufficient light to guide their way back to Antonia.

"Let's take the scenic path." Avitus took the lead and headed north, leaving the marketplace and Herod's palace behind them. They exited the city through the Garden Gate.

Just north of the gate, their path led them around a Roman pool. The moon reflected from its waters. "This is the Towers Pool," Avitus said. "It's fed by aqueducts that come from springs north of here. It supplies water to the people of the upper city. It's named for the three towers that rise above Herod's palace. At certain times of the year, in the late afternoon, the shadows of the towers stretch all the way to the pool."

Beyond the Towers Pool, the trio hiked through the scrubby hillsides from which Jewish farmers coaxed out a living.

As they rounded a curve, they were startled by dozens of Roman crosses that lined the road. Each cross held a man. Blood poured from their naked bodies. Most still moaned.

The three soldiers stood dumbfounded, mouths gaping. Then they continued walking, silent, cautious. Lucius had seen crucifixions before. In fact, he had performed such executions himself, driving spikes through criminals' hands and feet. Even so, this unexpected site in the moonlight turned his stomach. Vultures had descended on the crucified bodies and picked at their flesh and eyes.

"So, how'd we do?" The voice came from the shadow of one of the crosses, spooking Avitus.

Lucius recognized the gruff tone and arrogant undercurrents. "Septimus, how nice to see you on this pleasant evening."

"Quite the spectacle, huh?"

"When did this happen?" Decimus furrowed his brow.

"Just a few hours ago while you cowards were out on patrol. You could've been in on the fun if you hadn't stayed out so long." Septimus turned his head and spat on the ground.

"Who are they?"

"Rebels from Galilee. This morning they attacked one of our centuries that was training west of town. Our legionaries wiped out most of the rebels, but they brought these fifty back to Jerusalem. We wanted the Jews gathered in the city for the feast to see what happens when they defy Rome."

"Why are you still out here?" Lucius asked.

"Just wanted to make sure none of the Jews tried to help them. And I like to hear the victims whimper." Septimus picked up a rock and threw it at one of the rebels, hitting him square on the forehead. The rebel made no noise or movement. "That one's dead."

Decimus shook his head.

"Let's get back," Lucius said. Avitus started walking, and the two centurions followed. None of them spoke. As they walked away, they heard the thud of another rock hitting its target.

"That one rise in the landscape back there," Lucius said, "did you notice it? Where we stopped and talked to Septimus. The rock formations were spooky."

"Locals call it 'the place of the skull,'" Avitus said. "When we crucify people, we often do it there. Anything to instill fear."

Nona rose before her children. She was surprised to wake up. Well, surprised that she had slept. And pleased. *Today will be a better day.* She rubbed each of her arms to warm them. As autumn had progressed, mornings grew increasingly cool.

Paulla felt Nona stir. She sat upright on the bed and embraced her mother. Nona rested her chin on her daughter's shoulder, and smiled. "It's a new day," she whispered. "And we're going to make it. I don't know how, but we'll make it."

Moments later, Tullus woke and began the day not with an embrace but with a question. "Do we have any food?"

Nona chuckled. "Open my satchel. I saved some bread from last evening. Share it with your sister."

The other guests in the inn rose around the same time. The animals outside made certain everyone knew the sun had risen.

While her children divided and began eating the stale bread, Nona gathered their supplies and stuffed them into her satchel. "There is a stream just down the hill," she said. "Let's go and wash, and then we'll return to Jerusalem. Maybe we can find some work for the day."

The children nodded, picked up their satchels, and continued nibbling on the bread. Nona led them between rows of cots to the nearest door. She was thankful to get her children out of the putrid lodge and away from the leering guests with whom they shared it.

As soon as she passed through the doorway, her eyes fell on Lucius. He stood in the yard outside. She stopped. The children, following their mother and focused on their bread, bumped into her. Lucius's armor reflected the morning sun, and his winter cape fell gracefully from his shoulders. His powerful frame silhouetted against the blue sky.

The two locked eyes, just as they had they day before. Lucius didn't speak, but Nona saw that his gaze had softened, and watched as his lips curled, just barely, into the semblance of a smile. She needed no more encouragement. She dropped her satchel and leaped toward him, throwing her arms around his neck. He wrapped his arms around her waist. Her worry, tension, and aggravation that had been building for weeks, perhaps months, dissolved. "I missed you." She rested her head on his shoulder and breathed deeply. Her eyes grew moist and a smile stretched across her face.

Paulla squealed as she and her brother joined the embrace.

"How did you find us?" Nona whispered into Lucius's ear.

"You said you were south of town. I walked the road and stopped at each lodge. I was about to go inside this one to see if you were here."

Lucius stepped back from the embrace and walked the family to the edge of the yard, just inside the stone wall, and sat on the ground. Nona and the children followed. Lucius opened a sack that was slung around his shoulder. He pulled out a jar of fig relish and warm bread that had been baked that morning.

"Thank you, Father!" They tossed the stale bread they had been eating to a nearby donkey and tore into the fresh breakfast. Nona ate, as well.

When each had their fill, Nona put her hand on Lucius's knee. "What now?"

Lucius laid his hand on Nona's and looked at their children. He exhaled slowly. "As for the future, I don't know. As for today, I need to take you somewhere safe. You can't stay here anymore."

Lucius rose to his feet and brushed the dust from his uniform. Nona took the hint, stood, and helped Paulla to her feet.

"You don't need to worry about their safety, Father," said Tullus. "I've been watching out for them."

Lucius winked at Nona. "I know, son. And I appreciate it. But I'd feel better if you were staying somewhere else." The family gathered their supplies and marched from the courtyard, proud to follow their centurion father.

As they exited the gate, Nona drew closer to Lucius and whispered, "Did Decimus make you do this?"

Lucius's glare from the day before returned, but just for a moment. He chuckled and shook his head.

Lucius stood before Ephraim's inn. Nona and the children cowered behind him. He thumped the door three times with his knuckles. No one answered. He could see a pair of eyes peeking out the corner of a window.

"Let's just go back to the lower city," said Nona. "Maybe a bed has opened up there."

"No, you're not safe there. I met this couple last night. I think they'll help."

Lucius knocked again, this time with more force. A few seconds later, Ephraim opened the door, but just a few inches. "Mr. Centurion, it's so nice to see you again." His voice trembled.

"I need your help," said Lucius.

"But, sir, time is fast approaching for the Feast of Tabernacles, and Miriam and I need to prepare our inn for guests. Can you find someone else to carry your supplies?"

"No, no, you don't understand." Lucius realized he needed to soften his tone. He stepped to the side so that Ephraim could see his family. "These are my children and their mother. They have traveled to Jerusalem, and they need a safe place to stay. I was hoping—"

"Oh my!" Ephraim swung the door open and swooped out, his whole face smiling and his arms open. "I would be honored to care for your family. We have but one room vacant, but it is our best room. Miriam will prepare it and prepare a meal."

Ephraim smiled and bowed before Nona. "And you, ma'am, need not worry about anything. We will provide all your needs. We will pamper you like they do at the finest baths in Rome." Ephraim stepped back toward the entrance, and his long neck craned like a camel's around the corner. "Miriam, we have important guests."

Miriam burst out the door. She wore the same faded blue robe as the evening before, with a peach scarf over her head and a white belt mostly hidden by her ample midsection. "Oh, children. Just look at you. We must get you cleaned up. I have a barrel of water and some soap out back." Her boisterous voice raised and lowered in pitch with each word, sometimes with each syllable. Miriam grabbed hold of the children's hands and pulled them inside. Tullus's face turned red as he glanced back at his mother.

Miriam poked her head back through the doorway. She inspected Nona from head to foot. "And you, ma'am, will be next."

Nona stood speechless for a moment, then said, "Maybe I should go help." She hurried after her children.

Ephraim clasped his hands in front of his body. He tilted his head and wore a smile that seemed to never leave his lips. His eyes fixed on the centurion.

Lucius shuffled his feet and scratched behind his ear. Ephraim kept staring and smiling.

Ephraim finally broke the silence. "We'll take good care of them, sir."

"I appreciate it."

"Any friend of Avitus's is a friend of mine."

"Thanks."

More silence.

"Sir, it might help if I knew your name, in case I need to get in touch with you."

"I am Lucius Valerius Galeo."

"And you are stationed at Antonia, I assume?"

"Yes."

Lucius continued staring at the ground. Ephraim continued smiling.

"They have traveled a long way," Lucius said, finally looking up at Ephraim. "And they don't know their way around Jerusalem."

"I understand, Lucius Valerius Galeo." Ephraim's countenance and voice softened. "We will be honored to provide them a nice room and meals. And we will help them adjust to the city."

Lucius placed enough coins in Ephraim's hand for a week of lodging and meals, turned, and left.

"Please give my greetings to Avitus," Ephraim called after him.

Miriam and Ephraim's inn sat on the northern edge of the upper city's market. The previous evening, when Lucius visited with the other two soldiers, the market had slowed to a reasonable pace. This morning, vendors and customers flooded it with bartering, laughter, and arguments. A few soldiers from Antonia mingled among the throngs. Some shopped, some patrolled, and others bullied Jews just for the fun of it.

Lucius stood next to a legionary who kept a careful eye on the crowds. "Is it like this every morning?"

"Almost. Especially now, at harvest time. Merchants—mainly those selling fruits, vegetables, and fish—arrive early and try to get everything sold while their goods are still fresh. And a lot of the servants come in the morning to get supplies their employers need for the day."

Lucius stood silently, hoping he wouldn't have to step in and calm a ruckus that was brewing between a merchant and customer. Thankfully, the buyer finally succumbed and paid what the merchant demanded.

"Today is busier than usual, though," the soldier continued. "The Feast of Tabernacles is just a few days away. Jews are arriving from all over. The wealthier ones come here for supplies."

"I keep hearing about this feast. There isn't much good to say about these Jews, but I will give them this, they know how to celebrate."

The soldier offered a polite chuckle. "Yes sir. That they do."

Lucius strode away from the soldier and began the hike back to Antonia. He waded through the market, enjoying the wide berth always given him when the commoners saw a centurion drawing near. He exited the Garden Gate and followed the same path on which Avitus led them the night before. The path snaked around the Towers Pool and then into the hillsides northwest of the city.

A stench filled his nostrils, and a grotesque site filled his eyes. The crosses that lined the road now creaked under the weight of the dead bodies draped on them. The heaviness of the bodies lessened by the hour, however, as vultures and buzzards partook in their own celebratory feast. The midday sun warmed what remained of the corpses. Lucius lifted the collar of his shirt to cover his nose and mouth. Unlike the evening before, no moans or movements rose from any of the crosses. These rebels were dead. And gone. And wouldn't hide behind any more rocks to ambush any more soldiers. Lucius thanked the gods and kept walking.

He recalled what he said a few minutes before, to the soldier in the market: "There isn't much good to say about these Jews . . ." As time went on, he admitted to himself that the Jews left him less repulsed and more puzzled. Those old men at the hippodrome in Caesarea brazenly laid their necks bare before Pilate's threats and the soldiers' swords. He admired them. He'd allow that description into his mind now, even if he'd never say it aloud. He admired their zeal for their law and their dedication to Sabbaths and festivals. And these rebels, hanging from the crosses—they certainly believed in what they fought for. To assault the Roman Empire with their rudimentary weapons and such little training and organization, it's like a gnat attacking an elephant. It takes a courageous gnat—ridiculous and naïve, but courageous.

His own courage felt more contrived. Selfish. He acted bravely, but, he admitted, the act was intended to impress others, especially those who could boost his rank. There was little to admire in his courage. It wasn't noble or honorable; it was manipulative. Such as his ambition to bring Septimus down. To scheme his way to the command of the first century. It was more treacherous than courageous.

As he neared Antonia, an image seeped into his mind. The same image haunted his memory a few times each day. He couldn't shake it. That rabbi from Nazareth, Jesus, reaching out to touch the greasy paralytic who everyone else ignored. The paralytic's twisted, decrepit body straightening and strengthening. He stood up. Like a man with perfect legs, he walked. And the next day in the temple courts, the oddest conversation. The healing somehow displeased the Jewish officials. Why wouldn't they celebrate the healing? The paralytic was one of their own. Jesus's relationship with the Jewish leaders seemed complicated. Lucius fought back his own curiosity. He would watch the Jew closely.

16

January, AD 30

Nona rose while stars still sparkled in the sky. Predawn noises floated through her window. Carts clattered along the stone streets, mules brayed and grunted, and early-rising vendors greeted one another. Three months into her work for Ephraim and Miriam, she'd finally grown accustomed to the routine.

Tullus stirred.

"You don't need to get up yet, son." She pulled a blanket over his feet.

In the dark, she changed from her sleeping gown into a heavy, faded green robe that kept her warm. She tied a white belt around her waist and pulled her hair back with a scarf. She slid her feet into hardened leather sandals.

Nona crept from the room she shared with her children, down the stairs, and through the front door, careful not to wake anyone.

Her first step out the door landed her foot in a puddle. She ignored it, just as she ignored the drizzle that drifted from the gray canopy that hung over Jerusalem this time of year. The upper city smelled of mildew, smoke, and bread.

"Shalom!" came the cheery voice of a merchant.

"Shalom to you," Nona responded with the Jewish greeting. In the darkness he must not have noticed she was Roman, but certainly he detected her accent.

"Halt." He stopped the donkey he was leading. "I have candlesticks, ladles, and bowls." He waved his hand across his merchandise. "Might I interest you in anything?"

"No, thank you." He apparently didn't mind her ethnicity. Some Jews turned up their noses at Romans, refusing even to sell to them in the marketplace. Others, though, had become accustomed to people like Nona and tolerated their presence in the city. A few, like Ephraim and Miriam, even befriended the occasional Roman.

A woman, evidently the merchant's wife, walked behind him carrying a basket of bread on her head. "Those loaves smell awfully good," Nona said. "Might I send my son to get some later?"

"Yes, please. I will set aside a few loaves," the wife responded.

Nona noted what direction the Jewish merchant couple went.

She wished Lucius expressed the kindness to Jews that some of them had expressed to his family. She recalled the incident at the hippodrome, when he beat the Jewish man. Everyone in the settlement talked about how brutal he'd been.

Just a few weeks back, when Nona mentioned the possibility of working at the inn for Ephraim, Lucius responded sharply. "No woman of mine will ever work for a Jew."

"But Ephraim and Miriam have been so kind to us," she responded. "And the job will be convenient. We can live at the inn, work here, and eat here." She held his hand. "You're just a short walk away." And then the clincher, "Our children feel safe here."

As the weeks passed, Lucius's tone softened, and his glares toward the Jews became less frequent.

The sun crested the eastern horizon above the Mount of Olives and sent the day's first rays scampering across the Kidron Valley, bouncing from the gold-plated arches of the temple and tumbling into the upper city marketplace.

Nona shielded her eyes. Her breath crystalized in the frigid air and shimmered in the sun. She hurried to the side of the inn, into a narrow alley. She found a water jug, hoisted it onto her head, and joined the stream of ladies who marched out the Garden Gate to the Towers Pool.

When she arrived at the pool, she found women dispersed around its edges, filling water jugs. About half were Jewish. The others were Syrian, Roman, Greek, and other ethnicities. She'd been surprised by the variety of people in Jerusalem. The upper city, especially the homes and businesses around the market, reflected the diversity of trade that passed through the city.

Nona found an open spot in the midst of the ladies and lowered herself to her knees, which protested by cracking and popping—sounds she'd grown accustomed to.

She dipped the jug into the pool, and clean, cold water gushed in. She sat the container on the ground, then used all her strength to raise and rest it on her head. Her scarf protected her scalp from its rough edges. Water dripped down the back of her robe.

With a balanced, graceful gait, just as her mother taught her when she was a girl, Nona trekked back to the inn. One arm held the jug in place, the other swung at her side. The city had awakened, and the marketplace buzzed with the first transactions of the day.

"Here, let me help." Ephraim met her just outside the inn and lifted the container from her head. He sat it on the ground. Out of breath, Nona nodded her thanks.

Her appreciation for Ephraim grew daily. Just last evening, after dinner, one of the guests pulled Ephraim aside. "What's the Jew cost for the evening?" Nona overheard. This wasn't the first guest to misinterpret her role at the inn.

Ephraim responded firmly, "She is unavailable for such activities. Though, perhaps you would like to check with her husband, Lucius Valerius Galeo. He's a centurion at Antonia. Should I summon him for you?"

"No, no, that won't be necessary. My sincerest apologies to the lady and her husband."

Nona chuckled as she recalled the look on the man's face when he learned about Lucius.

By this time, the children had risen and joined Nona and Ephraim on the front porch.

"Take this water inside and fill wash basins for each of the guests," Nona instructed Tullus. "Leave the basins outside their doors. And take one basin to Miriam out back."

"Yes, mother."

"Then, go to the market and buy ten loaves. Look for a Jewish couple on the south side of the market. He's selling wooden crafts, and she has freshly baked bread. She's wearing a blue robe and a green scarf. They're friendly."

"Yes, mother."

"Ephraim will give you coins for the bread."

"Yes ma'am." Ephraim reached into the pouch on his belt for coins.

Nona yelled after her son, "And don't stop to talk to any soldiers." He didn't respond.

"Paulla, you'll help Miriam and me prepare the morning meal for our guests."

"Yes, mother."

Nona felt most secure when she barked orders. Everyone smiled and complied.

She and Paulla joined Miriam in the outdoor kitchen, an area covered with a canvas canopy immediately outside the back door of the inn. A small fire kept the ladies warm and heated fig relish, which hung from a tripod a few inches above the flames.

Nona checked the relish. "This will go nicely with the bread Tullus is bringing back."

Miriam nodded.

"Have the guests risen?"

"I heard them moving around, but I haven't seen them yet." Miriam stood on her toes to stir the relish. She tasted it and nodded her approval. "This time of year, I'm just happy we have guests. They're merchants from Syria trying to make connections in Jerusalem to expand their trade further south. They aren't the friendliest of people, but what do you expect? They're from Syria." She grinned at her own words.

Nona smiled. Miriam made such comments from time to time, but she treated everyone with kindness and hospitality, regardless of where they came from.

Nona dipped a ladle into a bucket that held red wine, which she'd purchased from her favorite winemaker in the market. She emptied the ladle into a pitcher until it was one-third full. She filled the remainder of the pitcher with water until the mixture was just right for the morning meal. She sent Paulla inside with the diluted wine.

"Didn't you say you have family visiting soon?" Nona asked Miriam.

"Yes." Miriam rubbed her hands on her apron. "From Caesarea. My brother and his wife. They live in the Jewish quarter there."

"Well, I look forward to meeting them."

"They're generous people who love Yahweh. You'll like them. My brother's sister is expecting a baby soon. They have no family in Caesarea. They're coming here so I can help take care of her." Miriam stoked the fire. "I worry about her traveling this far, but she's healthy, and my brother promised to travel slowly. They should be here in a few days."

"What are their names?"

"Tobiah and Deborah."

Nona shifted a lilac to the left of the tulips. Such flowers were difficult to come by this time of year. "In Rome they developed a way to grow flowers during the cold season," a shopkeeper had told her. "They have this structure that keeps them warm. A farmer south of Jerusalem is trying it, too." The flowers weren't quite as healthy as those grown when it was warmer, and they cost more, but special guests deserve special treatment. And Ephraim didn't pay attention to the finances anyway.

She stepped back and studied her arrangement. She'd found the vase stashed in a storage bin. A skillful potter fashioned it from clay and dyed it a deep shade of green. Likely, Miriam had purchased it at the market, and then cast it aside when its glimmer faded and a chip appeared on its rim. Yesterday, Nona spent an hour polishing it and filing down the sharp edge of the chip. The vase deserved to be used, to bring a smile to someone's face. She buffed a smudge from its side. Just because something got a little damaged was no reason to throw it out.

Nona enjoyed every minute she spent with Tobiah and Deborah. She felt blessed to be near them. She smiled. "Blessed" was a term she seldom used before getting to know these Jews. They said it all the time. That, and "shalom," which referred to a kind of peace and satisfaction. Wholeness.

The term was accurate. Tobiah and Deborah, and to a slightly lesser extent, Ephraim and Miriam, emanated shalom. Nona couldn't recall a single Roman so at peace. Her Roman friends obsessed over power and reputation. They lied and manipulated to get more clout, more prestige, more pleasure.

Not all Jews displayed such shalom, of course. But these four, the four Nona knew best, certainly did.

She took the flower arrangement downstairs and set it aside for the evening banquet.

A few hours later, Nona pushed Miriam from the outdoor kitchen. "I told you not to come out here."

"Yes, but what about the lamb?" Miriam asked. "Did you salt it?"

"Of course I did. I've been roasting lamb since my mother weaned me."

"And the bread? Will it still be warm when it's served?"

"Out. I told you, you're not the host this evening. You're a guest. Along with your husband, Tobiah, and Deborah. We will serve you."

"I don't know who you think you are. Throwing me out of my own kitchen."

Miriam turned in a huff and pranced back into the inn.

Paulla, slicing onions, raised her eyes toward her mother and smiled. Nona and her children were excited to serve this special meal to Miriam and her family. They planned it for days. Nona wanted their Jewish friends to know how much she appreciated their kindness.

"Tullus," she instructed, "get this bread out to the table. And don't forget the olive oil."

He removed four loaves from the oven, placed them in a basket, and disappeared into the inn.

"The oil!"

"Yes ma'am," he replied, reappearing with his chin on his chest. He picked up a small container and four saucers.

A few minutes later, Nona entered the dining room carrying a silver tray that spilled over with roasted lamb, onions, and potatoes. Her children stood to the side, out of the way, holding pitchers and ready to refill cups. She sat the tray in the middle of the table. Steam rose from the platter and filled the room with the aroma of lamb and vegetables.

"Nona," Deborah gushed, "you've outdone yourself."

"No one else from Jerusalem, Caesarea, or Rome itself could prepare such a delicious meal," Tobiah said.

Miriam scrunched her nose and inspected the tray. "And you used the good salt, correct?"

"Yes ma'am." Nona smiled.

"And what did this cost me?" Ephraim asked Nona.

"You'll never know, sir."

"That's what I was afraid of." Ephraim cackled. Laughter spread around the table.

Ephraim stood and raised his arms. The giggles quieted, but the smiles remained. "Blessed are you our God, Lord, and King. You bring forth bread from the ground and fruit from the vine. You nourish the world with goodness, kindness, and compassion. You sustain all whom you created. Blessed are you, Lord. Amen."

Ephraim lowered his arms, picked up a knife, and began slicing the lamb. He filled three plates with lamb and vegetables and passed them around the table. He then filled his own plate and sat.

Nona nudged Tullus. "Refill their wine." He obeyed.

Between mouthfuls, Miriam asked, "How are you feeling, Deborah?"

"I'm feeling big. And tired. And ready to bring this little one into the world."

"When do you think the baby will arrive?" asked Ephraim.

Tobiah piped up before Deborah could answer. "Soon, I hope."

Deborah laughed, then responded, "I feel like it could be any day. The trip here was difficult, but on the positive side, it may have accelerated the process."

"Well, we are here to help, whenever the baby comes," said Miriam. Though she seldom showed tenderness, her love for her brother and sister-in-law was evident. Her new nephew or niece would never want for anything.

The conversation paused while everyone enjoyed the lamb. Nona sent the children to the outdoor kitchen to prepare bowls of figs, dates, and almonds. She realized she'd forgotten the vase of flowers out back. She hurried to retrieve it, then waited next to the wall for an appropriate moment to place it on the table.

"And how about you, Tobiah?" asked Ephraim. "How is your recovery?"

Nona had noticed Tobiah's limp, and how, when he rose from a chair, he leaned gingerly to one side. She wondered why.

"I'm getting stronger by the day," Tobiah replied. "Still some pain in my leg and ribs, but I expect to be back to normal soon."

Deborah put her fork down, rested her hands on her stomach, and lowered her eyes.

Tobiah squeezed her shoulder.

Miriam glared at Ephraim. "I'm sorry I brought it up," he said.

"No, it's alright," Deborah replied.

"It was a traumatic experience for us all." Tobiah said. "I'd heard stories, and had seen some things, but I never imagined it would happen to me."

Nona leaned in.

Tobiah spoke carefully. "I've always enjoyed the games. I could do without all the drunkenness and violence, of course. But the races themselves, and the athletes. I just like the excitement, I guess." He sighed. "Late in the day people had grown bored. Some mocked the soldiers, saying things just to irritate them. I had a loaf of bread in my hand." He picked up a loaf from the table to demonstrate. "I raised my arms to cheer for the athletes, and I guess this centurion thought the bread was a rock and that I was about to throw it. He dragged me from the bleachers and—"

A vase of flowers shattered against the stone floor. Everyone turned toward the noise, toward Nona. Her face flushed white. Her hands trembled. She ran from the room.

17

L ucius glared at the slave who served the morning meal, ground wheat mixed with water to form a less-than-appetizing but sufficiently nutritious gruel. "Is that it? No second scoop?"

The slave returned the glare, held it for a moment, then scooped a second spoonful into Lucius's bowl. On most days Lucius would've responded with a backhanded slap, but on this day, he chuckled. The slave had spunk. He could appreciate spunk. At least he could today.

He searched the rows of tables in the recesses of Antonia, tables filled with soldiers who woke in bad moods that wouldn't improve as the day wore on. Lucius's gaze finally settled on Decimus, who sat with three other soldiers swapping grunts and one-syllable words. He weaved through the room and slid onto a bench opposite his friend.

Once they exchanged greetings, Decimus asked, "So, what do you think about the aqueduct?"

"Aqueducts in general or a specific one?"

"A specific one. Haven't you heard? Pilate already began construction." Decimus took a swig from his diluted beer.

"He's putting up aqueducts all the time, all over the place."

"Yeah, but not many to Jerusalem. And the Jews aren't happy."

"Aren't happy?" Lucius wasn't sure why this surprised him. "But it's almost impossible to find clean water around here. They build all these pools and reservoirs. They'll try anything to catch one more drop of rain. Why wouldn't they want a new aqueduct?" He put down his spoon, as if the conversation had robbed his appetite, but he picked it back up a few seconds later. "If Pilate is building them an aqueduct, they should bow to thank him."

Avitus slid into the seat next to Decimus. The slave had given him two spoonfuls of the porridge as well, but not because he'd asked for it. Lucius had instructed the cooks to give Avitus extra food any time he came through the line. Anything to push a few extra calories onto his skinny frame. "Good morning, sirs. The gods be with you."

"And with you." The centurions kept their eyes on their food.

Avitus took the hint and concentrated on his porridge, until he became uncomfortable with the silence and asked, "What do you think about the aqueduct?"

"What of it?" Lucius sighed.

"Oh, it's impressive." Avitus held each syllable a moment too long.

"You've seen it?" Decimus raised his eyes from his bowl.

"Just the other day. I was on patrol. We'd heard of a disturbance near Bethlehem, so we went to make sure everything was alright. It was nothing, just a little skirmish, but on the way back, on the western horizon, we could see the new aqueduct taking shape. We weren't in a hurry to get back here, so we hiked over to check it out."

"What'd you think?" Lucius asked.

"It's extraordinary. One of the more majestic ones I've seen. High arches, stone columns. Made me proud to serve Rome. The workers said it'll cover thirty miles by the time they're done. It'll bring cool water from the mountains southwest of here to supply Jerusalem."

Lucius wasn't overly impressed. Whatever aqueduct Pilate might build for Jerusalem was certain to be inferior to those delivering water to Caesarea. Still, he was curious. "Decimus said the Jews aren't happy."

"I've heard the same. It all seems absurd to me, but I guess they feel justified in their complaints."

"Why?" Lucius was learning that the Jews might lay dormant for a while, but when they decided to take a stand, they stood boldly.

"They're upset with how Pilate financed the construction."

Avitus raised another spoonful to his mouth. He obviously enjoyed being the one at the table with inside information, savoring this position more than he savored the gruel. The centurions watched as he chewed and swallowed.

Avitus continued. "It has to do with the corban."

"The what?" the centurions asked in unison.

"The corban. The sacred money. The priests tax the Jewish people from all across the empire, and the money that pours into the temple treasury is holy. They call it 'corban.'"

"What's it used for?" Decimus asked.

"Mostly it funds their ceremonies and feasts. Sometimes they'll use it for building projects or other things that will benefit the Jews."

"Like bringing clean water into the city," Lucius said.

"Yes, but the decision has to be made by the high priest and the Sanhedrin, their council. Our governors have always left the money alone. It's part of our agreement with the Jews to try to keep them peaceful."

"But Pilate took it without asking," Decimus surmised.

"You got it."

"And I imagine he needed most of their corban for something as extensive as an aqueduct."

"Right again." Avitus took a slow sip from his wooden cup.

Pilate elicited both admiration and frustration from Lucius. No one could needle the Jews like Pilate. But, he didn't know when to stop. One thing was for certain, the Jews wouldn't lie down for this. The image of those elders in the Caesarean hippodrome appeared in Lucius's memory again.

"And to top it off," Avitus sat his cup by his bowl, "the aqueduct passes through a cemetery. As clean as the water might look to us, the Jews say it's unclean because it comes near dead bodies."

"Did Pilate do that on purpose?" Lucius's frustration was gradually eclipsing his admiration for the governor.

"I'd never say such a thing." Avitus smiled. "But there's a lot of open land out there that doesn't pass through cemeteries."

Lucius grunted and stood. He left his dirty bowl and cup on the table and marched out of the dining hall.

Before he made it to his quarters, Septimus stopped him in the hallway. "Pilate will arrive late this afternoon. He'll have his guard with him, but he may need extra protection. Take forty of your soldiers and meet him outside the Garden Gate. Escort him to Herod's palace." Septimus swaggered away and Lucius growled. Just his presence, and his odor, caused Lucius's stomach to turn.

Later that day, as commanded, Lucius waited with forty of his most accomplished legionaries. He wished he'd brought more. The Jews were congregating in the market in front of Herod's palace, just inside the Garden Gate. They tried to be sly by moving in groups of two or three, but he could see what they were doing. Apparently, word had leaked that Pilate would stay at the palace on this trip, rather than Antonia. Probably some Jewish servants in the palace hadn't learned to keep quiet. Lucius would need to remind them what confidentiality meant.

The centurion stood outside of the gate, squinting in the midday sun as he surveyed the horizon. Half an hour passed. Then an hour. Then another. "Stay at attention," he commanded his soldiers.

"Yes sir." They were obedient but growing weary. They flanked each side of the gate, ready to protect the governor when he arrived.

The cloud-speckled sky emitted an orange glow. When the cavalry approached, its dark outline emerged as if from the setting sun. Their crimson banner crested the horizon first, then

Pilate's guard came into view, fully armored and riding proudly atop black steeds whose muscles rippled like the sea. Pilate's soldiers rode in an oval shape, two deep. The governor rode in the center, bouncing on the back of a white horse, with a sneer across his lips. Lucius couldn't see the sneer from that distance, but he knew it was there.

Lucius peeked over his shoulder and through the gate. He saw a Jew run into the market. Their lookout, obviously. The centurion looked to the ground, his eyes dancing from pebble to pebble. He wasn't sure how well organized the Jews were, and what degree of danger faced Pilate. He motioned to his soldiers. "Fall in line!"

The legionaries, moving in synchronous beauty, fell into four columns behind their centurion.

"Full pace!" Lucius instructed.

The soldiers marched away from the gate, toward the governor's entourage. When the two groups met, Lucius held his hand into the air. "Halt!" His soldiers and Pilate's guard stopped. The centurion saluted Pilate. "The gods be with you, sir."

"And with you," Pilate responded.

"Welcome to Jerusalem."

"And what kind of welcome will I receive?" Pilate knew this visit would be less than peaceful.

"You will receive a welcome worthy of your stature."

The governor chuckled. Then hissed. "Make sure I get to the palace unscathed."

"Yes sir."

Lucius motioned for his legionaries to surround Pilate's guard. Now the soldiers were four deep around Pilate, the two outer layers marching on foot and the two inner layers on horseback. Lucius marched at the front.

"Military pace!" Lucius ordered. The huddle of armor, muscle, and determination marched toward the Garden Gate. When they reached the gate, the oval remained intact but compressed to squeeze through. On the other side, the procession spilled into the market. The soldiers raised their shields to form a four-layered wall around Pilate.

Lucius glanced to his left, where he hoped Nona and the children remained safe inside of Ephraim's inn.

Seconds later, a stone smacked Lucius's shield. He scanned the buzzing crowd and saw others bending down to pick up rocks.

"Full pace!" Lucius ordered. The soldiers on foot lengthened their strides, and those on horseback nudged their steeds to keep up. They covered the distance from the Garden Gate to the entrance of Herod's palace in seconds. A few rocks thudded against soldier's shields, but most missed because of the soldiers' quick pace.

The oval compressed again to squeeze through the gate into Herod's palace. As soon as the final soldier passed through, guards emerged from inside the palace and pushed the mob back. "Move. Disperse. Go away!" The soldiers swung clubs and threatened with daggers.

Lucius turned to make sure Pilate was unharmed, but his guard had already rushed the governor into the depths of the palace. He quickly counted his soldiers. All had made it safely through the gate. They were fortunate.

He took deep breaths to slow his racing heart. He'd been a centurion for a long time, and a soldier for longer, but when an official as important as Pilate faced danger, even this seasoned soldier broke into a sweat.

The Jews' voices rose from the marketplace. "You took our corban. Tear down that unclean aqueduct!"

"Animals," Septimus growled. Lucius turned, surprised to hear his fellow centurion's scratchy and disgusted voice. Decimus stood beside him. The two centurions must've been waiting in the palace.

"Wearing your battle armor, I see," Lucius said.

Decimus crossed his arms and gazed at the gate, which, along with the soldiers just outside it, held the Jews at bay. "Oh, we heard there was a little get-together and thought we'd join the fun."

Septimus ignored his more casual colleague. His head remained stationary while his jaw flapped with rapid information. "Half the cohort is here. All three of our centuries. Our legionaries will take shifts protecting the palace through the night. The three of us will join Pilate at a banquet."

Septimus turned on his heels and marched back toward the palace. Lucius glanced toward Decimus, who knowingly tilted his head.

They followed Septimus. The gap between them widened as the two friends walked more slowly through the courtyard. The sounds of water sprouting from the fountains gradually drowned out the cries of the Jews.

"The next few hours could get interesting," Lucius said.

"You don't know the half of it."

Lucius shifted on his couch. He tried to scratch his back without being too obvious. The toga was too stiff, too clean. And the garland made his forehead itch.

"Where's Pilate?" he whispered.

Decimus shrugged. Septimus glared. Must be rude to ask such questions.

Lucius scanned the room, noting that Pilate's officials waited more patiently. They must be accustomed to the governor's tardiness.

They reclined on couches covered with purple blankets. The couches slanted upward toward a long banquet table, hewn from cedar and decorated with carvings of olive vines. Candelabras lined its center. Persian rugs of blue, gold, and crimson covered the floors. The walls were adorned with tapestries from Greek and Roman artists. Oil lanterns clung to the walls.

Two hours before, Lucius and his legionaries helped Pilate get safely into the palace. Soon after, he was assigned to a room and a servant to prepare him for the banquet.

"We don't have time to bathe you," the servant had said. Lucius was relieved. "But we will perfume you." The servant opened a bottle of oil with an aroma too sweet for Lucius's nostrils.

"That makes me queasy."

The servant frowned. "It's imported from Persia. The best in the empire."

"Do you have to?"

"Yes sir. And you must remove your tunic."

"Not a chance."

"Pilate's orders."

Embarrassed and irritated, Lucius stepped out of his tunic. The servant lavished the oil on his body until his skin glistened, then helped him into a white toga, and rested a garland crown on his head.

Now he waited in the banquet room. Still no Pontius Pilate.

A dozen slaves streamed into the room, all with olive skin, hair as dark as coal, and dressed in skimpy tunics. They sashayed around the table, hips swaying and seductive smiles crossing their lips. In pairs, they sauntered by the guests, brushing against them at every opportunity. They carried buckets and cloths.

A male servant stood next to Lucius. The centurion refused to return the servant's smile or look him in the eye.

"Your hand, sir?"

"What for?"

"We need to cleanse it to prepare you for the feast."

Lucius glanced around the table and saw others enjoying the hand washing. He extended his arm to the servant, who poured cold water over his hands. A female servant held an empty bucket beneath his hands to catch the water. The two then sat their buckets to the side, pulled perfume-soaked cloths from their belts, and massaged his hands with the cloths.

The servants streamed out of the room as orderly and as provocatively as they had entered.

Five minutes passed. Then ten.

Lucius nudged Decimus. "Do you think he's coming?"

"He'll be here. Be patient."

A trumpeter entered the doorway and blasted a brief refrain. Everyone stood. Pilate's guards marched into the banquet hall, flanked to the sides, and stood at attention. The governor swaggered in. He wore a white toga similar to those adorning his guests, except his flaunted purple and gold stitching around the edges. A crown of olive twigs rested on his brow. He looked no one in the eye, but marched to the head of the table and draped himself over a couch. His guards took positions around him.

"Proceed." Pilate snapped his fingers. The guests sat. The servants reentered carrying pitchers of wine and silver trays overflowing with loaves of bread and relish made with fish and olives.

Lucius felt as awkward as an ox in a crowded market.

Decimus grinned. "A little different from our meals back at Antonia, isn't it?"

"I'm not sure what to do. Or when."

"Just watch me. I'll guide you through it." Decimus had attended more banquets. He knew which cup to offer the servants for the wine, how to dip his bread into the relish so that nothing spilled on the table, and when to speak or remain quiet.

Lucius sipped his wine and dipped his bread in relish. "For these elites, eating is a game, a pleasure. For me, it's just necessary. We're wasting a lot of time. We could be training our soldiers or corralling those Jews out in the market."

"Maybe. But try to enjoy it. We don't get invited to these banquets very often."

When the guests had their fill of bread and relish, servants returned with wet cloths.

"Again?" Lucius asked. "My hands have been washed more tonight than in the last month."

Decimus grinned. "Just making sure you're clean, my friend."

Servants lined the center of the table with trays of boar and pheasant resting on beds of apples, celery, and dates. Their aromas intermingled and filled the room with scents of the wild and charcoal. Servants placed small bowls of honey next to each guest.

"We can never eat all that," Lucius said.

"Maybe not, but I plan to do my part." Decimus scraped generous portions onto his plate. He dipped a piece of pheasant into the honey with his fingers, then threw it into his mouth.

Lucius did the same. "This is sweet. Too sweet."

"You have to pace yourself. And be careful with the honey. Enough to flavor the meat, but not too much."

Servants remained stationed along the walls holding pitchers of wine.

As the alcohol took effect, Pilate's stern expression loosened. "Enjoy yourselves, men. This is how Romans feast." He pulled one of the female servants onto his couch. "Come here, lovely."

She smiled seductively and reclined next to him. She chose an apple slice from his plate, dipped it in honey, and placed it on his tongue. "How does this taste?"

Pilate licked the honey from her fingers. "Better than anything I've had in years."

The governor turned his attention to his guests. "This reminds me of the banquet Tiberius gave after the great battle of Weser River. I was a legionary rising through the ranks, and the battle gave me a chance to prove my worth." For the next half hour, Pilate entertained his guests with tales of battles won, the political wrangling of Rome, and his own outlandish successes. Lucius smirked. Some of the stories might have even been true.

"How long do these feasts last?" Lucius whispered.

"Sometimes four or five hours." Decimus sipped his wine.

Lucius's eyes grew wide.

"But this one won't be so long. We got a late start. And we need our rest for tomorrow."

"Tomorrow?"

"Just wait. I don't know the details yet, but something is in the works."

Servants cleared away the main course and replaced it with a variety of cheeses, nuts, and breads sweetened with honey and spices. Musicians and dancers entered the banquet hall.

Lucius grew more at ease. Not entirely comfortable, as were the others around the table, but relaxed enough to chuckle at the stories, gorge on the desserts, and return the smiles of the servants as they glided by.

Without warning, Pilate's mood changed. He waved his arm to the dancers and musicians. "Leave. Now." He gulped the wine that remained in his cup and slammed it on the table. When a servant stepped forward to refill the cup, Pilate delivered a back-handed slap that sent blood spurting from his nose. "Not now."

The governor glared at the three centurions, holding his gaze on each a few seconds longer than was comfortable. Then he threw his head back and cackled.

Lucius shuddered.

Pilate raised his arm into the air, his fist clenched. "Tomorrow the foul Jews of this city will meet the brute force of Rome!"

The men cheered.

"I bring clean water into the city, and this is the welcome I receive? After tomorrow, they will never grumble again."

Pilate addressed the centurions. "You will gather your soldiers and give them the precise instructions my men are about to give you. Neither you nor they will alter the slightest detail of this plan."

Pilate stood, wobbled until he found his balance, then staggered from the room accompanied by his guards and female servant.

One of Pilate's officials walked to the head of the table. He pulled a parchment from his belt, studied it, then described the plan. Lucius's eyes grew wide.

Lucius stumbled out of the palace gate and waded through the moonlit market, which smelled of livestock and Jews. The protestors had settled but hadn't left. They stood in circles around fires, whispering to each other and glaring at Lucius as he walked by. He still wore the toga, and his body radiated the aromas of Persian oils and alcohol.

He arrived at Ephraim's inn. Nona stood on the front porch with a broom in hand. "I could smell you before I could see you." She glared. "Must've been quite the celebration. I saw Pilate coming into the city. And the Jews throwing rocks. You're lucky you didn't get hurt. But it looks like he rewarded you well this evening."

Lucius's mind was a haze.

Nona resumed sweeping. "You're pale. How much wine did you have?"

"Not much."

"It doesn't usually affect you this badly. And your hands are shaking. Come inside and I'll get you some water."

Nona started toward the door and Lucius followed. But she stopped short of entering. Lucius stumbled into her.

"Sorry," they both said.

"You stay out here," Nona said.

"Why?"

She paused for a moment, then said sharply, "I don't want you to disturb the guests."

Before he could object, she disappeared through the door and closed it behind her. Her behavior puzzled Lucius, but his mind was too foggy to dwell on it for too long. He waited in the chilled night air. His eyes explored the market. His ears filled with the dull roar of Jewish voices and his nostrils with the smoke from their fires.

Nona returned and handed Lucius a cup of water. He drank slowly. He wasn't thirsty, but hoped the water would clear his mind and minimize tomorrow morning's headache.

Nona stood with her hands on her hips. "Are you going to tell me what's going on, or do I have to guess?"

"What makes you think something's going on?"

"You know me better than that, Lucius. I've heard the grumbling about this new aqueduct. And now the governor visits. Hundreds of Jews are camped in the market. And you stumble over here in the middle of the night, wearing that toga and smelling of wine and perfume."

Lucius took another sip of water, pretending to savor it to delay answering. He couldn't tell her about Pilate's plan, but he worried about her safety, and for the children. Especially Tullus. Once he saw the uproar, he'd want to jump in.

"Stay out of the market tomorrow," he blurted.

"I can't. I have to—"

"No, you don't understand. Stay out of the market tomorrow."

"But I—"

"And take the children with you."

"Lucius, what are you talking about? What's happening?"

Before Lucius could answer, the door opened. Nona spun around to see who it was. Her expression relaxed when she saw Ephraim emerge. He carried a bucket of water and hummed what Lucius assumed was some old Jewish song, exaggerating the rising and falling of the melody. The song held Ephraim's attention such that he didn't notice Lucius and Nona in the darkness. He carried the bucket to the side of the inn and emptied it.

When Ephraim turned around, his humming gave way to a gasp as he saw the two figures standing there.

"Good evening, Ephraim," Lucius said.

"Oh, it's you." Ephraim exhaled more comfortably than he'd inhaled. He studied Lucius's clothing and bloodshot eyes. "You haven't been around for a few days."

"Nona says you've been busy with guests, and that I'd be in the way." She'd been acting strange about his visits to the inn lately. As if she didn't want him there.

"We have been busy. Yahweh is blessing us. And some of our guests are family now. Have you met Miriam's brother and his wife from Caesarea? They're staying with us until their baby arrives. Their names are—"

"I'm sure Lucius needs to get back," Nona snapped. Ephraim looked surprised by the interruption. Lucius wondered why she was so abrupt, but maybe he was missing something.

Lucius finished his drink. "I'd like more water, please."

"Absolutely. Give me your cup and I'll refill it," Ephraim responded.

"No, don't worry yourself. Nona can get it."

Nona raised a brow, then took the cup from Lucius and disappeared into the inn.

Ephraim stood silently. Lucius cleared his throat and shifted from one foot to the other. Both turned their eyes toward the market.

"Tomorrow . . . " Lucius began, his eyes searching the darkness for a way to finish the sentence.

"Yes, tomorrow." Ephraim's voice lowered in pitch.

Lucius continued. "If you can keep Nona and our children away, I'd appreciate it."

"I will be busy, unfortunately, but I will ask Miriam to watch after them. They can visit the farms north of town and buy vegetables for next week."

"Thanks." Lucius locked eyes with Ephraim. Why did he have to be a Jew? He appreciated how Ephraim provided a job and a home for Nona and the children. He and Miriam showed them such generosity and compassion. "And perhaps you could go visit the farms with them?"

Ephraim smiled but didn't respond. Lucius took a deep breath, then nodded. He hiked back to the palace, weaving through the campfires and huddles of Jews who scowled as he passed.

Lucius drifted in and out of sleep. His dreams brought assorted images and sounds that had little to do with each other. Swords clashed and Jews chanted. Paulla giggled as she bounced on his knee. Blood spurted from pigs his father slaughtered on the farm. Men cried out from crosses. Nona's faced contorted into a worried expression. Pilate sneered. Ephraim hummed a jovial song.

The next morning, he sat with Decimus and Septimus in the palace banquet room.

"The food not good enough for you?" Septimus asked.

"Just not that hungry." Lucius picked at the porridge in front of him.

"You'll need your strength today. Eat up." Septimus shoveled another bite into his mouth, his appetite fully intact.

The banquet hall was void of the revelry that filled it the evening before. A single slave served them, an older man with a gray beard and a limp.

"Wine?" the servant offered.

"We'll take water," Decimus responded. "All three of us." Septimus shot him a glance but didn't argue.

After the morning meal, Lucius followed his fellow centurions through a corridor from Pilate's banquet room to the soldiers' rudimentary dining hall, where their legionaries finished the last crumbs of their meal.

"Attention!" Decimus commanded. The legionaries stood and saluted.

"Listen closely," Septimus began. "Today you have a chance to prove your strength. Rome's strength. You have a great opportunity to serve the empire. This is not a day for cowards but for heroes. For men. Men trained to kill." The soldiers cheered. The ranking centurion laid out the details of Pilate's strategy and fielded a few questions, then the room fell silent.

Servants filed into the dining hall and distributed Jewish garments to the soldiers.

"Here we go." Lucius glanced at Decimus. "They have no idea what's coming."

"May the gods protect us."

Lucius sighed. *We may see today whose god has more power to protect.* He watched the distribution of garments. "Where'd they get all the Jewish clothes?"

"From prisoners and markets, over the last few weeks. Not all at once so they wouldn't raise suspicion."

Lucius took a stack of clothes from a servant and returned to his room. He donned linen undergarments and a wool outer garment that draped across his shoulders and covered his body from neck to ankles. He completed the outfit with a rope belt, sandals stitched from camel's hide, and a wool head covering that shaded his face. He strapped a dagger to one hip and a club to the other, hiding them beneath his outer garment.

Lucius took a deep breath. He looked like a Jew, as long as he kept his head bowed and face covered. But he certainly didn't feel like one. He wasn't sure what he felt like, nor how he felt toward the Jews. One thing was certain, though—today he'd have to suppress any admiration that had been growing in his heart for the Jews. He was a Roman centurion. Dominant. Powerful. Violent.

Lucius stepped out of his room just as his fellow centurions emerged from theirs. He had to look twice to recognize them in Jewish garb.

Decimus scratched his arms. "These clothes itch. And I can't see well." He pushed the head covering from his eyes.

"I don't know why they wear so many layers." Lucius adjusted his outer garment.

"Quit complaining." Septimus sniffed. "We have a job to do. But first, we pray to the gods." He lumbered toward the end of the hallway where an ornate room glimmered with idols and icons. Decimus followed.

Lucius almost joined them, then stopped. *Just a waste of time.* He turned and weaved through the palace's corridors into the courtyard. He plodded past fountains and gardens and climbed a guard tower.

He nodded to a legionary. "Status?"

"More Jews by the minute. I've never seen them this agitated."

Lucius peered over the tower's wall, careful to remain hidden. The throng of Jews milled around fires and kept their eyes fixed to the palace gates.

By midday, Lucius mingled among them. He kept his head down but observed his surroundings through his peripheral vision, as much as his head covering allowed. Hundreds of other soldiers did the same. Their Jewish garb kept them inconspicuous, thus far.

Mist filled the air and fused with smoke from the Jews' fires. They roasted fish and vegetables over the flames. Vendors circulated through the crowd. The lack of breeze left the market stale with mingled odors and thick with fog.

Lucius shivered, grateful now for the long and thick Jewish clothing.

"Would you like some bread?" A young man extended a round, thick loaf toward Lucius. The boy looked about the same age as Tullus.

Lucius grunted, lest a spoken word give away his accent, and gratefully accepted the loaf.

"Do you think the governor will listen to us?"

Lucius shrugged.

"I just don't understand why he'd take the corban. My father says we shouldn't be surprised. 'Never trust a Roman,' he says. But maybe we'll get Pilate's attention today and he'll change his mind and give back the money from the temple treasury."

Lucius shook his head and walked away. He raised his eyes and scanned the perimeter of the crowd. This demonstration was significantly larger than the one in Caesarea. Maybe twice as many Jews, well into the thousands. They packed into the marketplace and spilled into surrounding streets. Likely, Jews from Galilee and elsewhere traveled to join their brothers. They continued to stream in from the countryside.

The anger in Jerusalem was reaching its crescendo more quickly than it had in Caesarea. The stories, conversations, and smatterings of laughter that marked the first few days in the hippodrome were absent in Jerusalem. This demonstration wouldn't stretch into days. It would boil over, and it would end, today. Lucius shuddered. His stomach turned. *I've never felt this way before.*

He stole a glance toward the inn, hoping Ephraim kept his promise to send Nona and the children away for the day. And maybe Ephraim reconsidered his own plans.

"Return the corban. Return the corban. Send your filthy water to the sea!"

Lucius chuckled. The Jews like their chants.

He adjusted his garments, yet again, and lifted what remained of his bread to his mouth. It hid most of his face, allowing him to raise his head and eyes and look upon the faces of the Jews. Every face contorted into a sneer. Hatred flamed from their eyes and spewed from their mouths.

"Return the corban. Return the corban. Send your filthy water to the sea!" They added another stanza, "Show your face. Answer for your sin! Show your face. Answer for your sin!" The chants rose from the mob and hung in the smoky mist above the market.

Lucius saw the determination in Pilate's glare the evening before. He could imagine how Pilate's spine stiffened today as he heard the Jews' chants, his eyes narrowing and his jaw clenching. By now, Pilate's servants had bathed him and were fitting his body with the royal tunic, armor, and cape. Surely he would wear his helmet.

The mob pressed toward the palace. Their chants grew louder. A couple dozen Jews weaved through the throng until they stood directly in front of the palace.

"The rabbis are at the gate," someone cried out. The crowd roared.

The rabbis banged on the palace's iron gate and chanted. "Answer! Answer!" The mob joined the chant. A few hundred protestors pressed toward the stone walls on both sides of the rabbis. The ground trembled, and the walls surrounding buildings, including Ephraim's inn, rattled. The mist in the air seemed to turn red.

Lest he appear conspicuous, Lucius joined his voice with the Jews. "Answer! Answer!"

Five minutes passed, then fifteen. Lucius knew Pilate planned to emerge, but evidently the governor wanted to let the frenzy build. It did. Hundreds more pressed toward the palace walls. The tide swept Lucius toward the palace until he stood just five paces from the gate, his fist raised into the air, the chant now bursting from his lungs. "Answer!"

The whole city, perhaps all Judea, pulsed with the protests.

Pilate emerged. Lucius heard the crowd's response before he saw the governor. Some jeered while others continued the chant. "Return the corban. Send your filthy water to the sea!"

Pilate stood in the guard tower above the palace wall. He stared forward and extended one arm in front of his body, his palm facing outward.

The howls and chants continued for several minutes until the crowd lifted a rabbi onto a cart. His long, speckled beard and sparkling eyes exhibited years of accumulated wisdom. The quieting of the mob attested to the respect he had earned from the Jewish community.

He raised both arms into the air. "Mr. Governor, our demands are two. We demand that you return the corban you stole from the temple treasury." The crowd roared. "And we demand that you tear down the aqueduct that pours unclean water into our holy city." The mob thundered its agreement.

Pilate remained in the same awkward posture, his right arm outstretched and palm facing outward. When the crowd finally quieted, he spoke. "The water will continue to flow. And with your corban . . . I will do as I please."

The throng erupted and pressed further toward the palace walls. Lucius began pushing back. *Can't these animals control themselves?* In the midst of the bedlam, he kept an eye on Pilate. Surely he would signal soon.

He did.

Pilate slowly moved his outstretched right arm until it pointed to the side. He then lifted his left arm so that it mirrored the right. He stood stiff, arms stretched to the sides, eyes staring forward, and his face set as stone.

Lucius and five hundred other Roman soldiers tore away their Jewish head coverings and pulled weapons from beneath their outer garments. The unarmed Jews panicked. They flailed, swinging fists, satchels, or anything else within reach that might serve as a weapon. But they were untrained and unprepared.

A soldier near Lucius thrust his dagger into the neck of a Jew. Blood erupted. The soldier spun and clubbed another Jew, smashing his skull. He continued spinning and assailing. All around him, Jewish bodies buckled.

Soldiers throughout the marketplace bludgeoned and beat Jew after Jew. The legionaries, so often constrained by their superiors, released years of pent up hatred. Every groan emitted and every drop of blood sprayed emboldened the soldiers all the more.

Lucius stood like a statue amid the bedlam, his feet wide, knees flexed, and arms ready to attack. One hand clutched a dagger and the other a club. The world around him slowed. His arms and legs paralyzed. All the noise blended into a dull roar. A tingling sensation, like needles emerging from his bones, prickled his skin, spreading down his spine to his fingers and toes. No sound fell from his lips. His club never landed on a Jewish skull and his dagger never penetrated a Jewish gut. His body remained motionless while his eyes wandered around the field of bloody slaughter.

A fleeing Jew ran directly into Lucius, drawing the centurion back to consciousness. The Jew's eyes filled with panic. Lucius pushed him toward the gate. "Get out of here while you can."

The Jews still alive darted about aimlessly, searching for a way out, any pathway to freedom. Some fell and were trampled. Others, with blood pouring from their midsections or throats, reeled and then fell, succumbing to the ocean of people that flowed over them.

Lucius stumbled through the masses, his feet sticking in the crimson sludge. He looked into the faces of those who ran. Terror filled their eyes and horror filled their screams. His arms fell to his sides as he stepped across yet another lifeless body. There must have been hundreds pressed into the mud in twisted, inhumane positions. Thousands.

As Lucius staggered through the carnage, his foot caught on a body, almost causing him to lose his balance. He looked down and his gaze fell on the dead, contorted face of Ephraim.

He dropped the weapons that had remained snug in his hands. He ran, weaving around trampled Jewish bodies and bloodthirsty Roman soldiers. He slowed to a walk when he passed through the Garden Gate, then stumbled to the wall beside the gate.

He hunched forward, rested his forehead against the wall, and vomited.

When the heaving stopped, Lucius rested his back against the wall. His face was pale and his eyes glassy. He gazed across the Towers Pool, and then his eyes rested on the scraggly hillside where soldiers crucified criminals.

He dug his fingers into his scalp. "What have we done?"

March, AD 30

The knock at the door startled Tobiah. In his drowsiness, he couldn't remember where he was. "Yes?" He roused. A muffled voice filtered through the door and brought him back to reality. "Get that baby up. It's time for Deborah to feed her."

Must Miriam be so persistent? Deborah knows when the baby needs to eat. Why does she have to be on such a strict schedule? Tobiah rolled over. "Go away."

Miriam banged on the door again. "Wake the baby. She's going to starve."

Deborah pulled a blanket over her head and groaned. Tobiah didn't know how many times she fed little Abigail during the night. Though Tobiah usually helped, he struggled last evening. Deborah, always the servant, didn't wake him.

"Just a minute, Miriam." Deborah spoke with a kinder tone than her husband. She nudged him. "Bring me the baby."

Tobiah grunted and obeyed. He trudged to the other side of the room where their daughter had begun to whimper.

Every time Tobiah looked at the crib, he thought of Ephraim. He had commissioned a carpenter to find the best wood from the highlands and fashion it into "the finest crib any baby ever had." At least that's how Miriam described it when she gave it to them, a few days after she buried Ephraim. Swirls, stars, and flowers were carved into its oak frame. Deborah gave birth to Abigail a week later.

Tobiah opened the door to let his sister in.

"You need nourishment." Miriam bustled into the room carrying a tray with fresh bread, sliced applies, and a pitcher of goat's milk.

When Tobiah reached for an apple slice, Miriam slapped his hand. "These aren't for you. They're for Deborah. You don't need anything. Get out of our way."

Miriam had always been a second mother to Tobiah. Their actual mother was a fine woman, but Miriam, ten years older, had cared for her younger brother from his infancy.

"Just like when we were children, huh?" Tobiah asked.

"I don't know what you mean."

"Slapping my hand. Correcting me. Bossing me."

"Rocking you to sleep. Feeding you. Holding your hand when you took your first steps. Always making sure your tunic was clean."

Tobiah grinned.

He was fourteen when Miriam announced she was leaving Galilee for Jerusalem. "Ephraim's uncle is sick and needs our help with the inn," she had explained. "When he passes away, he'll leave the inn to us. It's too good of an opportunity to pass up." Tobiah sobbed. She lifted his chin. "We'll still see each other from time to time." A lone tear dripped from the corner of her eye.

Beneath Miriam's bristly nature, she cared deeply. Tobiah knew that she loved him. She extended that love to Deborah when she joined the family, and now extended it, perhaps in even greater measure, to Abigail.

Once, a few years before, Miriam confided in Tobiah. "It seems Yahweh has chosen not to bless us with children." Her voice cracked. "It's difficult for me when families with children visit the inn. Ephraim bounces the youngsters on his knee and tells them stories. He would've been a marvelous father."

He would've been a marvelous uncle, too. Tobiah caressed his daughter's tiny head as she nursed. He brushed a tussle of hair from Deborah's eyes. He fed his wife an apple slice, then sneaked one into his own mouth.

"I saw that," Miriam said. She scuttled around the room exchanging dirty towels for clean ones, simultaneously coaching Deborah on proper nursing techniques. "Turn Abigail more toward you. Relax your shoulders. You're not doing it right. Hum a little to calm her."

Her arms full of towels and sheets, Miriam took a couple steps toward the door, then turned. "You take good care of that baby or I'll have to." Tobiah knew the words were more a hope than a threat. "I've got to go care for the guests." She exited the room in as much of a flurry as she'd entered.

Deborah looked up. "She means well?"

"Yes, I promise."

"I know. And we couldn't have survived these last couple of weeks without her." Deborah sat upright in the bed and lifted Abigail to her shoulder to burp her. "Get cleaned up and go help your sister. Your voice distracts Abigail, and she needs to eat well this morning."

Tobiah squeezed his wife's shoulder and kissed the top of Abigail's head.

Miriam had left the door partially open. Tobiah saw Tullus leave a small basin of water in the hallway. They locked eyes briefly but neither spoke.

Tobiah carried the basin into the room and washed his hands and face. He pulled on his woolen outer garment and slid a covering over his head. He descended the staircase that emptied into the back side of the inn and stepped into the outdoor kitchen.

"How's the morning meal coming along?" he asked.

"Just fine. No help needed." Miriam arranged fruit on a tray.

Nona stood a few feet from Miriam, transferring water from a basin into pitchers. She didn't speak. Nona hadn't spoken much since Ephraim's death. She and the children weren't in town the day of the massacre, but they were Romans. And the Romans killed Ephraim and hundreds of other Jews. Over the following few days, she quietly took care of the inn as Miriam, Tobiah, and Deborah mourned.

A week after Ephraim's burial, Nona approached Miriam in the dining room where the family ate together. Tobiah overheard. "Ma'am, I have finished all of the evening chores." Nona bowed her head.

"Thank you." Miriam didn't look at Nona.

Nona stood quietly for a moment. "You have been so welcoming and gracious, but if we need to leave, I understand."

Miriam didn't respond right away. Just as Nona turned to walk away, Miriam whispered, "That won't be necessary. I can still use your help."

A few weeks passed since the conversation, and, as far as Tobiah knew, no more words had passed between the women other than occasional bits of information necessary to keep the inn running smoothly.

The children's father, the centurion, hadn't visited the inn since Ephraim's death. Tobiah and Deborah hadn't met him, but before the massacre Nona and the children spoke of him often. Since the massacre, the centurion had not been mentioned.

Tobiah exited the inn and walked into the marketplace. It remained closed for a few days after the slaughter, but had now regained most of its activity. Ladies stood on the edges offering wine and treats. Some vendors sold animals, others crafts and tools. Tobiah found the booth he was searching for.

"I'll take six of your newest blankets, please." A few of the bed coverings at the inn were ragged and needed replaced.

"That'll be one denarius."

"Throw in an extra blanket and you have a deal."

"Deal."

Tobiah handed him a coin. The vendor had a couple dozen woolen blankets on display, dyed in various colors. Tobiah chose the seven he thought Miriam would like best and hoisted them onto his shoulder.

Tobiah knew Miriam appreciated his assistance, though she hadn't said so aloud. And he hadn't yet told her what he and Deborah decided. They would live in Jerusalem permanently. It wouldn't be safe for Miriam to manage the inn by herself. In a few weeks, Tobiah would travel to Caesarea to retrieve their possessions.

As Tobiah neared the inn, he saw Tullus standing next to the alley. He had draped a rug over the railing and was beating the dust from it with a broom handle.

His heart ached for the boy. Tullus obviously loved being Roman. He knew the history and the stories of the great wars. Not accurate history, necessarily, but what he'd picked up from the old soldiers in Caesarea. "One day I'm going to fight," he used to say, puffing out his chest. "Like my father. Like a Roman." Now he completed his chores at the inn but said little.

"Whenever you're finished with the rug, I could use your help." Tobiah's voice startled Tullus.

The boy nodded. "The rug needs a few minutes in the fresh air anyway. What can I do for you?" It was the most Tullus had ever spoken to Tobiah.

"Some of the blankets in the rooms are ragged. I bought these replacements. Walk with me through the rooms, and we'll collect the old ones and lay out new ones."

Tullus took four of the new blankets from Tobiah, hoisted them onto his shoulder, and followed the Jew into the inn. They proceeded through each of the inn's guest rooms and completed their task without speaking. They stacked the old blankets in a storage room near the back of the inn.

"Want something to drink?" Tobiah asked.

Tullus nodded. Tobiah filled two cups with water from a basin in the outdoor kitchen and handed one to Tullus. They walked to the front of the inn and stood on the front porch.

"How's the baby?" Tullus ventured into conversation, his eyes fixed on the marketplace.

"She's doing well. Deborah has been amazing. I don't know how she's functioning on such little sleep. But fortunately little Abigail is eating and sleeping and doing everything else like she's supposed to." He took a drink of water. "Everyone told us it would be an adjustment. We should've listened better. It feels like our whole world has been turned upside down. With the baby and then of course . . . " Tobiah's voice trailed off. He hadn't meant to bring up Ephraim's death or the massacre in the marketplace.

"Yeah, I know," Tullus offered quietly.

They stood silently, each sipping his water to avoid speaking.

"I'm just . . . " Tullus didn't complete his thought. Tobiah put a hand on the boy's shoulder and squeezed it. "I'm just not sure what to think," Tullus continued.

"What do you mean?"

Tullus sighed. Tobiah let the boy form his thoughts without interrupting.

"Ephraim, he treated us so well. And I don't know why. He let us stay here, let us work instead of paying. And he always made sure we had whatever we needed."

"Did that surprise you?"

"He was a Jew. And we're Romans."

"Maybe Ephraim could see beyond that."

"Maybe." Tullus swirled the water in his cup.

Tobiah watched him out of the corner of his eye, trying to read his expressions. He wanted to ask about his father, but feared the young man wasn't ready to talk about him yet.

"I'm Roman," Tullus finally said. He stood taller, as if trying to convince himself of what he was about to pronounce. "My allegiance is to Caesar, and I oppose all who oppose him."

Tullus disappeared into the inn, leaving Tobiah standing by himself on the front porch.

Tobiah sighed and smiled—not a smile of happiness but of resignation. Old prejudices pass from generation to generation, and the cycle seldom breaks.

Moments later, Deborah emerged from the inn holding Abigail in her arms.

"How's she doing?" Tobiah tugged on the corner of his daughter's blanket, revealing her face.

Deborah brushed his hand away. "She's resting. Don't disturb her." Deborah swayed and hummed. Abigail seemed to enjoy the steady noise from the marketplace and the fresh air. A contented smile covered her sleeping face.

"I just had a conversation with Tullus," Tobiah said.

"Really? An actual conversation?"

"Yes. A meaningful one." He paused, trying to form words that described the tension he sensed in Tullus. "I hurt for him. And I fear for him. He's trying to figure out how to be a man. And a Roman. And we're the first Jews he's spent any time with. Us and Ephraim and Miriam. I think he likes us but he doesn't want to." Tobiah took the last sip from his cup. "He's been told his whole life that Jews are dogs and that to support us is to oppose Rome. That Caesar is a son of the gods and anyone who doesn't bow before him deserves the sword." He drummed the rim of his empty cup with his fingers. "But then he met us. He wants to be strong, but he's trying to figure out how and where to show that strength."

Deborah continued swaying and humming. The baby cooed. Tobiah wanted to help Tullus, to provide some guidance to the confused young man. But he wasn't sure how to break through the wall that stood between them. This morning's conversation may've been a breakthrough. Maybe.

Deborah cleared her throat and interrupted Tobiah's thoughts. She nodded toward the marketplace. A centurion was approaching.

He was disheveled, unlike the typical centurion, and his gait lacked confidence. Taller than most, and wiry in frame, his shoulders drooped, and his feet shuffled on the dusty ground. His eyes remained lowered. He held his helmet in his hands, its once-gleaming bronze smudged and dull. He moved like a stallion that had once pranced gloriously into battle, but was now injured, shaken, demoralized.

Paulla ran from inside the inn, brushing past Tobiah and Deborah. She threw her arms around the centurion. "Father!"

Tobiah glanced at Deborah. She raised a brow.

The centurion wrapped his arms around his daughter as if he hadn't seen her in weeks. As far as Tobiah knew, he hadn't.

"My sweet girl, you look well," he said, releasing his embrace. He kissed her on the forehead.

"Well, you don't. Have you been sick?"

"Sort of. But I'm beginning to feel better."

Paulla noticed Tobiah and Deborah. "Have you met my father?"

"I don't believe we have," Tobiah responded.

"Tobiah and Deborah, please meet Lucius Valerius Galeo. The greatest centurion in the Roman Empire."

Tobiah and Lucius locked eyes. Pain surged through Tobiah's ribs and leg. Lucius turned ashen. Deborah looked at her husband and then the centurion. She took a step backward and held Abigail tight against her chest. Silence.

April, AD 30

Lucius brushed the shimmering coat of a black steed. The horse stood proud and tall, its muscles rippling. The centurion moved at the pace of a mule. He pulled a handful of grain from his satchel. "Here, enjoy." The steed neighed and nuzzled him.

They stood in the street on the north side of Antonia. The cold and rainy season had faded, and the mornings were warmer. The dew evaporating in the morning sun left a milky mist hovering above the ground.

Lucius pulled the brush from the horse's neck to tail. Such power, yet such grace. A worthwhile balance to pursue, not just for horses but for people. And empires. Rome wielded greater power than any empire in history. Nations trembled before them. But to what end? They caused so much pain. And what was true of the empire was true of its soldiers. *Including me.*

A month had passed since Lucius encountered Tobiah and Deborah at the inn, but he still shuddered when he remembered the fear in their eyes.

"So now you're doing the servants' work?" Septimus's gravelly voice pulled Lucius back to the present. He walked the center of the street toward Lucius. He ate an apple, chewing with his mouth open.

Lucius bristled, glared at Septimus, and resumed brushing. When Septimus reached the horse, he stroked its neck and belly, but not as gingerly as Lucius would have liked.

"You've not been yourself." Septimus spoke directly but wasn't as snide as usual. He searched Lucius's face for signs of an answer. Lucius didn't speak. "You're a centurion. Legionaries follow your example. The strength of Rome depends on the strength of its officers. And you . . . "

Septimus appeared unsure how to finish the sentence, so he took another bite from his apple. "I have a job for you. A messenger just arrived and said there's a demonstration, a parade of sorts, approaching Jerusalem from the east. It began in Bethany and gets bigger as it gets closer to the city."

"I'll investigate." Lucius's eyes remained on the stallion.

Septimus grunted his agreement and tossed the apple core to the street. Lucius watched him amble west toward the upper city. Not too many days ago, Lucius envied his superior. Wanted his rank. Schemed to bring him down and steal his position. Now? The thought of more power, at least that kind of power, made him nauseous. He was puzzled as to why.

A couple hours later, Lucius sat atop the steed he groomed that morning. Decimus mounted a horse next to him.

"Two columns," Decimus said. A dozen legionaries on foot hurried into formation behind the centurions. "Follow." The soldiers headed eastward from Antonia, with the temple to their right and the Pool of Bethesda to their left.

Lucius motioned to Avitus. The young soldier, struggling beneath armor too large for his skinny frame, scrambled to the front of the columns and marched alongside the centurions.

"What do you know?" Lucius asked.

"Why do you think I know something?"

"Don't you?"

"Well . . . yes."

Decimus chuckled.

"I hear it's that teacher from Nazareth," Avitus said. Lucius's ears perked. "Jesus, who they say works miracles. Some of the Jews think he might be their Christ. Or they use the word 'messiah.' They think he's anointed by their god."

"Anointed for what?" Decimus asked.

"Well, that's the question that's making our people nervous. A lot of the Jews, maybe most of them, believe he's going to rally their people and drive Rome from city. Maybe from the whole region." Avitus adjusted his ill-fitting helmet. "This talk has the rebels from Galilee sharpening their swords. I hear hundreds are on their way. And the chatter from the rebels has Pilate worried."

"So, what's happening today?" Lucius asked.

"Nobody is sure. Jesus stayed last night with friends in Bethany. Today he and his disciples started toward Jerusalem, and people followed along. More and more are joining them, and apparently it's grown into quite a mob."

Decimus scanned the horizon. "We should've brought more soldiers."

"You may be right." Lucius squinted in the midafternoon sun. Hadn't the Jews learned anything from their last revolt? Must more good men die in this naïve effort to oppose Rome? The image of Ephraim's bloody, contorted face haunted his mind.

The soldiers continued in silence as they descended the Kidron Valley, which was covered with tents.

"Didn't they just have a feast?" Lucius asked.

"Seems like it, doesn't it?" Avitus responded. "It was a few months ago. Jews pilgrimage to Jerusalem for three festivals a year. The last one was the Feast of Tabernacles. This one is Passover. In a few weeks, they'll celebrate Pentecost. Not every Jew travels to every feast. Men in villages take turns."

Pilgrims scurried throughout the valley gathering supplies they'd need for the coming days. Some had already built fires, filling the air with smoke and the aroma of roasting meat.

"What do you know about this festival, Passover?" Decimus asked.

"They'll have a feast later this week and then keep celebrating for seven days," Avitus said. "They say that several hundred years ago their god did a miracle, rescuing their ancestors from slavery in Egypt and taking care of them in the wilderness for forty years. They've been celebrating every year since. Passover is a time when they all rally together. It's part of their identity as a people."

"How many?"

"Thousands are already here, tens of thousands more are on their way."

Decimus sighed. "I'm hearing all the ingredients for a rebellion."

The soldiers weaved through pilgrims' tents until they reached the floor of the Kidron Valley, then they began ascending the Mount of Olives. The mob crested the hill above them. Lucius and Decimus veered their horses into Gethsemane, a garden on the lower slope of the mount. Their legionaries flanked to either side.

Jews who had camped in the valley saw the procession approaching and streamed toward it. The mob grew and numbered in the hundreds.

"They don't look angry," Lucius said. "They're smiling. They look hopeful."

"Hopeful for what, though?" Decimus fixed his gaze on the approaching parade. "That's what worries me."

Just down the slope from the soldiers, a group of Jews broke branches from trees, stood to the side of the road, and waved them. Others laid cloaks and blankets on the road as the parade approached. "Hosanna!" they shouted. "Blessed is he who comes in the name of the Lord. Peace in heaven and glory in the highest. Blessed is the coming kingdom of our father, David!"

When the centurions heard the Jews say "kingdom," they looked at each other. Then Lucius shot an inquisitive glance toward Avitus, who shrugged. Pilate might unleash the wrath of the empire when he heard of this.

As the parade descended the Mount of Olives, Lucius caught his first glimpse of the teacher at the center. Jesus wore the same dingy white robe and blue sash that he wore when Lucius first saw him.

"Is he riding a donkey?" Lucius rubbed his eyes and looked again.

"And it's not even a mature, sturdy donkey," Decimus said. "It's wobbly. A foal. Barely able to hold the grown man on its back."

A dozen men clung closely to Jesus and tried to create a path through the crowd. "Clear the way. The teacher is coming through. Step to the side." While Jesus wore an expression of peace, even resolve, these men bustled and jostled, as though they hadn't expected their journey to the city to create an uproar, and they didn't want anyone touching Jesus.

When the procession reached Gethsemane, just a few paces from the soldiers, it stopped in the middle of the road. A few Jews stood in the way with their arms raised.

"Those men are called 'Pharisees,'" Avitus whispered. "They're teachers, and the most righteous of the people."

The Pharisees, all bearded, dressed like typical Jews except their outer garments had long, blue fringes attached, and they wore black head coverings that draped around their shoulders and halfway down their backs. They had fastened boxes to their foreheads with leather straps. Lucius had seen other Jews wearing such boxes, but those worn by the Pharisees were more ostentatious.

Lucius pointed toward his own forehead and whispered to Avitus, "What are the boxes?"

"They put scraps of parchment in them, with some of their Scriptures written on them."

The procession came to a full stop, and the people stopped singing. The eldest Pharisee spoke. "Teacher, rebuke your disciples. Their words are blasphemous!"

Jesus, still sitting atop the donkey, smiled. Then he gestured toward the crowd. "I tell you, if they keep quiet, the stones will cry out."

The crowd cheered. The Pharisees grumbled.

Lucius wondered if Jesus would push the procession onward and trample the Pharisees. Instead, the teacher's face formed a contented smile. He scanned the people, his eyes seeming to rest on each person, one after the other. As the people felt Jesus's gaze, they grew silent.

Jesus turned toward the Pharisees. The smile faded from his face.

Then, his eyes shifted to the city behind them. Jerusalem. A tear appeared in the corner of his eye and was soon followed by a steady stream.

Lucius followed Jesus's gaze to the city. Pilgrims' white tents dotted the Kidron Valley. On the hill opposite the Mount of Olives, the temple glistened in the afternoon sun. Its white marble pillars and gold-plated, emerald-studded domes sparkled with such brilliance that Lucius shaded his eyes. Within the temple courts, religious leaders hurried about preparing for Passover activities. Downhill of the temple, the lower city hummed with afternoon business. On the far side of the temple, Herod's palace loomed over the upper city. Lucius had not yet seen the Jerusalem from this perspective. For a moment, his mind wandered through its streets.

"If you, even you, had only known on this day what would bring you peace. But now it is hidden from your eyes." Jesus's voice interrupted Lucius's thoughts and brought his attention back to the scene before him. Weeping, the rabbi continued,

"The days will come upon you when your enemies will build an embankment against you and encircle you and hem you in on every side. They will dash you to the ground, you and the children within your walls. They will not leave one stone on another, because you did not recognize the time of God's coming to you."

Lucius heard the legionaries behind him unsheathe their swords. He motioned for them to stand down. What did Jesus mean? Was this a call to battle? Surely not. Such rallying cries never came through tears, at least not through tears of compassion, which is certainly how Jesus appeared. But enemies? Embankments? Hemmed in on every side? Dashing people, including children, to the ground? Those weren't words of peace.

Lucius could sense Decimus bristling beside him.

Jesus went silent. He wiped the tears from his cheeks. Then his head turned, and his gaze rested briefly on Lucius. The centurion looked immediately to the ground. *What is it about this teacher? What does he know about me?*

"Let's continue," Jesus said. The Pharisees stumbled to the side. One of Jesus's disciples slapped the donkey on the backside, and it resumed its wobbly trek down the Mount of Olives. The procession followed, less exuberantly than before, but continuing to sing praises and lay blankets before Jesus, until he entered the temple on the other side of the valley.

"What do you think?" Decimus pulled the reigns of his horse, guiding it out of Gethsemane. "Do we need to tell Pilate?"

"We should tell him something." Lucius's horse came aside. "The question is what exactly to tell him." The legionaries, including Avitus, fell into two columns and followed the centurions. They descended the valley toward Jerusalem, toward Antonia.

"Is this the early stages of a rebellion?"

"Most of the elements are there." Lucius patted his horse on the neck. "The people are hurting. Many are furious after the riot in the market. Pilate continues to goad them. Jesus gives them a figure to rally around. There is a religious undercurrent." Lucius waved his hand toward the tents in the valley. "And, thousands of Jews are coming for Passover."

"You said 'most' of the elements are there. What's missing?"

Lucius's mind swirled. He didn't know how much of his inner struggle to reveal to Decimus. He'd once despised the Jews; now he admired their courage. He appreciated their compassion. He'd seen their pain. He'd caused their pain and regretted it. Deeply.

Centurions weren't supposed to regret, they were supposed to exert power, to oppress, to dominate. But power and domination meant less to Lucius each day. And Jesus, so intriguing. And appealing. The way he talked to people, and touched them. And taught them. He exuded peace, kindness . . . love. Yet, he confronted people when they needed it, like the Pharisees. On the Mount of Olives, he wept. This was no tyrant, no insurgent.

"It didn't seem like Jesus wanted a rebellion," Lucius finally said. "He talked about enemies and embankments, but it was like he was warning the Jews, pleading with them, not calling them to arms."

"We certainly need to keep an eye on him." Decimus nudged his horse into a trot.

"Yes. Yes, we do."

Lucius rotated between Antonia's four towers, each filled with soldiers. "Let me know if you see anything unusual. We can't let this get out of hand." The city below buzzed with tens of thousands of pilgrims. According to his superiors, the number could swell above a hundred thousand by week's end.

Septimus assigned him to this duty when they met early that morning. "Keep an eye on these Jews," he grumbled. "I smell trouble." In addition to the legionaries stationed in the towers, a few hundred circulated throughout the city, especially near the temple.

The afternoon was warm but comfortable. A salty breeze wafted to Jerusalem from the Dead Sea. The soldiers stationed in the towers wore full armor. Lucius rapped a dozing legionary on the back of the leg with his baton. "Wake up, soldier."

A group of legionaries in the next tower heckled the people below. "We can smell your stench all the way up here. Or is that the sheep dung? We can't tell the difference!" Lucius shook his head. The jeering continued. "Go back to where you came from. Or are you smart enough to find your way? Come up here, and we'll point you the right direction!"

Lucius cupped his hands and yelled, "Show some respect, soldiers." The reprimand surprised both the soldiers and himself. A few months ago, he'd have participated in the heckling.

Twenty-four hours had passed since Jesus rode into Jerusalem on the back of a foal. After the parade, he strolled around the temple courts, then returned to Bethany to stay the night with friends. No one in the city had seen him today.

According to Lucius's scouts, the gossip about him swept through the city like dust in the desert wind. Peasant Jews hoped he was their Messiah, while Jewish officials plotted against him. Romans worried he would incite a rebellion. No one could ignore him.

Lucius moved to the southeast tower, which rose above the temple and gave him the best view of the courts below. Avitus arrived for his shift.

"What's all the ruckus?" Lucius asked. The temple had remained in a state of commotion all day. "A lot of money changing hands down there."

"The Jews have to pay a tax to the temple to fund its upkeep and operation. But they have to pay it with Jewish coins."

"Why?"

"Roman coins have the images of emperors stamped on them. The Jews say it's blasphemous to bring these images into the temple's inner courts. So, money changers station themselves in the outer courts." Avitus pointed to the far side of the temple. "Pilgrims exchange the Roman coins they earned back in their hometowns for Jewish coins that they can take into the inner courts."

"What about all the animals?"

"The Jews sacrifice them to their god during Passover. They don't want to travel with them, so smart businessmen in Jerusalem sell them goats, sheep, and doves."

The stench of the animals rode the breeze, taking Lucius's breath.

"The money changers and the animal sellers hike up their prices at festival time," Avitus continued. "Sometimes the pilgrims get upset about it, but there's really nothing they can do. They gripe, but they pay."

Lucius pulled a canteen from his belt and downed a mouthful of lukewarm water. He surveyed the four towers to make certain the soldiers were behaving. Most were.

"Sir, you might want to keep an eye on this." Avitus nodded toward the south. A small group of Jewish peasants entered the temple.

Lucius squinted his eyes. They looked familiar. "It's him, isn't it?"

"I think so. Faithful pilgrims enter from the south. The steps on that side were built with varying heights and depths, forcing them to climb slowly. They say it encourages contemplation and prayer."

Jesus reached the money changers and animal sellers. He crossed his arms and watched as a money changer and a pilgrim haggled. He then moved a few paces north, closer to Lucius, observing another pilgrim negotiate the cost of a goat. The rabbi slowly shook his head. He spoke to his disciples.

Once the pilgrim surrendered to a price and led a goat away, Jesus approached the animal seller. He cocked his head. As he talked, his arms uncrossed and gestured. The conversation grew animated. Lucius wished he could hear what the rabbi was saying. The animal seller shook his head, rubbed the back of his neck, then put his hands on his hips and barked at Jesus. The rabbi's gestures grew more vigorous, and Lucius could just begin to hear his voice, and the seller's voice, as they yelled simultaneously.

As the seller continued to scream, Jesus took hold of the front edge of his table, and with a brisk, forceful motion, flipped the table upside down. The seller dashed to the side. A bucket of coins crashed to the pavement. A cage of doves hit the ground and broke open. The doves, liberated from their prisons, flapped their wings and rose into the air, shrieking. Behind the seller, goats bleated and pigeons in cages squawked.

Everyone near Jesus stopped and stared. "It is written," he bellowed loudly enough for Lucius to hear, "'My house will be called a house of prayer.' But you are making it a den of robbers!"

Jesus stormed to the next table, and the next, toppling them and sending their attendants cowering. He stopped and thundered a second time, "My house will be called a house of prayer!" He flipped more onto their sides.

Those whose tables remained upright rushed to secure their money and parchments. But he was finished. The Jewish pilgrims applauded. Jesus turned toward the pilgrims, who surrounded him. They bowed, raised their arms, and sang praises, "Hosanna to the Son of David." Jesus talked with them, his gestures less forceful now, and more open, inviting.

The outburst shocked Lucius. This wasn't the peaceful teacher who wept over the city yesterday. He glanced at Avitus. "What do you think?"

"I think it's great entertainment." The legionary laughed. "I guess it's justified, though."

Lucius scratched his chin. "In what way?"

"The people were being treated unjustly, cheated by the greedy. He stood up for them."

"This Jesus we see today isn't a pushover, that's for sure." Lucius contemplated the implications of what they'd witnessed. "He took a stand."

As the soldiers continued to watch, a Jew led a blind man to the rabbi. Jesus paused from teaching and touched his eyes. The man blinked in the bright afternoon sun, then swung his head to the left and the right, absorbing the spectacular views of the temple's gold, precious stones and white marble. Lucius could see the man's glowing expression all the way from the guard tower. He rubbed his own eyes and stared at the scene unfolding below.

Next, a group of men carried a friend on a mat and laid him before Jesus. The teacher knelt, brushed the lame man's hair from his eyes, and put a hand on his shoulder. Then he placed a hand on the man's thigh. The lame man stood. Shaky at first, but he grew stronger by the second. Finally, he stood tall and embraced Jesus. The crowd of Jewish pilgrims cheered.

Lucius watched dumfounded. "Again?"

A few hours later, Lucius sat in Antonia's dining hall before a loaf of stale bread and a plate filled with rotten fruit. The evening meal usually brought better options, but this evening, either because supplies were low or Septimus was in a bad mood, the soldiers, even the centurions, would endure less appetizing fare.

"What do you think?" Decimus sat across from Lucius.

Lucius usually enjoyed his friend's company, but he'd hoped to eat alone this evening. He sat in a dark corner of the room assuming people would take the hint. He needed to think. But Decimus found him and wasn't good at taking hints.

"What do I think about what?" Lucius replied.

"You know. Him. The rabbi. I was watching from another tower today."

Avitus sat, as well. Centurions didn't typically let their subordinates get so familiar, but Lucius enjoyed the young soldier. He was funny. And helpful.

"You talking about Jesus?" Avitus asked with his typical raised brows and Syrian accent.

"I wasn't talking about anything." Lucius focused on his fruit.

Avitus's cheeks turned red.

"We were just getting ready to discuss him," Decimus said.

Lucius shoved a handful of wilted grapes into his mouth.

"Here's what has me puzzled," Decimus ignored his obstinate comrade. "That spectacle today. It doesn't make sense. Yesterday he paraded into the city with all the Jews waving branches, laying down their cloaks, and worshipping him like he's their Messiah." He gestured with a piece of bread in his hand. "But if he's going to rally the Jews against us, he needs the backing of their leaders. The priests, Levites, Pharisees, Sadducees, all of them. But his antics today, attacking the money changers and animal merchants, was certain to anger any Jew with any authority. And Jesus knew that would happen."

Lucius nodded, now curious what Decimus was thinking.

"On the other hand," Decimus continued, "if he was trying to make some kind of connection with Rome, maybe trying to impress us by bullying the Jews, he went about it all wrong. We want peace, especially during Passover. The last thing we want is turmoil in the temple. So basically what he did today makes him an enemy of everybody, except maybe the peasant Jews, but he's going to need more than the peasants to get anything done."

Avitus grinned. "You're learning, sir. These are complex dynamics between the Jews and Romans."

"And what do you think, my fellow centurion?" Decimus looked to Lucius.

"I don't think anything."

"Sure you do. I can see it on your face. You've done nothing but think about it for the last three hours. Maybe longer." Decimus picked at his food. "Maybe you've been thinking about it for a few weeks."

Lucius stiffened. Twice Decimus began to say more but then pursed his lips. Lucius appreciated that his friend was treading carefully, but wished he'd drop the subject altogether. He wasn't ready to talk. The seconds felt like minutes. Avitus kept sneaking peeks at the centurions as he lifted his cup to his lips.

"Something has changed with you, my friend." Decimus spoke quietly, slowly. Lucius stared at the table and didn't even pretend to eat.

"I think what the rabbi did today was bold. And brave." Lucius hoped to take the conversation back to Jesus and off of himself. He knew, though, that the two topics of conversation, Jesus and himself, were somehow intertwined. He just didn't know how. "He stood up against corruption. Those money changers and animal merchants were taking advantage of people. He knew it would make the Jewish leaders angry, and that it would make Rome suspicious, but he took bold action anyway. People just don't stand up against the powers and politics like that." He nodded toward the room full of legionaries. "That kind of courage is in short supply around here."

Lucius took a final swig from his cup and slammed it on the table. He took what remained of his bread, left the fruit half eaten, and trudged from the room. He climbed a staircase that spiraled to the guard tower on the southeast corner of Antonia, the same tower from which he watched Jesus that afternoon.

The full moon spilled its light into the temple and reflected from the golden domes to create a brilliance different from that of the daytime. What had gleamed in the sunshine appeared frosted by the moon. Lucius breathed deeply. *What are you doing here, Jesus? And what does it have to do with me?*

Nona swept the front porch of the inn. As she finished this morning chore, she saw Lucius approaching.

Since he had met—or was reintroduced to—Tobiah and Deborah a month before, he had returned to the inn only once. During that visit, she asked, "You figured out who they are, didn't you?" Lucius nodded in response, looking at his hand, balling it into a fist. "Well, there's no need to talk about it," she announced.

Nona buried her feelings as deeply as Lucius did. She realized who Tobiah and Deborah were the evening she served them dinner and heard them describe the beating. But she saw no need to bring it up, lest she threaten the peace of the inn. Or lose her job. As far as Nona knew, no one had told Miriam. She hoped it would stay that way.

"Greetings, stranger. Do you need a room?"

Lucius smiled at the obvious jab. He held her shoulders and kissed her forehead. More affection than he usually showed in public. Or in private.

"I hope you're well this morning," he said.

He seemed a little better. His eyes brighter, stride more purposeful.

The last few weeks had been unlike anything Nona had experienced with Lucius. The always self-assured centurion, one of Rome's finest and proudest, walked slower, and his shoulders drooped. He wouldn't look people in the eye when he talked with them, even when he talked with her. His voice was quieter, sometimes shaky.

And the questions he asked. "What if the Roman way isn't the only way? Would you still care about me if I wasn't a soldier? What do you think the children, especially Tullus, would think about me?" And perhaps most disturbing, "What do you know about the Jewish god?" She had picked up a few things from Ephraim and Miriam about their religion, but not enough to satisfy Lucius's curiosity. In all the years she'd known him, he seldom asked her about anything. He always had the answers, not the questions.

The change began after the riot in the market, when Ephraim was killed. Nona wondered if Lucius had taken a blow to the head during the revolt, but he said he didn't. Or, perhaps he had contracted a sickness about that same time. Other than his change of demeanor, though, she saw no symptoms of sickness.

"You stay here and I'll get you some water." Nona wanted to keep Lucius on the porch. He nodded and sat on a bench.

She ducked through the doorway and hurried to the water basins at the back of the inn, hoping not to see anyone along the way. She didn't. Her children stood in the outdoor kitchen cleaning dishes from the morning meal. "Your father is on the front porch."

"Wonderful!" Paulla darted toward the front of the inn. Her brother followed.

Nona grabbed a cup that Tullus had just cleaned. She dipped a ladle into a barrel and took a deep breath. She poured water into the cup slowly, watching it fill to the brim. She'd give the children a moment to catch up with their father, and she wanted to collect herself. Nona wasn't accustomed to worrying about Lucius, at least not in this way. Sure, she was nervous when he went to battle. But this was different. When he was in battle, she was concerned about his safety, but now she worried about him. His confidence, his ability to function.

But he looked a little better this morning, she reminded herself.

Nona returned to the front porch and smiled at the scene before her. Paulla sat on her father's lap, her arms wrapped around his neck. She talked incessantly. "And last week Miriam let mother roast the lamb for the evening meal. For the first time! And Miriam didn't even have a single bad thing to say about it. It was the best lamb I've ever had. I sneaked a few bites after the guests were finished."

Lucius nodded attentively. Nona handed him the cup of water.

"And three days ago, Tobiah and Deborah's friends from Caesarea arrived. They came for the Jewish festival. Their names are Benjamin and Esther, and they're so nice." Her tone grew more serious. "Benjamin told me that I am a great hostess. The best he's ever seen, for a young girl, at least. And someday I should go back to Caesarea and start my own inn there. Do you think I can do that, Father?"

"Of course you can, sweet girl. Maybe the rest of us can go back with you and help."

Paulla laid her head on Lucius's shoulder and beamed.

"And what news do you have for me, Tullus?" Lucius took his son's wrist and pulled him close.

"There was some good action in the market yesterday. I went to get loaves of bread for the guests. On the way I heard a Jewish merchant telling a Roman soldier, 'Your days are numbered!' The soldier took his baton and beat the Jew until there was blood all over his face and he was unconscious. It was really something."

"I imagine so."

"What did the merchant mean, Father, when he said, 'Your days are numbered?'"

Nona looked to Lucius. She was curious to hear his answer, too. Lucius took a drink of water before responding. "I'm not sure, Tullus. He may've just been trying to scare the soldier. The Jews always get a little more defiant at feast time."

The evasive answer frustrated Nona, so she pressed further. "Speaking of the feast, what's been going on at Antonia and the temple? I hear the city is in an uproar."

"There's always an uproar around the festivals." Lucius chuckled awkwardly.

The conversation paused while Lucius took another sip. Paulla climbed off his lap to investigate a bug that had crawled onto the porch.

Voices came from within the house, muffled at first, then they grew clearer. Nona could pick out Tobiah and Benjamin's voices. Then their wives'. Finally, Miriam spoke up. Nona shot a glance at Lucius. She hoped the Jews would stay inside. Fortunately, they did. They sat in the room just inside the entryway and continued a conversation that had already begun.

"Children," Nona said, "go see if Miriam and the others would like some water, and then continue cleaning the dishes." The children entered the inn, offered water to those inside, then retreated to the back of the inn to get cups.

"I've longed for this day since I was in an infant in the cradle." Tobiah's voice trembled. "My mother would quote to me from the prophets:

The people walking in darkness
have seen a great light;
on those living in the land of deep darkness
a light has dawned.
For as in the day of Midian's defeat,
you have shattered
the yoke that burdens them,
the bar across their shoulders,
the rod of their oppressor.

The others joined, and they quoted the passage in unison:

For unto us a child is born,
to us a son is given,
and the government will be on his shoulders.
And he will be called Wonderful Counselor, Mighty God,
Everlasting Father, Prince of Peace.
Of the greatness of his government and peace
there will be no end.
He will reign on David's throne
and over his kingdom,
establishing and upholding it
with justice and righteousness
from that time on and forever.

The group fell silent. Nona couldn't see them, but imagined expressions of wonder on their faces.

Tullus interrupted the silence. "Here is your water."

"Thank you, children," Miriam said.

"Would you like any bread? Or fruit? I can bring a bowl of figs and nuts." Benjamin was right. Paulla was a good hostess.

"No, we are fine, thank you," Miriam responded. "You can continue with your cleaning."Another moment passed while the children finished passing out cups of water and left the room.

Benjamin broke the silence, "From among all the nations on earth, Yahweh chose us."

The others chimed in their agreement. "By his grace, in his mercy, he called us out from the nations."

"But," Benjamin continued, "in my lifetime I certainly haven't felt chosen. And neither did my father, or his father. The sword of the Romans, and before them the Greeks, pressed us to the ground. But the words of the prophets and the hope of our fathers still ring in my ears. Every time I see a soldier backhand a brother, I remember, and I have hope. Yahweh will not fail us. We are the children of the covenant. The Messiah will come. He will redeem us."

The words sounded so egotistical to Nona, so arrogant. They were chosen? Out of all nations? Ridiculous.

Deborah spoke up, quoting again from the Jewish prophets:

Rejoice greatly, Daughter Zion!
Shout, Daughter Jerusalem!
See, your king comes to you,
righteous and victorious,
lowly and riding on a donkey,
on a colt, the foal of a donkey.

Lucius's eyes grew wide and he turned to Nona. "Did she say the king comes riding on a donkey?" he whispered.

"Yes, I believe so. Why does that matter?"

Lucius didn't respond but turned his attention back to the conversation coming from inside.

"But so many have come," Miriam said. "They claim to be the Messiah, and we get our hopes up. But then they just go by the wayside like the rest."

"We can't lose hope," Esther spoke, as if reminding herself. "I just wish we knew when he was coming, and how, and who it will be."

Tobiah reentered the conversation. "These questions are debated every day in the temple, in the synagogues, and on street corners all across the land. He will be king. Of the Jews. A warrior greater than David and wiser and more marvelous than Solomon." Lucius leaned forward. Nona could feel her anger rising. Tobiah continued, "And he will lead us to freedom. Like he led our fathers from Egypt, he will bring us from under the sword of Rome. And he will lead us to conquest, to power, delivering justice to our oppressors."

Tobiah began the next refrain. The others joined in:

I will take away the chariots of Ephraim,

and the warhorses from Jerusalem,
and the battle bow will be broken.
He will proclaim peace to the nations.
His rule will extend from sea to sea
and from the River to the ends of the earth.

Nona stared at Lucius until he finally felt her eyes and glanced up. "Aren't you going to do something? Shouldn't you put a stop to this? This fantasy, it's absurd. But if other Jews are talking this way, too, it could be dangerous. You need to tell the other centurions. And Pontius Pilate."

Lucius grumbled something she couldn't understand and turned his attention back to the conversation inside.

"But is he the one? The Nazarene?" Esther asked.

"I don't know," Benjamin answered. "He's certainly not acting the way I thought the Messiah would act. And he's not a great warrior like David. I can't imagine someone like him overthrowing Rome. But those miracles, and the authority of his teaching. The way people are drawn to him. I'm curious to see what happens over the next few days."

From the look on Lucius's face, Nona could see that he was curious, as well.

Lucius stood with Decimus in Antonia's guard tower. The sun drifted behind the Mount of Olives, casting rays of orange and purple across the sky. He felt secure with Decimus by his side. His old friend knew when to speak, when to question him, and when to stand in silence to watch the sun set.

When the sun disappeared, the centurions turned their attention back to the temple below. "Been a quieter day?" Lucius asked.

"Fortunately." Decimus sighed. "Your men report any problems?"

"Nothing significant."

Septimus emerged from the top of the stairwell, huffing. He marched to his two subordinates. He had to catch his breath before speaking. "Pontius Pilate is coming tonight. When he gets here, he wants an update on the Jews and the ruckus caused by the Nazarene rabbi. I told his messenger that the two of you would bring him up to date."

"Yes sir," Lucius said with more respect than he'd ever shown Septimus.

Decimus wasn't as quick to agree. "Why us?"

"You were there when he entered the city a couple days ago, with that mob of Jews. And, from what I hear, your comrade here has taken special interest in the rabbi."

Decimus ignored the jab at his friend. "Why is Pilate staying here instead of the palace?"

"Herod is coming to town tonight, also, and will stay in the palace. Pilate wanted to stay at Antonia to keep a close eye on the temple and the Jews." Septimus ambled from the tower and back down the stairs.

"Herod's coming, too," Lucius said. "Must be an important feast." He crossed his arms. "What do you know about him?"

"Herod Antipas. Son of Herod the Great, who built the palace, temple, and most of Caesarea." Decimus rattled off biographic information. "Antipas has been governor of Galilee and Perea for three decades. He's not quite the leader his father was, isn't as accomplished. Though he did build Tiberius, his capital on the Sea of Galilee. He has an affection for drink and women. Can be brutal, from what I hear. A little paranoid."

Lucius raised a brow.

Decimus laughed. "I sit at the feet of Avitus of Syria."

Later that evening, the two centurions stood at attention at the bottom of the stairs that led to Antonia's entrance. They heard Pilate's entourage before they saw him emerge from the darkness, accompanied by his wife, numerous attendants, and a cohort of soldiers from Caesarea.

"A hectic week is about to get more hectic," Decimus said.

"And cramped." Lucius sighed. The legionaries from Caesarea would worm their way into every corner of Antonia, inconveniencing and irritating the soldiers already stationed in the fortress.

The two centurions, adorned in full armor, held spears in their left hands and extended their right arms in the Roman salute. As Pilate's attendants and soldiers ascended the stairs into Antonia, the comrades remained still.

Then Pilate himself approached, perched atop his favorite stallion. He stopped just before he reached the stairs and dismounted. A servant took hold of the horse's reins and led it away. Torches lined the stone stairs. In their light, Pilate's breastplate shimmered, and the crimson mantle draped over his shoulder looked the color of blood. He stepped toward Lucius, who continued staring forward.

Pilate stopped inches from Lucius's face, the governor's eyes even with the taller centurion's chin. "I need to see you two centurions. Come to my quarters in an hour. Apprise me of the events of the week. I especially want to hear about the rabbi."

"Yes sir."

Pilate ascended the stairs, his wife a few paces behind him. Soldiers surrounded them.

Lucius pursed his lips. He'd have to think carefully about what to say at this meeting, and what not to say. He was glad Decimus was going with him.

An hour later, Lucius, with Decimus at his side, marched down a dingy corridor. Guards posted outside Pilate's quarters saluted the approaching centurions. Lucius returned the salute, then rapped on the door three times. A guard inside opened the door. "You may enter. The governor is expecting you."

Lucius ducked his head to step through the doorway. He scanned the room. Lanterns lined the walls and brightened the room like midday. Tapestries hung from the walls and multicolored Persian rugs covered the floors. Chairs hewn from oak and cedar provided seating throughout the room. A dozen attendants bustled in and out.

Pilate and his wife reclined on a purple couch next to a table, which held silver platters overflowing with fruit, cheese, and steaming loaves of bread. An attendant entered carrying a tray with carefully arranged meat delicacies. Pilate and his wife grazed. A servant stood ready with a pitcher to refill their goblets of dark wine.

Lucius remembered the stale bread and weak beer he'd consumed earlier that evening.

"Enjoy." Pilate waved the two centurions toward the table. Decimus chose an apple slice, but Lucius ate nothing. Both accepted a goblet of wine from a servant and sipped carefully. They remained silent, waiting for Pilate to begin the conversation.

"And how is everything in our fair Jerusalem?"

"Normal for festival time," Decimus replied. Lucius was glad his friend took the lead. "Most of the pilgrims have already arrived. A few stragglers may come in tomorrow. They will gather in families for the Passover feast tomorrow evening."

"Any disturbances?"

"None more than usual."

Pilate tore a piece of bread from a loaf and placed a slice of cheese on it. He took a bite and chewed with his mouth open. The governor looked at Lucius, who had yet to speak. "And what about this rabbi from Galilee?"

"We have our eye on him," Lucius replied quietly.

"And what have you seen with this eye you have on him?"

Lucius shifted his weight from one foot to the other, attempting to formulate a response that would neither alarm the governor nor leave him open to the accusation of withholding information. "On the first day of the week, he entered the city from the Mount of Olives, surrounded by what appeared to be an impromptu parade. His followers sang praises, waved branches, and laid their cloaks on the road in front of him. The rabbi rode a donkey. Once inside the city, he looked around the temple for a while and then left." Lucius cleared his throat. "The next day, Jesus returned to the temple and appeared angry. In the outer courts he screamed at those who were exchanging money and selling animals, and turned over their tables."

"Why would he do such a thing?" Pilate inquired.

"We're not sure," Decimus injected. "But we could hear him say something like, 'This is supposed to be a house of prayer and you've turned it into a den of thieves.'"

"Odd behavior." Pilate paused from eating.

"We thought so," Lucius responded. "But the last couple of days, yesterday and today, were calmer. He came to the city each day and spent most of his time in the temple and on the Mount of Olives, teaching his followers and debating the Pharisees and Sadducees."

"Any signs of insurrection?"

"Not that we've seen," Lucius continued. "We worried after the parade a few days ago. But the tantrum in the temple and his teaching and debating since seem to be confronting the Jews more than rallying them. At least, confronting the priests and other leaders. The peasants appreciate his teaching. And he's kind to them, unlike the temple officials."

"Where is he staying?"

"With friends in Bethany," Decimus spoke up again. "One of them, named Lazarus, claims that Jesus raised him from the dead."

"Raised from the dead?"

"Yes, that's what he says. We haven't been able to confirm it. There are additional reports of Jesus healing people. The lame, the blind, lepers. Those Jews like to tell their tales."

Pilate tore a leg from the duck and took a bite. He glanced back at Decimus. "What do the Jewish officials think of him?"

"They're not happy. Our contacts tell us that the Pharisees, priests, and Sanhedrin have been conspiring against him for some time. They say he is a heretic and blasphemes their god. But you know how they are." Decimus smiled. "Any time a rabbi gets more popular than them, they howl about heresy and blasphemy."

Pilate sipped from his goblet of wine. "Have they done anything more than howl this time?"

"Well, we think so." Decimus swallowed. "There is a rumor that they have turned one of his followers, one of the dozen who are closest to Jesus. This disciple is willing to betray Jesus and help them arrest him."

Lucius tried not to let his shock show on his face. He'd not heard this rumor. His mind traced through the images of those twelve men who were always around Jesus. He wondered which of them had agreed to betray their rabbi. Should he warn Jesus?

How could he get word to him? What if he tried and was found out?

"And you believe the rumor?" Pilate asked.

"Yes, I do," Decimus responded.

"Who will arrest him?"

"The temple guards."

Pilate rolled his eyes, then turned his attention to the tuna. The fish was so tender that pieces flaked off with barely a pull. He savored a few bites and sipped his wine before speaking again. "The temple guard is inept. Laughable, really. I don't trust them to handle the arrest. And these Jews will look for any reason to rebel. We can't allow any chaos that would give them an excuse." He thought for a moment. "Find out whatever details you can. Where, when, and how the temple guard plans to arrest him. And then the two of you follow along. Take some legionaries with you. Just make sure the incident doesn't cause an uproar. Keep everything quiet and calm."

Pilate waved his hand to indicate the conversation was over.

"Yes sir," Decimus replied. "We serve at your bidding."

Pilate didn't respond; his attention returned to the tuna.

Lucius followed his comrade back into the dingy corridor. "I didn't know about the arrest. And that they've turned one of his disciples."

"I just found out myself, right before our meeting. I'm sorry I didn't have a chance to tell you."

"What does this mean?"

Decimus stopped and faced his friend. "Are you asking what it means for Rome or the Jews?" He paused. "Or what it means for you?"

Lucius sighed. He wasn't ready to answer the question, either aloud or in his heart. "Pilate was wise to ask us to go. We can keep it peaceful."

He nodded to his friend, then returned to his quarters, his mind racing. *Why does Jesus continue to dominate my thoughts?*

Who is this man? Lucius couldn't yet formulate a response, but he knew one thing for sure—the time had come to find out.

Well after sunset, Lucius hoisted himself onto his steed. Dew covered the ground and his leather saddle. The full moon, obscured by the occasional wisp of cloud, cast a glow across the city and the surrounding mountains and valleys. Chill bumps appeared on the centurion's bare arms and legs. Decimus came alongside him. Twenty-four hours had passed since they met with Pilate.

Two columns of legionaries fell in line behind the centurions. "Military pace," Lucius commanded. The soldiers headed east. At the northeast corner of Jerusalem, outside the city walls, a few dozen temple guardsmen waited for them.

Avitus, marching just behind the centurions, spoke up. "The temple guards are really just priests, Levites, and servants who occasionally perform guard duty. We'll have to watch them closely. This could go bad quickly."

Lucius assessed the temple guardsmen. They carried clubs, swords, and torches. They held their weapons awkwardly, as though they'd never been trained. Probably, they hadn't. Their ill-fitting armor consisted only of metal chest plates strapped over woolen robes. Instead of helmets, they wore cloth head coverings.

"We can do this without you," said the captain of the temple guard.

"We're not sure you can," Lucius replied.

The two stared at each other. Lucius shook his head. "You go and we'll follow. We'll stay out of your way unless things turn ugly."

"We want a peaceful evening," said Decimus, speaking loudly enough for the whole guard to hear. "You Jews have your skirmishes. Make sure this one doesn't boil over into something we'll have to deal with."

The captain of the Jewish guard nodded and marched southeast toward the Mount of Olives. He held a torch in his left hand and a sword in the right. The rest of the guard followed in no particular order or formation.

"What a mess," Decimus said.

Lucius chuckled.

Once the temple guard was on its way, the Romans followed in tight formation. They descended the Kidron Valley, zigzagged between pilgrims' tents, and ascended the Mount of Olives on the other side.

The temple guard bumbled its way toward the Gethsemane gates. Lucius tugged the reins of his horse, turning it toward Jerusalem. The temple and the city behind it gleamed in the light of the moon. The glow had assumed an ominous, red tint. Lucius let his mind wander through the streets of the city to the marketplace in front of Herod's palace. He squinted, trying to see Miriam's inn, but it wasn't visible from this vantage point. His mind meandered through the inn's front door. He imagined Nona and their children sleeping peacefully in their room. He wanted to hold them.

"You coming, soldier?" Decimus interrupted his thoughts.

"Right behind you."

The two centurions followed the temple guard through the gate, their legionaries behind them. A stone wall enclosed the garden. Gnarled trees that brought a sense of peace, even wonder, during the daytime appeared eerie by the light of the moon. An olive press sat on a stone platform beneath a thatched roof, its crushing stone awaiting the harvest that would arrive in a few months.

The Jewish captain stopped, as did guardsmen behind him. Just ten paces from the captain stood a group of men with Jesus at their center. Lucius, perched atop his horse, could see above the guardsmen as the confrontation unfolded.

"Who do you want?" Jesus asked.

"Jesus of Nazareth," the captain replied.

"I am he."

Several of the guardsmen gasped. Perhaps they assumed he would deny his identity.

"If it is me that you want," Jesus motioned toward his followers, "then let these men go."

At that moment, a man stepped forward from among the guards. He didn't carry any weapons. Lucius hadn't noticed him during the march. When the man turned back toward the captain for reassurance, Lucius recognized his face. He had been with Jesus when the rabbi entered the city on the donkey. *Must be the traitor.*

He kissed Jesus on the cheek. "Greetings, Rabbi."

"Judas, you betray me with a kiss?" Jesus placed his hand on Judas's shoulder and stared into his eyes. The betrayer and the betrayed. "Do what you came for, my friend."

Lucius's jaw dropped. Jesus is just going to accept this? Not order his other disciples to assail the betrayer, or defend him against the guard? How could he just submit?

Judas turned toward the guard and nodded. Three of them stepped forward. One held a torch and the other two carried ropes. The torchlight revealed the expression on Jesus's face—resignation, gentleness. Even pity. He held his hands forward; the guardsmen bound them. No one spoke. Then they bound his feet, allowing enough leeway for Jesus to take small steps.

His followers, paralyzed by fear to this point, unfroze. "Should we defend you, Lord? This can't happen!"

A disciple pulled a sword from its sheath.

"Peter, no." Panic crossed Jesus' face.

Lucius leaped from his horse. "Stop. Stand down!" He drew his own sword and rushed forward.

Peter swung wildly toward one of the temple guards, aiming for his skull. The guard ducked his head at the last moment. The sword caught his ear and sliced it from his head. The guard screamed. "What have you done?!" He fell to his knees and covered the wound with both hands. Blood gushed through his fingers and down his arms.

Lucius reached the guardsman and knelt next to him. He pulled a cloth from his belt and pressed it to the man's head. The blood drenched the cloth and covered Lucius's hands and forearms.

The captain of the guard stepped toward the disciples, his sword raised. "Not another move." The other guardsmen followed, ready to attack. Jesus' disciples stepped back, their eyes wide, arms tensed but at their sides. Peter dropped his sword.

"No more," Jesus said. Strangely, everyone stopped. "Put your weapons away. Those who draw the sword die by the sword."

Jesus turned to his disciples. "This is a part of my Father's plan. Don't you think, if he wanted to, he could send legions of angels to protect me? He isn't sending the angels because the Scriptures must be fulfilled."

Jesus reached to the ground, his hands still tied, and picked up the gory ear. He knelt next to Lucius and the injured guardsman. Lucius continued holding the cloth to man's head. Jesus brushed Lucius's hands away and pressed the ear into place. The bleeding stopped. The guard stood and touched his ear. His eyes bulged and his mouth gaped. He looked to his arms. They were clean. He touched the side of his head. No blood.

Lucius looked to his own arms and hands, and the cloth he held. The blood vanished. He stumbled backwards. This was no illusion. No rumor. Not the wishful thinking of gullible religious fanatics. It was a miracle. "Who are you?"

Jesus smiled at Lucius. The centurion staggered back to his horse, alternately staring at his arms and the rabbi.

Jesus turned his attention to the temple guard and Roman soldiers. "Am I leading a rebellion? You've come out with swords and clubs to arrest me. Every day this week I've been teaching in the temple courts, yet you didn't lay a hand on me then. Why now? Why tonight? Why under the cover of darkness?"

No one responded. Instead, the Jewish captain marched toward Jesus with more confidence than Lucius thought was merited. The captain whispered something to the rabbi, spat on the ground, then shoved him toward the other guardsmen.

Jesus stumbled when shoved, but then, resigned to his fate, walked toward the gate with strides as long as the ropes around his feet allowed.

Lucius kept a close eye on Jesus's followers, wondering if they would now fight for their rabbi. They didn't. They didn't look at the guard, the legionaries, or Jesus. Instead, beginning with Peter, each disciple took a few steps backward, turned, and ran from the garden into the darkness.

Judas's face filled with confusion and terror, then he ran as well.

Jesus, abandoned, continued toward the gate. The temple guardsmen shuffled to the sides to create a path for him. Lucius motioned for his legionaries to do the same. The captain of the guard followed Jesus, prodding him with the tip of his sword.

As Jesus passed Lucius, he paused, reached up, and grasped the centurion's hand. Decimus tensed and reached for his sword, but Lucius motioned for him to stay back. "It's OK."

Jesus looked into Lucius's eyes. "Believe," he whispered. He held the gaze until the guardsmen nudged him to continue.

Lucius stared at his hand. *Believe what? Who are you? Where did you come from? Why do your eyes haunt me? What do you want from me?*

The group started toward the city, their pace constrained by the ropes around Jesus's feet. Their torches threw shadows on pilgrims' tents as they passed through the valley.

Lucius dismounted, handed the reins of his horse to a legionary, and shivered. The night had grown colder. He stood before an extravagant, Roman-style home in Jerusalem's upper city. Servants milled around fires warming their hands. Fountains, flowers, and statues adorned the courtyard.

The captain of the temple guard prodded Jesus toward a portico that extended from the house. "Move. More quickly." The portico boasted columns of white marble and floors decorated with colorful mosaics.

Lucius looked to Decimus. "What are they waiting for? Or who?"

Decimus shrugged. "Whoever it is, I'd wish he'd hurry."

Lucius stared. His mind elsewhere.

"Want to tell me what happened in the garden? You looked like you saw a ghost. And what happened with that guard and his ear?"

"I was . . . did . . . I don't know. It was strange." He held up the hand once bloody from the guard. *White as snow.*

"Did the rabbi threaten you? You backed away, almost terrified."

Lucius grew impatient. "I told you. I'm not sure what happened. It was strange. Leave it at that."

Lucius had never experienced such a feat. His hands trembled, but more so, his heart, his mind . . . raced. What was this rabbi trying to say to him? He felt confused, but now wasn't the time to discuss it with Decimus. Not today. Not until he understood it himself.

A half hour passed, then an old man, obviously accustomed to being asleep at this hour, opened a door and shuffled onto the portico. Two servants assisted him. He wore a purple robe. He sat in an ornate, throne-like chair, and took a deep breath.

"Who's this?" Lucius asked.

"Don't know."

A servant nearby overheard the centurions. "It's Annas. He was the high priest for a while. Now his son-in-law, Caiaphas, is high priest, but Annas still has a great deal of influence."

"Why did they bring Jesus here?" Lucius asked.

"Not sure," the servant answered. "But a lot of people still respect Annas. Maybe the temple officials want his backing before they go further."

Lucius turned his attention to the portico.

"I understand you're causing quite a stir," Annas said.

Jesus looked Annas in the eye but didn't respond.

"The high priest asked me to speak with you. Why at this late hour, I don't know." He chuckled. "But it seems they want my opinion before you stand before them in the morning."

Annas continued, "I hear that a group of Galileans—a dozen or so—have been sitting at your feet for some time now. Is this true?"

"Yes."

"And I understand that it's quite the eclectic group. Some fishermen. A tax collector." Annas paused. "And perhaps a zealot or two?"

Ah, yes. Now Lucius could see where this was going. He exchanged a glance with Decimus. Annas was trying to figure out if Jesus was inciting a rebellion.

"My disciples are learning the ways of the kingdom of God."

"Ways they can't learn from priests or Pharisees?" Annas's tone grew sharper.

Jesus remained silent.

"What exactly are you teaching them?"

Jesus studied the ground at his bound feet, then raised his eyes. "I've spoken openly. I always taught in the synagogues or at the temple, where Jews gather. I said nothing in secret. Why question me?"

"Because I need to know what you taught."

"Ask those who heard me. Surely they know."

The captain of the guard stepped forward and slapped Jesus with the back of his hand. "Is this the way you answer the high priest?"

Blood appeared on Jesus's lower lip. "If I said something wrong, tell me what was wrong. But if I spoke the truth, why did you strike me?"

Annas looked to the servants who stood to his side, as though they would have an answer to Jesus's question. He then motioned for the guard captain to come closer. The two spoke in hushed voices. Then Annas commanded, "Take him to Caiaphas."

Decimus sighed. "Sounds like our long night is going to spill over into a long day."

Perhaps, Lucius thought, *but it may be the day that changes everything.*

"Y ou can nap for an hour or two. I'll keep watch," Lucius said.

"Thanks." Decimus yawned. "Wake me if you need me."

Lucius turned to their legionaries. "Take turns sleeping through the rest of the night, but make sure half of you are always awake and ready to act."

He glanced across the courtyard of Caiaphas's house, an extravagant palace similar to Annas's. The temple guard had taken Jesus inside. Every few minutes, cries of agony erupted from the palace and pierced the night. Jesus received no break from the torture.

A few hours later, when dawn broke, dozens of Jewish officials wearing ceremonial garb drifted from the surrounding streets into the courtyard. Temple soldiers emerged from Caiaphas's house dragging Jesus, bloodied and frail.

When the officials saw Jesus, they glared. One near Lucius whispered, "You've embarrassed us for the last time, you worthless peasant from Nazareth."

The guard poked and jabbed Jesus. "Move along. Pick up your feet." He pushed the rabbi onto the portico. Jesus stumbled, his hands and feet still tied.

Everyone waited. The Jews murmured among themselves. Lucius dismounted his horse and stood next to one of the fires that glowed in the courtyard. Smoke filled his nostrils and made his eyes water. He glanced to the east. The morning sky's orange and purple hues gradually yielded to grayish blue. Sunrise at last.

"You were with him," came a girl's voice. Lucius turned to see who spoke. She wore the tattered tunic of a servant. Her voice sharpened and her finger pointed to a Jew. "You . . . you were with Jesus!" The Jew lifted his head only briefly, enough that Lucius recognized him. He was one of Jesus's followers, Peter.

"I don't know him," Peter mumbled and turned away. He walked to another fire closer to the gate. Lucius followed.

"You look familiar." A Jew near the gate nodded toward Peter. "You're one of his disciples, aren't you?"

Lucius leaned in, his curiosity growing.

"No, I don't know that man," Peter replied.

Lucius tilted his head. A few hours before, in the garden, the disciple risked his life for Jesus. He drew his sword before a band of temple guardsmen and Roman soldiers. This morning, before peasants, he wouldn't even admit that he knew the rabbi. *Odd.*

Minutes later, another servant spoke up. "You're Galilean. I'd know that accent anywhere." The servant took a step toward Peter. "I was at the garden last night. Didn't I see you there?" He furrowed his brow. "You were the one who cut off the guardsman's ear."

Lucius tensed and slid his hand toward his sword.

Peter cursed and pointed toward Jesus. "I'll tell you again, I don't know that man!"

When the disciple's voice rose, Jesus turned. The two locked eyes. A rooster crowed. Peter's eyes filled with tears and he ran from the courtyard.

Lucius watched Peter escape through the crowd. *Why did the disciple act that way? Such a drastic change, from courage to cowardice.*

A large, oak door to Caiaphas's palace creaked open and drew Lucius's attention back. Servants and priests streamed onto the portico, flanking to either side. They faced the door and stood at attention.

A priest appeared in the doorway, adorned in a sleeveless, blue robe, with scarlet tassels swinging from its hem. An embroidered vest rested over the robe, and atop the vest hung a woven breastplate gilded with twelve gems.

A legionary leaned toward Lucius and whispered, "Caiaphas."

The Jewish captain grabbed Jesus from behind and forced him to his knees. "You will bow before the high priest."

Caiaphas scanned the crowd, then his eyes settled on Jesus. He stepped down from the portico and stood before the rabbi. He extended his foot, hooked the toe of his sandal under Jesus's chin, and lifted his head. Dried blood clung to Jesus's upper lip.

"What a surprise to find you in my courtyard this morning," Caiaphas said.

He orchestrated this whole thing, Lucius realized. The entire mob is against Jesus, including the officials who were supposed to make sure he was treated fairly. He had no chance.

Caiaphas addressed the crowd. "Why do you bring this man to me? What charges do you wish to bring against him?"

The captain of the temple guard stepped forward. "This man has committed blasphemy against the temple." The other officials nodded their agreement. Murmurs rumbled through the crowd. Lucius and the other Romans remained stoic.

"Do any witnesses support this accusation?" Caiaphas scanned the courtyard.

The captain grasped the arm of a man behind him and shoved him forward.

"Speak," Caiaphas said.

"I heard this Jesus of Nazareth say the temple would be destroyed," the peasant said. "Not a stone would be left on top of another." He slinked to the back of the crowd.

"Are there others who would condemn this man?"

A second peasant cautiously stepped forward. "Yes, but I heard him say he'd destroy it himself, and that he'd rebuild it in three days." A different account.

Caiaphas shot a sharp glance toward the captain, who, in turn, cast the same menacing look toward the second witness.

Lucius smiled. *That didn't go as planned.* The planted witnesses didn't get their stories straight. Both accusations had to do with destroying the temple. Jesus must've said something about that. *Gutsy. What can he do? What are his limits?* Lucius looked at his hands and forearms. Jesus is a miracle worker. But he's more than that.

Caiaphas returned his attention to Jesus. "What do you say, Jesus of Nazareth? Which of these testimonies is true? Or are they both? What have you said about the temple? How do you answer?"

Jesus didn't respond.

Caiaphas frowned, then changed tactics. He steeled himself, glared at Jesus, and demanded, "I charge you, under oath by the living God, tell us if you are the Messiah, the Son of God!"

The Jewish officials stiffened. The crowd grew silent.

"I am," Jesus said.

The crowd gasped. Relief crossed the high priest's face.

Lucius remembered what he and Nona overheard on the porch of the inn, when their Jewish friends quoted their prophets about the Messiah. He gazed around the crowd, wondering if Tobiah and Benjamin were among the Jews gathered, but didn't see them. What would they think about Jesus's confession?

Jesus raised an arm into the air. "I say to all of you: from now on, you will see the Son of Man sitting at the right hand of the Mighty One and coming on the clouds of heaven."

Caiaphas's face fell at Jesus's brash response. The high priest looked to the heavens, grasped the edges of his blue robe, and tore the garment. "He has spoken blasphemy. Why do we need any more witnesses? You all have heard from his own lips!" Caiaphas glared at the Jews before him. "What do we do with him now?"

"Death to the blasphemer!" The Jewish officials cried out in unison, as if they'd practiced.

Temple guardsmen rushed forward and pulled Jesus to his feet. They spit into his face and battered his ribs and gut with their fists. "Prophesy to us, Messiah. Who hit you?"

Roman legionaries started toward the rabbi to keep the scene from escalating, but Decimus held them back.

"What are you doing?" Lucius took a step toward Jesus. "They'll kill him."

Decimus put a hand on his comrade's arm. "This isn't our fight. At least not yet."

The Jews pushed Jesus out of the gate. The throng spilled onto the street outside of Caiaphas's house. They weaved northeast through the city, with Jesus stumbling along at the center.

The Romans followed. "Are they going to Antonia?" Lucius asked.

"Sure looks that way," Decimus said.

"Pilate won't be happy. With them or with us. We were supposed to keep this from getting out of hand."

Decimus sighed. "With the few soldiers we brought, I'm not sure we could've stopped it anyway. I'll send a messenger ahead to get more legionaries ready at Antonia."

"Maybe that'll help." Lucius nudged his horse to keep up with the mob. "But I wonder if there are larger forces involved than we realize."

The sun had fully risen and taken the chill from the air. The agitated mob stood outside of Antonia. They pushed Jesus to the front. Lucius, on horseback, milled around the edge of the crowd. Decimus and other centurions did the same.

Lucius motioned toward a group of legionaries. "Disperse throughout the people. Keep the peace, as best as you can."

Pontius Pilate emerged from Antonia and stood on the landing at the top of the stairs. The murmuring of the crowd crescendoed, then quieted when Pilate raised his arm. "What charges do you bring against this man?"

"He's a criminal." A Jewish elder stepped forward. "Otherwise we wouldn't bring him to you."

Another shouted, "We have found him subverting our nation. He opposes payment of taxes to Caesar and claims to be the Messiah, a king."

A wise approach. Lucius didn't understand all the dynamics at play, but did know that Pilate could only act if he was convinced Jesus was a threat to Rome.

Pilate frowned. He descended the stairs, pulled a club from his belt, and used it to raise Jesus's chin. "Are you the king of the Jews?"

"You have said so." The rabbi spoke through swollen and bloody lips.

Lucius's heartbeat quickened.

"Do you hear the things they're saying about you?" Pilate continued.

Jesus stared at the governor, but gave no response.

Pilate pulled his club from beneath Jesus's chin, looked toward the Jews, and ascended three stairs backwards. "I find no basis for charges against this man. Take him yourselves and judge him by your own law."

Lucius leaned toward Decimus and whispered, "Does this end it? Where else can they go from here?"

Decimus shrugged.

The Jewish leaders conferred with one another, then one spoke up. "We have no authority to execute. And he stirs up people all over Judea by his teaching. He started in Galilee and has come all the way here."

Pilate cocked his head. "Did you say Galilee?"

"Yes. He began in Galilee, then came south."

Pilate scratched his chin. "Galilee is Herod's jurisdiction." He turned to ascend the remainder of the stairs, waved his hand, and commanded over his shoulder, "Take him to Herod."

The Jews pulled Jesus to his feet and pushed him to Herod's palace in the upper city.

Lucius and the other centurions patrolled the fringes of the crowd on horseback. As they passed through the marketplace outside of Herod's palace, Lucius glanced toward Miriam's inn and wondered if Nona and the children were inside. Perhaps they were preparing the morning meal for their guests. He felt a twinge in his heart and held his gaze on the inn's front door, hoping his family would come outside. He couldn't speak to them, but he could at least see them smile. It was a strange dynamic— the more he felt drawn to Jesus, the more he felt drawn to Nona and the children, and the less obsessed he was with scheming against Septimus and amassing power.

Evidently, those in the inn hadn't heard the crowd coming. No one came outside. Or if they had heard the disturbance, Miriam may've gathered everyone into a back room. After Ephraim's death, she feared any public demonstration.

The horde passed through the gate into Herod's palace and marched through the courtyard to the portico. They shoved Jesus to his knees. Herod waited with a gaping smile. Lucius inched his horse close enough to hear.

"Jesus of Nazareth," Herod Antipas bellowed, rubbing his hands together, "I've heard stories about you. I've wanted to see you."

Jesus raised his head.

"I hear that you've awed the crowds by your deeds. Healing leprosy? The demon possessed? Making the lame walk? I understand you're quite the miracle worker."

Lucius nudged his mount a step closer. This reception from Herod surprised him.

"So, how about a miracle for me? Impress me." He waved his hand before the crowd. "Impress us all."

Jesus refused to answer and Herod's smile faded.

"Sir," a Jewish official said, "This man has blasphemed our God. And Rome. He claims to be king and speaks of destroying the temple. He has caused riots from Galilee to Jerusalem. He's from Nazareth. As governor of his region, you must put a stop to this."

Herod stared at the prisoner, and his smile turned more sinister. "A king, you say?" Herod motioned to the soldiers who stood beside Jesus. "Show this prisoner how we treat false kings in Galilee." A legionary stepped forward and raised a club in the air. When it landed in the center of the rabbi's back, the thud made Lucius's stomach turn. Jesus slumped over. Lucius looked away. Part of him wanted to help, to intervene, but he couldn't. Herod would have him flogged for insubordination. But Jesus didn't deserve this treatment. He'd been kind, helped people.

"How's that feel, King of the Jews?" A half dozen legionaries stepped forward and taunted. "Aren't you a miracle worker? Heal yourself of this wound. You're a king, call your army to protect you!" A soldier grabbed Jesus and lifted him from the ground. Jesus was conscious but dazed. He moaned. Another legionary draped a purple robe around his shoulders and announced, "All hail to the king!" Just as the word "king" left his lips, the back of his hand crashed into Jesus's jaw, spraying blood and teeth across the pavement.

Herod scowled. "Take him back to Pilate."

Lucius maneuvered his horse quickly through the crowd. He ducked into an alley and slid off his saddle to his knees. He removed his helmet, his hands trembling. He wiped sweat from his brow. Cruelty never bothered him until Jesus. He feared it might get worse.

L ucius caught up with the procession. "How's he doing?"

"Guardsmen had to carry him for a while," Decimus responded. "Then he regained consciousness, got his footing."

Lucius scanned the mob until he found Jesus. The rabbi lurched and hobbled, but managed to walk on his own.

When they reached Antonia, Pilate waited with his arms crossed. He motioned for the two centurions. They dismounted and marched to the top of the stairs.

"Bring him inside." Pilate disappeared into Antonia.

Each centurion slipped an arm around Jesus and helped the rabbi ascend the stairs. They found Pilate waiting in a room just inside the fortress. They eased Jesus into a chair before the governor. Pilate paced. Jesus raised his eyes, scanned his surroundings, and watched the governor.

The centurions stood guard at the door.

"What's he going to do?" Lucius whispered.

"He's in a tough spot," Decimus said. "A political dilemma. Maybe this Jesus of Nazareth is just another in the long line of rebels who've tried to stir up the Jews against Rome."

"But the Jewish priests and elders are determined to see him prosecuted." Lucius crossed his arms. "From what I hear, they didn't pay so much attention to past rebels. They're more scared of Jesus."

"And, what they're saying to Pilate is true. He can't allow an insurrection against Rome. Or a threat to his own rule." Decimus flicked a piece of dust from his tunic. "If Jesus calls himself king, he has to be dealt with."

Pilate stopped in front of Jesus and opened his mouth to speak, then closed it. He continued to pace.

Lucius watched the governor, then turned to Decimus. "I don't think Pilate is convinced Jesus is a threat to Rome. He hasn't raised up an army. He doesn't seem interested in that kind of uprising. When his disciples started to fight back in Gethsemane, he stopped them. And the guardsmen's ear—"

"That was impressive, wasn't it?" Decimus smiled, then sighed. "To complicate Pilate's dilemma even more, as much as the officials despise Jesus, the Nazarene has a following among the peasants. And the governor may not want another riot from the Jews, at least not now. With such confrontations, timing is everything."

Lucius dropped his gaze to the stone floor. Riots, confrontations. He hoped to never participate in such massacres again.

"He just needs to figure out a way to keep this from getting out of control," Decimus concluded. "Or at least, no more out of control than it is already."

Lucius took a deep breath. For the past several hours, he had functioned as a soldier. He'd tried to bury thoughts of himself or questions about Jesus beneath duty. But now, as he watched Pilate pace and Jesus wait, questions crept into his mind. *Why has Jesus caused such an uproar? Not only in Jerusalem, but in me? Is he the Jews' Messiah? If so, what would that mean for Rome? For me? And those miracles that Herod talked about. The lame walking and the blind seeing. The guardsmen's ear. These weren't rumors but wonders I witnessed.* "Believe," *Jesus whispered in the garden. Believe what? Who is he?*

Pilate stopped and faced Jesus. "Are you the King of the Jews?" Lucius stood taller now, surprised by Pilate's directness.

"Is that your own idea?" Jesus's voice was hoarse. "Or did others talk to you about me?"

"Am I a Jew?" Pilate spoke briskly. "Your own people and chief priests handed you over to me. What is it you have done?"

"My kingdom is not of this world." The rabbi's voice grew in strength. "If it were, my servants would fight to prevent my arrest by the Jewish leaders." *A good point,* Lucius conceded, though his use of the word "kingdom" was still worrisome. Pilate couldn't let such language pass.

Jesus emphasized a second time, "My kingdom is from another place."

"You are a king, then." Pilate put his hands on his hips.

"You say that I am a king. In fact, the reason I was born and came into the world is to testify to the truth. Everyone on the side of truth listens to me."

"What is truth?" Pilate sounded impatient and disgusted. He crossed his arms and stared at the prisoner. Lucius remained still, and pale, his eyes fixed on Jesus. Decimus took a deep, impatient breath.

"Where do you come from?" Pilate demanded.

Jesus didn't respond.

"Do you refuse to speak to me? Don't you realize I have the power either to free you or to crucify you?"

"You would have no power over me if it were not given to you from above." Jesus leaned forward. "The one who handed me over to you is guilty of a greater sin."

Pilate shook his head, then rolled his eyes. Exasperated, he stormed out of the room.

"Stay here with him," Lucius instructed Decimus.

Lucius followed Pilate out of Antonia, to the landing outside its entrance. His eyes widened. The crowd of Jews had doubled.

Pilate raised his arm. When the mob quieted, he announced, "I find no basis for a charge against him." The Jews hissed. Pilate regrouped and revealed a concession that, apparently, he'd been considering. "It's your custom for me to release one prisoner at the time of the Passover. Do you want me to release 'the King of the Jews,' or Barabbas?"

Lucius was shocked. Tales of Barabbas circulated throughout Judea. He led a violent rebellion in Jerusalem, which left a number of Romans and Jews dead. Surely Pilate didn't want him roaming the streets again. But the Jewish priests feared Barabbas as much as the Romans did. Lucius smiled. The governor, cunning as always, made a calculated move. Certainly, the Jews would choose to release Jesus. What's turning over a few tables in the temple compared to the carnage that Barabbas caused?

The Jews shouted in unison, "Give us Barabbas!"

Lucius whipped his head toward Pilate, whose mouth gaped. Unfathomable.

Pilate scanned the crowd, as if searching for a single Jew who made sense. None did. Their cry continued, "Release Barabbas!"

Pilate nodded toward Lucius, who hurried to the governor's side. "Release Barabbas. Flog Jesus." Pilate marched into the fortress and disappeared into its dark corridors.

Lucius's heart raced, but he had a job to do. He pointed to a few legionaries who stood near the front of the crowd. "You two, release Barabbas from his cell. The rest of you, come with me." Lucius marched into the room where Decimus guarded Jesus. The centurions and legionaries circled the Nazarene.

On the stone-paved courtyard outside of Antonia, Lucius nodded to two legionaries. They stripped Jesus of his tattered robe and strapped his arms to a post. Jesus stood, bent at the waist, with his bare back arched and his head tucked into his chest. Soldiers pushed the crowd back and cleared a semicircle, allowing the Jews to observe and jeer but not to participate in the flogging.

"Proceed," Lucius choked out the command. The legionaries grasped leather whips and stood to either side of Jesus. Each whip had three strands, each strand three feet long, studded with lead balls and sharp fragments of bone and pottery. Lucius and Decimus stood a few feet away.

When the first whip struck Jesus's back, his cry filled Jerusalem and echoed from the Mount of Olives. The lead balls whiplashed round his body and cracked his ribs. The shards of bone and pottery lodged into his skin. The soldier yanked the whip back toward himself and shredded the rabbi's back. Blood poured. Lucius winced and turned away. Decimus remained stone-faced.

"You turned away," Decimus prodded. "Have you grown a soft spot for the rabbi, or have you recently developed a sickness for discipline?"

Lucius frowned. "I'll be fine."

The soldiers alternated blows, one focusing on Jesus's upper body and the other on his lower body. His cries lessened with each lash, and then faded into involuntary moans through gritted teeth.

Lucius was awed by the rabbi. He didn't scream curses like most prisoners. He didn't call upon the gods for mercy or for their wrath upon the soldiers. Despite unspeakable agony, Jesus remained at peace until he finally lost consciousness, his mangled body slumping over the blood-soaked post.

Lucius's heart slowed, as did the world around him. His vision blurred. The Jews' sneers and the Romans' laughter merged into a roar. He felt as though he floated above the street, suspended in the air looking down upon the grotesque spectacle. The scene was familiar to a centurion of his experience, but this time, it sliced like a knife through his soul.

"Halt," Decimus instructed. "That's enough."

Lucius snapped back to reality.

The soldiers with the whips stepped back, breathing heavily. Sweat dripped from their brows, and their armor and tunics were spattered with the prisoner's blood. Additional soldiers stepped forward, laughing. One pushed a crown of thorns onto Jesus's head, forcing it down with such force that the thorns sank into his skull. Another legionary placed a scepter in his hand. "Hail, King of the Jews!" They bowed in mockery and then spat on him.

"Isn't that enough?" Lucius choked out.

"Pick him up," Decimus ordered. Two legionaries untied the ropes that tethered Jesus to the post, draped his arms across their shoulders, and carried his limp body. His feet dragged behind, leaving a trail of blood. They carried the rabbi to the top of the stairs and dropped his body onto the landing. Lucius followed, with Decimus just behind him.

Pilate emerged from Antonia. He raised his arms to silence the crowd. "Here he is!" He pointed to Jesus. "I find no basis for charges against him. You said he was inciting a rebellion. I have examined him in your presence and have found no basis for your charges. Neither has Herod, for he sent him back to us. He has done nothing to deserve death."

Lucius felt a twinge of hope. Perhaps Pilate would spare the Nazarene's life.

The elders and chief officials began to chant. "Crucify him! Crucify him!" Others joined.

Pilate lifted his eyes to the horizon, sighed, and then said, "Alright. Take him. He's yours. Crucify him."

Lucius shot a glance at Decimus. The Jews didn't have the authority to crucify prisoners. Pilate knew that. So did the Jews. He was continuing to play games with them.

"Our laws require that he dies because he claimed to be the Son of God," sneered the Jewish leaders. "Your laws apply, as well. If you let this man go, you are no friend of Caesar. Anyone who claims to be a king opposes Caesar."

Pilate pulled Lucius close. "Get me a bowl of water." *A strange request*, Lucius thought, but he hurried into Antonia and returned with the water.

"He is your king," Pilate announced.

"Take him away. Crucify him!"

"You want me to crucify your king?"

"We have no king but Caesar," the chief priest answered.

Pilate gazed across the crowd, then immersed his hands in the water. "I am innocent of this man's blood. It is your responsibility."

"His blood is on us and on our children."

Pilate turned to Lucius and Decimus and sneered, "Crucify him."

L ucius squinted in the midmorning sun, physically and emotionally exhausted. He took a swig from his water pouch. "Ready to move, soldiers?"

"Yes sir." Avitus sighed.

"Let's get this over with," Decimus grumbled.

Each soldier grasped an end of a crossbeam, which was as long as a man was tall. They held it above Jesus, who, on his knees, struggled to stay upright.

"He's lost a lot of blood." Lucius steadied the rabbi. "I don't think he'll be able to carry this by himself."

"Rise, prisoner." Septimus barked. "Carry your cross."

Lucius spun around, surprised to see Septimus. *When did he arrive?* Lucius would have to concede leadership of the crucifixion to his superior. He'd hoped to speed the process and minimize the rabbi's suffering, but Septimus was certain to feel otherwise. He recalled Septimus's hunger for blood when he crucified the Jewish rebels. He liked hearing the victims groan.

Lucius grasped Jesus beneath a shoulder and pulled him to a standing position, as much as the Nazarene's battered body allowed. Jesus winced and grunted. His pale, mangled skin hung from his bones. His eyes appeared hollow. Blood that streamed from his wounds had dried and crusted. The crown of thorns remained embedded in his head.

As the rabbi stood, Decimus and Avitus positioned the wooden beam across his shoulders. Lucius draped Jesus's arms across the beam. The soldiers stepped back.

"March," Septimus ordered.

Jesus managed a step. Then another. The beam teetered. Lucius stepped forward and balanced it. He whispered, "Rabbi, I want to help you."

Jesus managed a smile. "And I, you."

The centurion stepped back. *What did that mean? How could Jesus help me?*

Jesus found his balance. He moved slowly, but he moved, his shuffling feet leaving trails of red on the stone pavement.

Lucius remained just out of arm's length, lest he reach out to help again. He ached to ease Jesus's burden, but knew Septimus would punish him if he saw. Decimus walked beside Lucius. Avitus and Septimus marched in front of the prisoner. A few dozen legionaries formed an oval around them to keep the growing mass of people back. The crowd consisted mostly of Jews, a few weeping but most mocking Jesus.

The beam swayed again. This time Jesus fell beneath its weight. It tumbled from his shoulders and thumped against the stone pavement. Jesus lay face down.

Lucius stepped forward, but Septimus arrived first. He lifted the rabbi's chin with his boot. "Up." Jesus struggled to his knees. Decimus motioned to Avitus, and together they returned the beam to his shoulders. But Jesus couldn't rise to his feet. "I said stand!" Septimus struck the prisoner's face with the back of his hand. Jesus toppled, and the plank crashed to the ground.

Lucius's heart ached. He scanned the crowd, then pointed to a man who looked sturdy. "You, carry the beam." Septimus glared at Lucius, but didn't stop him or the man.

Now free of the burden, Jesus managed to stand. He hobbled amid the soldiers as the procession crept westward from Antonia, along a busy thoroughfare that skirted the northern wall of the city. The sun behind them cast long shadows.

"You have to admire his fortitude," Decimus said.

"Not many of us could endure what he has and keep walking." Lucius settled his gaze on Jesus. "The scourging was severe. I don't imagine he'll last more than a few hours on the cross."

He perused the crowd. Some threw rocks. Others spat. The spittle seldom traveled far enough to reach Jesus, but the mockers made their point. "Blasphemer. You deserve this, you who mock the Lord. You're no king of ours!"

Decimus stopped Lucius, took him by the arm. "Can you do this? If you need to leave and let us handle this one, I can tell Septimus you got called away."

"I'm a soldier. A centurion of the Roman Empire. That's all that matters right now." He was sure Decimus didn't believe his pronouncement any more than he believed it himself. But he felt he had no choice. *Just do my job. Put my head down; get through this. He's going to be crucified no matter what I do, or don't do. Maybe I can somehow lessen his suffering along the way.*

The centurions resumed the march. Minutes passed more quickly than steps. The procession rounded the northwest corner of the city and turned south, arriving at the rise in the landscape where sinister rock formations jutted from the sandy soil. The place of the skull. A chill skirted Lucius's spine.

Septimus raised his arm. "Halt." The procession stopped in the middle of the street. He pointed to the man carrying the crossbeam. "Bring the plank to the legionaries." Avitus and Decimus lifted the beam from the man's shoulders and sat it perpendicular on a longer beam that already lay on the side of the road. Avitus produced tools from his belt. He hammered spikes into the beams where they intersected, then tied a rope around the intersection to ensure the cross was secure.

Lucius stood back, uninvolved.

"Step up, centurion." Septimus grunted and waved him and Decimus toward Jesus.

Lucius gritted his teeth, annoyed yet obedient. He stepped forward, puzzled why he felt such fright. Lucius grabbed hold of the

Nazarene's left arm. Decimus clutched the other. They stretched his arms across the beam and fastened them with ropes.

Avitus handed the hammer and spikes to Decimus. "Give me those, soldier." Septimus yanked them away and pressed them against Lucius's gut.

"You do the honor," he dared.

Lucius glared. This was a test. For once, he wished he could fail. He laid Jesus's hand flat against the crossbeam and positioned a spike in the center of his wrist.

"Are you sure?" Decimus whispered.

"I'm sure." Lucius knelt next to Jesus. He took a deep breath. *You can do this. You've done it a hundred times before. This is no different. He's a prisoner. Maybe a rebel against Rome. Maybe.*

The sharp point pricked the rabbi's skin and released a tiny stream of blood. Jesus turned his head toward Lucius. The centurion felt the stare but kept his eyes fixed on the spike. Tears welled in Lucius's eyes. His vision blurred. *Something is different about this one. He's not like the others.*

Memories erupted. His fist landing on Tobiah's jaw. Life returning to the paralytic's legs at the pool. Ephraim's dead body in the mud. The guard's ear. "Yahweh will not forget us," Benjamin said at the inn.

Lucius clenched his jaw and raised the hammer. "I'm sorry," he whispered. He yanked the hammer downward until it connected with the spike, and sent it, in one forceful thrust, through Jesus's wrist, pinning it to the crossbeam. What little blood that remained in his body squirted.

Lucius rose, stepped back, and slammed the hammer into the chest of Septimus. "You dare doubt my loyalty? You were wrong."

Septimus rolled his eyes, then handed the hammer to Decimus, who finished the job.

With each blow, Jesus shuddered. Lucius did too.

Septimus motioned Avitus to the other side of Jesus. They lifted the cross that bore his limp body and dropped its base into a hole. When it struck the ground, Jesus's body jerked; the spikes ripped into his hands and feet. He cried out.

Lucius stood back, dazed, as events unfolded around him. Soldiers raised additional crosses on either side of Jesus, each holding a criminal. Legionaries cast lots for Jesus's robes. The crowds continued mocking until they grew weary and their numbers thinned. Passersby spat in the direction of the crosses and screamed insults. "Get yourself off that cross if you're God's Messiah!"

The minutes passed slowly but Lucius felt them deeply.

Jesus pushed upward with his feet, alleviating the strain on his lungs and allowing a breath. "Father, forgive them, for they do not know what they are doing." The whispers pricked Lucius's heart. *Is he praying this for me? For my forgiveness?*

A couple of legionaries lifted a vinegar-soaked sponge to the rabbi's lips. After one taste, Jesus turned his head. The soldiers laughed. "If you're the King of the Jews, save yourself!"

"You heard them," said one of the criminals on a cross next to Jesus. "Aren't you the Messiah? Save yourself. And us."

The other criminal rebuked him. "Don't you fear God?" His words came slowly, between shallow breaths, with anger and then resignation. "We're under the same sentence. Except we deserve it. This man has done nothing wrong." He swung his head toward Jesus. "Remember me when you come into your kingdom."

"Today you will be with me in paradise." The rabbi choked on the blood that filled his mouth.

Lucius watched and listened, intrigued and moved. He felt a compassion he'd never before experienced.

Jesus looked down at a couple of women and a man who had remained quiet. Unlike most of the bystanders, these three grieved. Lucius recognized the man as one of Jesus's disciples. "Woman, here is your son," Jesus said. And to the disciple, "Here is your mother."

His mother. The horror of the moment cut into the centurion's heart. He imagined how Nona would feel if that was Tullus or Paulla.

The world darkened. Lucius looked to the disappearing sun. It wasn't covered by clouds; it just faded. Midday became as night. Lucius remembered the legends he'd heard as a boy. When the greatest of men die, the world grows dark.

"Eloi, Eloi," Jesus cried out. "Lama sabachthani?" Lucius didn't understand the language but he felt the agony.

Time passed. All three of the crucified moaned less. Insects clustered around their open wounds. Birds of prey circled above.

Jesus slumped further. His arms separated from his shoulder sockets, and his elbows and wrists dislocated. His breathing grew shallow and less frequent. "Father, into your hands I commit my spirit." His voice gurgled.

Jesus raised his head. His eyes opened, slightly. They settled on the weeping women who remained beneath him. His gaze then moved to Lucius. Lucius couldn't turn away. Jesus's eyes poured into Lucius's soul a warmth, a feeling of grace he'd never experienced.

Jesus lifted his eyes toward the sky. "It is finished." His head dropped and his breathing ceased.

The earth quaked. The women wailed and the disciple dropped to his knees.

Lucius stumbled toward the cross. He stared at the limp body hanging there. "Surely this man was the Son of God!" The words erupted from his mouth before they passed through his mind or heart. But he didn't want to take them back. He couldn't. He believed.

Nona was clearing dishes from the table when she heard a knock at the door. She wiped her hands on her apron and hurried to answer. Lucius stood on the porch.

"I was worried." She wrapped her arms around his neck.

Lucius returned the embrace. "I'm fine."

She inspected him from head to foot. He looked tired, but not as despondent as in recent weeks. His tunic was laundered and he'd shaved. His eyes were more welcoming, and he even smiled a little.

"The whole city is buzzing," she said. "Were you there? Did you help with the crucifixion?"

He sighed. "Yes."

Nona hugged him again and took his hand. She kissed his knuckles. Beneath the armor and the uniform—the façade of strength—he was a man.

"The ordeal began night before last," Lucius said. "After sundown, we followed the temple guard to a garden on the Mount of Olives. They arrested Jesus. Through the night and into yesterday morning, he stood trial before the high priest, Pilate, and Herod. The whole time, it was obvious what the Jewish officials wanted. Finally, Pilate let them have their way, and ordered him beaten, whipped, and crucified. By late afternoon yesterday, he was dead."

"Why was this one different? You've crucified before." The words came out more directly than Nona intended. She could feel herself slipping into her default, mothering mode. She needed to be careful. She'd never seen him so vulnerable.

"I'm not sure I can explain it." Lucius spoke slowly. He searched the dirt at his feet for answers. "He didn't act like most. He told his followers to stand down, not to fight back. The rabbi was resigned and submissive to us. Respectful, even. He didn't yell curses or threats. And while he hung on the cross, he prayed that we, the very ones who nailed him there, would be forgiven."

Nona let him gather his thoughts, then probed further. "Some people are saying that the darkness and the earthquake had something to do with his death."

"Maybe." Lucius furrowed his brow. "I've seen so much I can't explain over the last few weeks."

He stepped away from Nona and gazed across the marketplace. It was Sabbath, so the market was tamer than usual, but it was also feast week, and the non-Jews and the less-than-faithful Jews still conducted some business.

Nona straightened her apron. "Now he's gone. Dead. Things will return to normal. Yes?"

"Right. He's dead." Lucius turned toward Nona. "Avitus put a sword in his side to make sure. We didn't even have to break his legs like we sometimes do. A wealthy Jew got his body and buried it in his tomb." He hung his head. "It's over."

But she could tell it wasn't over for him. He sounded more puzzled than resigned or relieved. She rested her head on his shoulder. Nona knew many sides of Lucius, and how to deal with these various aspects of his personality. She could calm him when he was angry, bring him back to earth when he was arrogant, and encourage him when he was down. But the Lucius standing before her today—moved, contemplative—she wasn't sure how to deal with.

"Something is still bothering you," she said.

He exhaled slowly. "There were a couple of times when he looked at me. Spoke to me. Even touched me. No one has looked at me that way before. It's like he knew me. Deeply."

"I know you deeply." She squeezed his hand.

"Yes, but even you have to dig through layers, these walls I've built over the years." He squeezed her hand back. "It's like he can see through all that."

"I'm not sure I understand."

He paused to gather his words. "When we were on our way to the crucifixion, he stumbled. I helped him balance the cross on his shoulders. I told him, 'I want to help you.' He looked up, all beaten and bloody, on his way to be crucified, and said that he wanted to help me. A man on his way to die wanted to help me."

Nona struggled to make sense of Lucius. The rabbi had affected him profoundly, but she couldn't understand why. She'd never seen Jesus or heard him teach, but to her, he sounded like just another Jew who thought too much of himself. Or, someone without a firm grasp on reality. But she knew Lucius, loved him. He wasn't easily fooled. And he certainly didn't open his heart hastily.

"Why would he say that he wanted to help you?" She shrugged. "That doesn't make sense."

"It doesn't. That's just it. He was in no position to help me. Still, it was like something inside me changed . . . healed. I can't let go of this feeling that my life will never be the same again. He's changing me in some way that I can't imagine." He held both of her hands. "I think he was more than just a rabbi."

"What do you mean?"

He stared into her eyes. "I believe he was more than human." She was flabbergasted. "Like a god?"

Before Lucius could answer, Benjamin came out of the door, his head down. He didn't see the centurion and almost bumped into him. "Oh . . . please excuse me."

Lucius gave him a nod. He neither smiled nor scowled at the Jew.

Benjamin turned and saw Nona. He greeted her, then looked back to Lucius. "I was about to take a walk."

"Alright," Lucius said.

Benjamin remained still. "But I don't have to."

"That's alright, too."

Benjamin leaned against the porch post. He turned toward the market. After a few seconds of silence, he addressed Lucius. "I was there. Yesterday."

Lucius didn't respond but kept his gaze locked on Benjamin.

"How about I get you men some water?" Nona stepped into the inn but remained just inside the door so she could hear. More silence.

"Was Tobiah with you?" Lucius asked.

"Yes."

"Your wives, or Miriam?"

"No."

Nona had seen Tobiah and Benjamin leave the inn early yesterday morning, but she didn't know they were going to a crucifixion. They had an earnest conversation when they returned. She didn't hear much of what they said, but sensed the seriousness of their tone.

She hurried toward the back of the inn and returned carrying two cups. Nona slipped through the door, handed the water to the men, then sat quietly on a bench. Normally, she'd dismiss herself and allow the men to talk, but she wouldn't let social convention prevent her from hearing this conversation. She had to know what made such an impact on Lucius.

Lucius sipped his water. "Was he your Messiah?"

Nona gulped, surprised Lucius asked so bluntly. The conversation must have progressed quickly while she was inside. Though, Lucius never was one for tact.

Benjamin frowned. Nona could tell he struggled how to answer Lucius's question. "I had hoped. But now, I don't think so."

"Why not?"

"Yes, there was something different about Jesus, something significant. The way he taught, the miracles he performed. He was unlike any rabbi I've ever seen. But," he sighed, "he didn't do the things our prophets said the Messiah would do."

Nona knew that Lucius wouldn't let the Jew remain so vague. He didn't.

"And what did the prophets say he would do?"

Benjamin lifted his cup and took a long drink. He spoke with measured words. "Our prophets picture the Messiah as a great leader. Powerful, influential. He will restore our people."

Nona stiffened. She knew that "restore our people" really meant "defeat the Romans and expel them from Judea."

Benjamin continued, more boldly, "'Of the greatness of his government and peace there will be no end. He will reign on David's throne and over his kingdom, establishing and upholding it with justice and righteousness from that time on and forever.'" He chuckled awkwardly. "So said Isaiah, anyway."

"But since Jesus was a peasant," Lucius continued what Benjamin implied, "he couldn't have been the one your prophet described."

Benjamin nodded.

"And his followers were peasants. He didn't raise up an army. He had no interest in government. When he was arrested he didn't even fight back." Lucius seemed determined to get clarity.

"Exactly," Benjamin said. "Jesus lies in a grave. The Messiah will rule from a throne." He took a deep breath. "So, no. I don't think Jesus was the Messiah." He didn't try to hide his disappointment.

Benjamin finished what remained of his water and handed his empty cup to Nona. "I think I'll go for that walk now."

Nona watched Benjamin disappear into the marketplace, then rose from the bench and stood next to Lucius. She put her arm around his waist, anxious to resume the conversation they had before Benjamin interrupted. "A god? The Jews' Messiah? What exactly do you believe?"

He leaned into her. "I can't put it into words. I believe he was more than a man. A god. Divine. Of the gods. Of the Jews' god.

Messiah. I don't know." He shook his head. "I can't figure it out. And most perplexing, his body is in the grave. He's dead. The priests and Pilate won. That's not how the story ends for a god."

Lucius dipped stale bread into water and threw it into his mouth. He stared into the half-full cup. Soggy bread crumbs floated on top. His sleep was unsettled last night. Each time he woke, his mind replayed the crucifixion and his conversation with Benjamin.

As hopeful as Benjamin and his friends had been that Jesus was their Messiah, Lucius was surprised how quickly they gave up on the possibility. Even Jesus's closest disciples had scattered, except the one who stayed at the foot of the cross with his mother. The Jews had seen numerous would-be messiahs come and go. Despite their aspirations for this one, when the first spike pierced Jesus's wrist, they returned to their fishing nets and synagogues.

Lucius lifted the cup to his mouth and finished his drink. As he sat the cup on the table, Avitus appeared in front of him. The legionary's face was pale. His lip quivered and mouth gaped, but no sound came out.

"Spit it out, soldier," Lucius said.

"He's gone."

"Who?"

"The rabbi."

"I know he's gone. We saw him take his last breath. You pierced his side. I reported it to Pilate, and that rich Jew put the body in his tomb. This isn't news."

"No," Avitus's voice cracked, "you don't understand. "His body is gone from the grave."

Lucius's pulse quickened. "But you were guarding it. You and another soldier. And we sealed it with a stone." He felt lightheaded.

Avitus looked down and his shoulders slumped, like a child caught stealing a treat in the marketplace. Worse, like a legionary caught sleeping while on guard.

"Who took it?" Lucius asked in a panic.

Avitus searched for words to respond but couldn't find them.

"Go ahead," Lucius prodded.

"You're not going to believe me."

"Try me." After all he'd seen in recent days, Lucius was open to whatever story Avitus proposed. And he trusted the young Syrian. The story could very well be true.

"The earth quaked," said Avitus.

"At the cross? I know, I was there."

"No, again. At the tomb. And a man appeared. He just materialized. Out of the quaking. And the light. It was so bright I couldn't look at it. Or him. His robes, they were like lightning."

Lucius shifted in his seat. He studied Avitus's face. Soldiers had tried to lie to him before. Avitus wasn't lying.

"Then he waved his hand and the stone rolled away from the entrance. Like it was a feather in the wind. After that . . . " Avitus searched for the words to finish the sentence.

"Yes?"

"After that, I don't remember. I blacked out."

"For how long?"

"I don't know."

"And the other soldier?"

"He blacked out, too." Avitus looked Lucius in the eye. "We woke up at the same time, and the man in bright robes was gone. The stone was still pushed aside. We ran into the tomb and it was . . . empty. Except for the cloths they'd wrapped around his body."

Lucius saw Decimus enter the dining hall and waved him over. "You need to hear this." He instructed Avitus, "Tell him everything you told me." The legionary repeated the story, more quickly this time.

"Simple," Decimus concluded. "The man in the white robes stole the body."

Avitus grew animated. "But how did he move the stone by waving his hand? How did the other soldier and I both pass out at the same time?" His voice raised. "And he wasn't just wearing white clothes—this blinding light radiated from him. I've never seen anything like it." His eyes grew wide. "In some of their stories, the Jews talk about angels. I think that's what I saw. An angel."

"Impossible. These were tricks, illusions. I'm sure there's an explanation." Decimus didn't seem concerned. "You haven't told anyone else, have you?"

The young Syrian hesitated.

"Who'd you tell?"

"When we were coming back, we saw some priests from the temple, some of the same priests who brought Jesus before Pilate. They could see we were upset and asked what happened."

"What did you tell them?" Decimus asked.

"The same thing I just told you."

Lucius could tell the legionary didn't want to say more, so he pushed, "And how did they respond?"

"They told us to wait while they went off to the side and talked. They came back and said, 'Tell people that his disciples came during the night and stole his body while you were asleep.'"

"Have you told anyone this story?" Decimus asked.

"I haven't. I wanted to talk to you first. But I don't know about the legionary who was with me."

"Just keep your mouth shut," Decimus ordered. "You can go now."

Avitus hurried away.

The two centurions sat in silence, Decimus eating his bread and Lucius staring into his empty cup. Decimus tilted his head and caught his friend's gaze. "Could it be?"

"Who knows?" Lucius replied. "We've seen so many unexplainable things over the last few weeks."

An hour later, Lucius sat on the threshold of an empty tomb. His horse grazed nearby, searching for grass in a sea of dirt and rock. He held his head in his hands, his feet rested on the track where the stone had rolled. The sun warmed his skin. Birds sang their greetings. The scents of spring filled his nostrils. Mysteries of life and death, and of religion and the divine, swirled in his head.

Behind him, in the tomb, lay the linens and head cloth that had shrouded Jesus's body.

In that moment, he believed Jesus was alive.

L ucius trudged through the corridor of Antonia, headed for a shift of guard duty. A few days had passed since he sat before the empty tomb of Jesus. He attempted to continue business as usual, but was distracted, wondering what might happen next. His mind swirled like driftwood in the waves of the Great Sea.

"Sir, I need to speak with you." Avitus's voice echoed from the stone walls.

Lucius turned and watched the legionary jog the remaining steps between them. "Yes, soldier, what is it?"

"There are rumors." Avitus caught his breath. "Stories going around that you need to hear."

"What stories?"

"Some of the Jews say they've seen Jesus . . . alive."

Lucius felt his heartbeat quicken. "Alive again, or alive still?"

"I don't know."

"Or do you think they've seen him at all? Could they be lying?"

Avitus shook his head. "I can't answer that, either. I just thought you should know the stories are circulating."

Lucius bit his lower lip. "I need you to take my shift of guard duty."

"Yes sir."

Lucius turned on his heels, hurried through the corridor, and descended the stairs that unfurled from Antonia's entrance. He had to talk to Benjamin. He chose the more congested route through the city, avoiding the road that passed by the place of the skull, and marched west.

Thoughts rushed through his mind like a tornado. *Maybe the rumors of a risen Jesus are just that, and nothing more—the disciples spreading the story in an effort to deceive. But why? What would they gain from the deception? Or, maybe they're trying to gain power. But unless they can prove he's alive, any power gained from the deception would fade in days, even hours. Perhaps they're trying to save face. That wouldn't last long either, though. With so many people involved, someone will give up the truth eventually.*

He scurried through narrow passages on stone streets, the stale air filled with the odors and bustle of the city. He arrived at Miriam's inn and knocked on the door. Tullus answered.

"Father!" The boy hugged his father. "Come join us. The guests are gone and we're finishing their bread and fruit."

Lucius followed his son into the dining room. Paulla bounced toward her father and wrapped her arms around his waist.

"What a pleasant surprise." Nona spoke as cordially as she was capable. "Have you eaten?"

"I have."

"Well, eat more." She motioned toward the table, which held partially eaten loaves and a platter of fruit and nuts. She poured him a cup of water.

Lucius reclined on a pillow next to the table, chose an apple, and bit into it. "How have things been here?" He would be kind to Nona and the children, but he really wanted to talk to Benjamin.

"Still busy, but less hectic," Nona replied. "The Jewish feast is winding down. All the guests left the inn this morning, so we'll have a day or two to clean and rest before anyone else comes."

Lucius smiled. He knew that "rest" was a relative concept for Nona.

"And for you?" Nona asked carefully, tearing bread from a loaf.

"It's been an interesting few days."

"So I hear."

Lucius took another bite of his apple. He didn't want to pursue this conversation any further in the presence of the children. "I was hoping to speak with Benjamin."

"Miriam sent him to the market to buy vegetables and fish for the evening meal. He should be back soon." Nona began clearing dishes away.

"I'll wait on the porch." Lucius took another swig of water and left his half-eaten apple on the table.

As the centurion exited the front door, Benjamin approached with a basket in each hand. The two men acknowledged each another with a nod. "Let me put these away and I'll be back," Benjamin said.

Moments later, they stood on the same porch where they'd talked a few days before, when Jesus's body still lay in the tomb.

"Have you seen him?" Lucius jumped straight into the conversation.

"No." Benjamin sighed. "I'd give anything to see him myself. But I've talked to some who have. A woman from Magdala, Mary, went to the tomb early on the first day of the week to put spices on his body. A friend was with her. When they got there, the stone had been moved from the entrance."

Lucius leaned forward.

"And there was an angel. Sitting there. His clothes were so bright they had to shield their eyes. He told them Jesus had risen."

These details sounded familiar.

"A little later, she saw him."

Lucius gulped.

"She was crying and thought he was a gardener. When he spoke her name, she looked up. It was him. Alive!"

Lucius studied Benjamin's face. The Jew believed what he was saying. "Who else has seen him?"

"That same day, two disciples left Jerusalem and were hiking to Emmaus. Jesus came and walked beside them. He taught them from the Scriptures and explained how all the prophecies and laws taught about him. Like Mary, these two didn't recognize Jesus at first, but when they sat to eat, they realized it was him. He disappeared. They ran back to Jerusalem to tell Jesus's closest eleven."

Please, let this be true.

"It was night when they got back to the city, and they found the eleven meeting in a room behind locked doors. The two told the others that they'd seen Jesus, and then . . . " Benjamin took a deep breath.

"What is it?"

"Jesus appeared right there with them. In that very room. They touched him—he wasn't just a vision. He was standing right there. He even ate some fish." Benjamin whispered, "And his body had the scars."

Lucius remembered the thorns sinking into Jesus's brow. Lashes whipping across his back. Spikes driven through his hands and feet. A sword piercing his side. Scars.

"Then, Jesus explained to the group how Moses, the prophets, and the Psalms all point toward his life and his death. And, they point to his resurrection three days later."

Lucius absorbed what Benjamin was saying. Things had certainly changed since the last time they talked. Those disciples of Jesus who had scattered at his arrest now made outlandish, and brave, claims.

There was something else Lucius needed to know. "Five days ago you didn't think he was your Messiah." He sounded more accusatory than he intended, so he softened his tone. "What do you think now?"

Benjamin ran his hand through his hair. "I think . . . maybe . . . Jesus is the Messiah."

Lucius could feel the weight of Benjamin's pronouncement. He and the other Jews endured centuries of desperation and disappointment with only occasional glimmers of hope. And now, through Jesus, that hope surged like a sunbeam through a dark cloud.

"And what about the prophecies?" Lucius asked. "Last time we talked, you didn't think they were about Jesus. He made no move to establish a kingdom."

"Maybe the kingdom is something different than we thought. When he was teaching, Jesus said things like, 'The coming of the kingdom of God is not something that can be observed, the kingdom of God is in your midst.' And, 'My kingdom is not of this world.'"

Benjamin grew more excited as he talked. "And what Jesus taught the disciples put all the other prophecies in a new light. He fulfilled them, but in ways we didn't know to expect." He began pacing. "One of our prophets said, 'The eyes of the blind will be opened and the ears of the deaf unstopped. Then will the lame leap like a deer, and the mute shout for joy.'"

Lucius remembered the healings he had witnessed. His heart raced.

Benjamin continued, "One of our psalmists said he would be betrayed: 'Even my close friend, someone I trusted, one who shared my bread has turned against me.'"

Judas's kiss.

"Another prophet wrote, 'I offered my back to those who beat me, my cheeks to those who pulled out my beard. I did not hide my face from mocking and spitting.'"

The legionaries and the Jewish officials.

"And another, 'They divide my clothes among them and cast lots for my garment.' And, 'They gave me vinegar for my thirst.'"

Lucius's jaw dropped.

"One more prophecy," Benjamin said. "'They pierce my hands and my feet.'"

Lucius stood dumbfounded. He had been an instrument in the hands of the Jews' god. Carried out his will and helped fulfill his prophecies. Completely unaware.

"They even spoke of a resurrection." Benjamin's eyes sparkled. "A psalmist wrote, 'You will not abandon me to the realm of the dead, nor will you let your faithful one see decay. You make known to me the path of life.'"

Lucius had no words to respond. The two men stood in silence, the gravity of these revelations settling in their souls. Jesus fulfilled prophecies made about the Messiah centuries before, prophecies the Jews desperately and hopefully quoted and sang in their synagogues for generations.

"So, what does all this mean?" Lucius asked, now finding his words. "I mean, why would your god send this Messiah to live, die, and resurrect, but not to establish any kind of kingdom here? He's no threat to Rome. Neither are his followers. What's all this about?"

"I don't have a good answer. It's still coming into focus. One of the prophecies that keeps rolling around in my mind comes from Isaiah: 'He was pierced for our transgressions, he was crushed for our iniquities; the punishment that brought us peace was on him, and by his wounds we are healed.'"

How could one person's death bring peace and healing to someone else? What was Isaiah talking about? What kind of kingdom is this? Peace. Healing. Hope. Lucius felt like the answers were just out of his grasp. Benjamin must've felt the same, as he said nothing more. They both stared into the night.

Finally, Lucius bid goodbye to the Jew and hiked back to Antonia. His mind raced. He believed, but as odd as it sounded, he didn't know what he believed, why it mattered, or what to do about it. Jesus was . . . is . . . divine. But what does that have to do with him? Romans believed in many gods. He'd always been skeptical but indifferent. Even if they did exist, the gods didn't affect his life much. He trusted in Rome, and in himself. But now he believed in Jesus. Other beliefs melted away. He couldn't understand it, but for the first time in his life, he felt free.

May, AD 30

T he sun crested the eastern horizon and cast its rays across Caesarea. Tobiah circled the cart that held most everything he and Deborah owned. He tightened the ropes and patted the mule that would pull the cart. It wasn't the stoutest beast in town, but it should have enough strength to make the journey to Jerusalem without keeling over.

He'd planned this trip for some time, but delayed until he could convince Deborah he'd healed enough to travel without her.

"And you promise you'll be careful," she'd said for the sixth time.

"Yes, dear."

"And you'll stop to rest whenever you feel tired?"

"Uh-huh."

"Don't try to look stronger than you are just to impress the other men. It's not worth it. Get whatever rest and help you need."

"I will."

"I need to talk to Benjamin once more before you leave."

"Alright, he's in the dining room and I'm sure he'd be glad to talk . . . again." Tobiah had chuckled then and did so again as he recalled the conversation. Her worry was endearing. He loved her. These few days he'd been away only magnified that love.

Tobiah gave the mule a handful of hay, then planted his feet next to Benjamin. "Thanks for making this trip with me."

Benjamin squeezed his friend's shoulder. "You're my friend. My brother." He shoved a satchel into an open space on the cart. "Besides, Esther and I needed some things from our house, too."

"It's kind of you to stay in Jerusalem. I know it's only for a few more weeks, but it's been good to have you around."

Benjamin nodded. "I admire what you're doing for your sister. She wouldn't be safe managing the inn by herself. When you told her that you would live in Jerusalem permanently, her eyes brightened like I've never seen them."

Tobiah smiled. "She's mostly excited about Abigail staying."

"She does love that baby."

The two men stepped back and looked over the cart. "All is secure," Tobiah said. The caravan wasn't ready to leave, so they sat.

"I'm glad we were able to make this trip at Pentecost time," Benjamin said. "I've always enjoyed the comradery, traveling to Jerusalem with our brothers. The long hikes, evenings around the fire. Conversation reaches a depth that isn't possible day-to-day in the village." He paused. "And we have a lot to discuss this year."

A breeze from the Great Sea cooled their backs. Tobiah gazed inland, toward the eastern horizon. Flowers bloomed, fields displayed the lush greens of early summer, and the difficult work of spring planting and cultivation had been completed. "This year's first harvest was bountiful. Pentecost at the temple should be exceptional. The feasting, the music, the dancing."

"We'll honor Yahweh with the firstfruits," Benjamin said, "and he'll bless the rest of the year."

Benjamin picked up a rock and threw it at the cart's wheel. "You did pretty well on the trip here. Are you strong enough for the return?"

"I'll be fine. The caravan will move slowly, and I shouldn't have any trouble keeping up."

"You're still limping."

Tobiah sighed. "Probably always will. A lifetime reminder of . . . that day." He traced his finger in the dirt. The attack no longer dominated his thoughts, or his dreams at night, but once or twice each day he would see or hear something that brought the memory to the surface.

Benjamin cleared his throat. "The centurion has been around the inn more. Has that been strange for you?"

"Yes, strange. Aggravating. Confusing."

"He's becoming more kind. And he's asking a lot of questions about our faith, about Jesus."

Tobiah glanced at Benjamin. "Do you think the questions are legitimate? Or is he trying to get information to use against us?"

"Legitimate, I think. I believe."

Tobiah stood. "But he's still a Roman centurion. Even more, he's *that* centurion."

A village elder raised his hands and dozens of men grew silent. "Arise," the elder announced, "and let us go up to Zion, to the house of the Lord our God!" The men cheered. The elder led an ox to the front of the procession, its horns wrapped in gold leaf, and its head adorned with an olive wreath. A flutist followed and began to play.

Carts similar to Tobiah's were scattered throughout the caravan, heaped with grains and fruits from the first harvest. Wives, children, and a few men who would remain in the village bid their goodbyes. "Be careful on your travels and watch out for bandits. Enjoy the feast at the temple!"

Tobiah tugged the rope attached to his mule's harness. He and Benjamin merged into the caravan near its middle, and the procession began its slow trek out of Caesarea's Jewish quarter. Jerusalem and Pentecost awaited.

On the fifth morning of the journey, Tobiah munched on crusty bread, then washed his face in a nearby stream. He checked the ropes on the cart, fed the mule, then coaxed it into their place in the caravan. He turned to Benjamin and blurted, "If he's alive, he could be the Messiah."

"I've been trying to have this conversation with you for five days." Benjamin laughed. "Every time I brought it up you kept changing the subject back to our families or the inn."

"It changes everything."

"Yes, it does." Benjamin looked at his friend. "But isn't this what we've wanted?"

Tobiah knew that by "we," Benjamin referred to generations of Jews who suffered slavery, war, and oppression, aching for Yahweh's promised redeemer. For centuries, grandfathers bounced grandchildren on their knees and told of the Root of David, the Son of Man, the Anointed One of God who would restore his people.

"It is what we wanted." Tobiah hesitated. "But he's not who we expected."

Benjamin stopped and faced his friend. "And isn't that how Yahweh has always worked?"

"I guess so."

They walked in silence. A breeze carried the scents of the scraggly countryside and kept the heat bearable. Dozens of indecipherable conversations rumbled in their ears.

Tobiah sensed that Benjamin felt more assured about Jesus's identity. Tobiah's heart and hope moved that direction, and his head followed closely behind, but it was a lot to digest. "If he is the Messiah, what now?"

"Before he ascended into the heavens, he commissioned his disciples to tell the world about him. But first, he told them to go back to the city and wait." Benjamin tilted his head. "I don't really know what for. But I guess we'll wait."

They crested a hill and caught their first glimpse of the mountain range on which Jerusalem perched. A group of men behind them began to sing. Such music filled the air sporadically throughout the trip, psalms particularly suited to their ascent into Jerusalem. Their frequency and volume intensified as they drew nearer to the city.

> I lift up my eyes to the mountains—
> where does my help come from?
> My help comes from the Lord,
> the Maker of heaven and earth.

> Those who trust in the Lord are like Mount Zion,
> which cannot be shaken but endures forever.
> As the mountains surround Jerusalem,
> so the Lord surrounds his people
> both now and forevermore.

> The scepter of the wicked will not remain
> over the land allotted to the righteous,
> for then the righteous might use
> their hands to do evil.

After this stanza, Tobiah cheered along with the rest of the men, envisioning the downfall of their wicked oppressors, the Romans.

> If you, Lord, kept a record of sins,
> Lord, who could stand?
> But with you there is forgiveness,
> so that we can, with reverence, serve you.

> Israel, put your hope in the Lord,
> for with the Lord is unfailing love
> and with him is full redemption.
> He himself will redeem Israel
> from all their sins.

As these stanzas flowed from Tobiah's mouth, their emphasis on forgiveness and mercy intrigued him. He'd sung these psalms since he was a boy. Yet, he wondered if he'd missed something significant. Perhaps they all had. Yahweh's forgiveness centered on the temple, its ceremonies and sacrifices. The Messiah would conquer their oppressors and return the Jewish people to prominence. The two, at least Tobiah had thought, had little to do with each other. Maybe he was wrong. Isaiah's prophecy about the Messiah popped into his mind. "It was the Lord's will to crush him and cause him to suffer. . . . The Lord makes his life an offering for sin . . . he will bear their iniquities . . . he bore the sin of many, and made intercession for the transgressors."

He raised his voice again.

For the Lord has chosen Zion,
 he has desired it for his dwelling, saying,
"This is my resting place for ever and ever;
 here I will sit enthroned, for I have desired it.

"Here I will make a horn grow for David
 and set up a lamp for my anointed one.
I will clothe his enemies with shame,
 but his head will be adorned with a radiant crown."

Tobiah belted the words with a smile and a shake of his head. Incredible.

As the caravan approached Jerusalem's Garden Gate, Tobiah took a basket of grain from a cart and carried it on his shoulder. The flutist continued playing and the men kept singing. A priest met the procession at the gate and led them through the upper city market. Craftsmen cleared a path for the caravan and announced, "Brothers, men of Caesarea, you have come in peace."

Tobiah looked to his left. On the porch of the inn, Deborah held their daughter and stood beside Esther and Miriam. Deborah raised Abigail's tiny arm and waved it toward her father. He grinned and waved back.

Benjamin nudged Tobiah, then pointed toward the other side of the market. The centurion was approaching. Tobiah felt a twinge in his rib. Apparently Lucius had been patrolling and saw them in the caravan. He looked eager to talk.

"Greetings, Lucius," Benjamin said as the centurion came alongside.

Tobiah fell a step behind. He wanted to hear the conversation but not participate in it.

"We have much to talk about," Lucius said.

"Indeed."

"I have more questions."

"I may have some answers. Not all the answers, but things are growing clearer to me."

"I feel so . . . different. But I don't know what it means for me. As a person, as a soldier. For my future. I don't know what happens next."

Benjamin grinned. "Me neither. Today we must continue to the temple. But we will talk very soon."

"Yes, soon." Lucius smiled. "Thank you." The centurion drifted back to the edge of the crowd to patrol.

Tobiah rejoined Benjamin and raised his brow. Benjamin draped his arm across his shoulders. "And you and I will talk more, too. Yahweh is on the move!"

They followed the priest through the upper city to the temple. Levites greeted the procession by singing, "I will exalt you, Lord, for you lifted me out of the depths and did not let my enemies gloat over me."

Tobiah sang, danced, and feasted until his body and voice grew weary. He and Benjamin bid a good evening to their brothers, with the promise to renew the Pentecost celebration the next morning. They returned to the inn, unpacked the cart, then retired to their rooms with their wives, exhausted.

Despite his weariness, Tobiah stared at the ceiling. "How's Abigail been eating?"

"Better." Deborah sat in a chair next to their bed and held their daughter to her breast. "She's settled into a good routine the last couple weeks."

"I'm sorry I've been gone." Tobiah lifted himself onto his elbow.

"We survived. I had a lot of help. Miriam would hold this baby every hour of the day if I let her." She gave Tobiah a reassuring smile. "I appreciate you making the trip to get our things. And I know how you enjoy traveling with the Pentecost caravan." Deborah lifted Abigail onto her shoulder. "Did you and Benjamin talk about anything important?"

Tobiah smiled. She was tactful, but he knew she was eager to have this conversation. "We did. We talked about the harvest. It's been a good year so far. And Benjamin had some good ideas for the inn. More efficient processes for our food purchases and cleaning schedule."

She threw a cloth at him. "You know what I'm asking."

He raised to a sitting position, and chose his words carefully. "Benjamin believes he's the one."

"Jesus is the Messiah?"

"Yes."

"And do you believe?" She bit her lip.

Tobiah took a deep breath. The question had dominated his thoughts for days. "Maybe. I'm not ready to say. But every prophecy I quote, every psalm I sing, every prayer I utter . . . " He could say no more.

Deborah placed Abigail in her crib, then lay next to her husband. He wrapped his arms around her and they drifted into sleep.

Tobiah lifted his crying daughter from her crib. He cradled Abigail to his chest and hummed the same Jewish melody that his mother hummed when he was a baby.

"It's gracious of Nona to care for Abigail today." He handed the baby to Deborah. "I'd hate for either of us to miss Pentecost, especially this year."

"She won't have to do much for the guests, fortunately." Deborah stood and swayed with their daughter, calming her. "The inn is full, but they're all attending the festival."

Tobiah sifted through a pile of clothes that Deborah had cleaned. He chose his finest robe and slipped into it. "I'll go help Miriam with the morning meal."

An hour later, they stood on the front porch of the inn. Deborah placed Abigail in Nona's arms. "She eats every three hours. And then sleeps. When she wakes, she likes to be held and sung to. Then you can play with her for a while before she needs to eat again."

Nona nodded and repeated the instructions back to Deborah.

"This isn't the first time Nona has kept a baby." Tobiah winked. "I'm sure she'll be fine."

"I can help, too," Paulla added.

Tobiah appreciated Nona's willingness to help. Their relationship had become less strained over the last month. It was still awkward from time to time, but respectful and progressing toward cordial. She was Roman, but she wasn't her husband. And she was a good worker at the inn, as were her children. He hoped to deepen his relationship with Tullus, but thus far had been unsuccessful.

Benjamin, Esther, and Miriam joined them on the porch. "We'll be back by nightfall," Miriam said. "Just have the rooms clean and basins full."

"Yes ma'am," Nona responded. "Don't worry, we'll take care of everything. Enjoy your feast."

Tobiah and Deborah kissed their daughter on the forehead, Deborah left one parting instruction, then the Jews merged into the river of their brothers and sisters flowing through the city toward the temple. Pentecost festivities would begin soon. Aromas of bread baking and fish grilling filled the air, and the buzz of excited pilgrims echoed from the stone buildings that lined the streets. Roman guards were posted throughout the city to quell any disruptions. Tobiah wondered if Lucius was on duty.

The parade of worshippers approached the southern steps to the temple. Those in front of Tobiah stopped abruptly, causing some who weren't paying attention to bump into each other. Tobiah grabbed Deborah's hand. "What's going on up there?"

"I can't see." She craned her neck.

"Someone is at the top of the stairs." He stood on his toes. "He's making a speech." He pulled Deborah near and the two snaked through the crowd to get closer. Their friends followed.

"Fellow Jews and all of you who live in Jerusalem," announced the man at the top of the stairs, "let me explain this to you. Listen carefully to what I say."

Tobiah squinted his eyes in the morning sun. He recognized the man speaking as one of Jesus's disciples. Someone next to him whispered, "It's Peter."

A flame rose above Peter's head, and above those stood around him. Tobiah rubbed his eyes. Were the flames just reflections from the golden domes of the temple? Perhaps, but they sure looked real. The longer he stared, the more tangible they appeared. "Do you see that?" Tobiah pointed. With wide eyes, his wife nodded her response.

Peter grinned, "We are not drunk, as you suppose. It's only nine in the morning!"

Benjamin nudged forward and stood next to Tobiah. Jews from numerous nations crowded around them. Tobiah recognized their attire and the languages they spoke—Parthians, Medes, and Elamites. Others hailed from Asia, Egypt, and even Rome. They looked bewildered.

Tobiah turned to an Egyptian behind him, hoping he was bilingual. "Why all the confusion?"

"We hear him in our own languages," the Egyptian gushed. "He's Galilean, but we hear his words in our native tongues."

Tobiah and Benjamin exchanged an inquisitive look.

The crowd's murmur lessened and Peter spoke again. "What you are witnessing today was spoken by the prophet Joel. 'In the last days,' God says, 'I will pour out my Spirit on all people. Your sons and daughters will prophesy, your young men will see visions, your old men will dream dreams.'"

Tobiah recognized these words. Jews found great hope in the prophecy. He mouthed the next phrases along with Peter, "I will show wonders in the heavens above and signs on the earth below." Others joined in, "And everyone who calls on the name of the Lord will be saved."

Tobiah let his gaze drift to the edges of the crowd. His eyes rested on Lucius. While other soldiers scattered about mocking and bullying Jews, the centurion stood motionless, his eyes fixed on Peter. Enthralled. What might be going through his mind? Did the centurion have any sense of what was going on? What Peter proclaimed? It was confusing enough for Jews. Tobiah still tensed any time he saw Lucius. After that day in the Caesarean hippodrome, he hoped he'd never cross paths with the centurion again. Apparently, Yahweh's plan differed from his own. And Yahweh's plans will not be foiled.

Miriam pushed her way between Tobiah and Benjamin. "What is all this?"

"Something monumental," Benjamin replied. "Jesus said to wait. Maybe this is what we were supposed to wait for."

Peter scanned the crowd. His eyes sparkled. "Fellow Israelites, listen to this. Jesus of Nazareth was a man accredited by God to you by miracles, wonders, and signs, which God did among you through him, as you yourselves know."

Tobiah squeezed Deborah's hand. Here we go.

"This man was handed over to you by God's deliberate plan and foreknowledge. And you, with the help of wicked men, put him to death by nailing him to the cross. But God raised him from the dead, freeing him from the agony of death, because it was impossible for death to keep its hold on him."

Silence enveloped the crowd. Some—many, perhaps—in to-day's throng had jeered and mocked Jesus as he went to the cross. And their leaders had orchestrated the execution.

"But God raised him from the dead." Stories had circulated. Witnesses spoke behind closed doors. But now, here in the open, Peter unashamedly proclaimed the good news. Tobiah's heart-beat quickened.

"Fellow Israelites, I can tell you confidently that the patri-arch David died and was buried, and his tomb is here to this day. But he was a prophet and knew that God had promised him on oath that he would place one of his descendants on his throne." The disciple paused. "Seeing what was to come, he spoke of the resurrection of the Messiah, that he was not abandoned to the realm of the dead, nor did his body see decay." Peter was build-ing momentum. "God has raised this Jesus to life and we are all witnesses of it. Exalted to the right hand of God, he has received from the Father the promised Holy Spirit and has poured out what you now see and hear."

Tobiah nodded his head. Everything that had been fuzzy was coming into focus.

Peter raised both arms. "Therefore, let all Israel be assured of this, God has made this Jesus, whom you crucified, both Lord and Messiah."

Peter's eyes danced from person to person, resting on each individual in turn.

Tobiah faced Deborah. He held both of her hands, rested his forehead against hers, and whispered, "The prophecies . . . the Messiah . . . his miracles . . . his crucifixion . . . the empty tomb. Jesus of Nazareth."

"I know." A tear fell from her cheek. "It's him. He's the one."

Tobiah took a deep breath, then spoke above the crowd. "Brothers, what should we do?"

Peter replied with a smile and open hands, "Repent and be baptized, every one of you, in the name of Jesus Christ for the forgiveness of your sins. And you will receive the gift of the Holy Spirit. The promise is for you and your children and for all who are far off—for all whom the Lord our God will call."

Tobiah looked around. Others did the same. Be baptized? Here? Now? Priests bathed themselves before they offered sacrifices. Jews were immersed in the ritual pools if they'd become unclean. Tobiah had heard of a zealous community near the Dead Sea whose members dipped themselves in water in a quest for purity. And a prophet named John called people to repent and be baptized to prepare for the coming kingdom.

Now that kingdom had arrived.

Peter and other disciples made their way to the cleansing pools on the southern side of the temple. They descended stairs into the water. "Brothers and sisters," the disciples encouraged, "repent of your sins and follow Jesus. Receive forgiveness and the Holy Spirit. Come and be baptized."

A few pushed their way through the crowd. The disciples greeted them with hugs and pats on the back. One by one, the disciples lowered these new followers of Jesus into the water then raised them, soaking and elated.

Tobiah was ready. He believed and he would follow. He turned to Deborah. She beamed. Hand in hand, they strode to the nearest pool. Benjamin and Esther were already there. Miriam wasn't.

After Tobiah was baptized, he greeted and assisted others. By now, people were streaming to the pools. Hundreds of them, perhaps thousands.

Tobiah caught Deborah's eye. She also helped new believers in and out of the water. "It's mayhem!" He grinned. "Joyous, divine, grace-filled chaos."

As Tobiah helped a woman out of the pool, he sensed someone was watching. He looked up to see Lucius standing a few paces away. His arms rested at his sides. His head tilted. On his face, no expression. He didn't interfere, didn't hassle, he just watched. The two locked eyes.

The centurion stepped toward the Jew. "I believe. Jesus is your Messiah. He resurrected. I believe, but I don't understand. And I don't know what to do."

Tobiah smiled. "We'll help. Come see us at the inn."

The centurion nodded, then stepped away, disappearing into the crowd. Tobiah welcomed another new believer into the pool.

June, AD 30

Lucius strolled from one wall to another in Antonia's southwest guard tower. He felt drawn to this spot any time he needed to think. It offered respite from the noise and busyness of the soldiers' quarters and a stunning view of the city and surrounding countryside.

To the east, the orchards on the Mount of Olives had grown green and lush. They reminded him of his boyhood years on the farm. The olives would mature for a few more months, then harvesters would scour the fields and lug basketfuls to the presses in Gethsemane, which extracted the oil that found its way onto the tables of peasants and royalty across the region.

Gethsemane. Lucius's mind replayed the scenes of the arrest. The kiss, the healing of the guard's ear, the rabbi's resolve. The images moved slowly through his memory, felt hazy, looked milky. *These things haunt me.* He rubbed his eyes trying to ease the memories.

His gaze shifted to the south, where dust hovered in the summer humidity above the lower city. The Jewish lower class scuttled around, attempting to fashion an agreeable existence for themselves. Lucius could see a few of his soldiers scattered throughout the lower city. "Keep the peace," he'd instructed them that morning. "That begins by being peaceful. Don't start any skirmishes." From what he could see, they'd listened.

Lucius's stare remained south but focused nearer, on the temple immediately below him. Levites carried out their duties under the watchful eyes of priests, keeping the daily ceremonies functioning smoothly. The more he understood the Jews, the more glorious their temple appeared. Gleaming gold, precious jewels, deep purple curtains. The majesty of the temple reflected the majesty of their god.

In the temple's outer courts, followers of Jesus huddled around a teacher, as they had most days over the last few weeks. Lucius sometimes lingered around the edges to hear what they said. The disciples who traveled with Jesus did most of the teaching. These men who scattered like mice at the rabbi's arrest now preached like lions. They retold what Peter preached at Pentecost. "Jesus was the Anointed One of God," they repeated. "The Messiah, foretold by the prophets, from the line of Abraham and David. He lived, died, and was resurrected according to God's plan." They prayed and sang psalms from their Scriptures. Those ready to repent of their sins and follow Jesus were baptized, often in the same ritual cleansing pools south of the temple used at Pentecost.

Pentecost. On that day, his heart pulled him toward the pool where Tobiah helped with baptisms. But his mind wasn't ready.

One afternoon, when he milled around the perimeter of the Christians' gathering, people began asking questions of the disciples. He inched closer. When he summoned the courage, he asked a question of his own. "Why do you dip people in the water?"

The disciple, startled to hear a question from a centurion, answered meekly. "It's a cleansing from sin and a submission to a new life in Jesus."

"Isn't there more to it than that?"

"Not really. Well, maybe. But I don't think you'd understand."

Lucius decided not to push the issue further. He'd save the deeper discussion for Benjamin.

After they fielded questions from a few others, the disciples turned to walk away. Lucius stepped next to one of them. The disciple tensed. Maybe he recognized Lucius from the night Jesus was arrested. The centurion spoke quietly. "I am not here to harm you."

The disciple didn't appear convinced.

"Can a Roman become a follower? A centurion?" Lucius gulped. "Even the one who crucified Jesus?"

The disciple stopped. His demeanor softened. "Yahweh's heart is for all nations. He longs for everyone to bow to him. And his mercy is never ending."

Lucius appreciated the disciple's openness, but left the conversation unsatisfied. Too many questions remained unanswered.

From Antonia's tower, he focused his eyes on the upper city, to the west, where Herod's palace loomed. Deep in its maze of corridors sits the banquet room where he feasted on Pilate's delicacies and learned of his plans for the massacre. It felt like the banquet happened a lifetime ago. So much had changed.

In front of the palace, the market. The massacre. Ephraim. *That's the moment I knew my life could not continue as it had been. Its quest for power was an empty quest. Its goals were futile, its consequences deadly.* A bead of sweat appeared on his brow.

He squinted to see Miriam's inn, where his family lived. Yes, he would call them that now. His family. They meant more to him than ever before. He loved them. But he needed to be a better husband, a better father.

Ephraim and Miriam had been so kind to welcome them. He'd never experienced such generosity. Especially from Jews. Then came Benjamin—his guidance was invaluable. And Tobiah. Lucius looked at his fist. Tobiah.

His gaze drifted north of the city wall, to the place of the skull. A tear streamed down his cheek. He could look no more.

He recalled a couple days before, when Avitus stopped by his quarters. "I hear they're gathering in homes now," he reported.

"All over the city. They eat together, sing, and pray to their god." He paused.

"What is it?" Lucius asked.

"I also heard something . . . strange. Disturbing." He raised his eyebrows. "Something about them eating flesh and drinking blood."

Lucius forced a chuckle. "Just rumors, I'm sure. Thanks for the update. Let me know if you hear anything more." Lucius needed to ask Benjamin about the flesh and blood.

His stare dropped to the street immediately below, on the west side of Antonia, and rested on a Roman woman and two children approaching the fortress. Nona held the hands of Tullus and Paulla. She walked briskly, with purpose, but not anger. At least that's what Lucius hoped.

Women and children weren't typically welcome at the fortress. Nona knew this, so she must have something significant on her mind.

As she reached the bottom of the staircase leading to Antonia's entrance, Decimus met her. Decimus—always in the right place at the right time. He hugged Nona and saluted Tullus.

Nona didn't notice Lucius watching from above. He hoped to keep it that way. He backed away from the edge of the tower, but remained close enough to peer over. Decimus talked with Nona, shaking his head every few seconds. A couple times he pointed back toward the inn. Likely, he was encouraging them to go back, assuring them that Lucius would visit soon.

Lucius chuckled to himself. If Nona came to Antonia to see him, she wouldn't leave until she had. As expected, Decimus finally turned and led Nona and the children into the fortress. Soon, they emerged in the guard tower where Lucius stood, with Decimus sheepishly leading the way.

"Father!" Paulla squealed and ran toward Lucius, her arms outstretched.

"My beautiful girl." He lifted her from the ground and swung her around. "Seeing you is the best thing that could happen today." He squeezed her then sat her back down.

"Hi, Father." Tullus smiled wide.

Lucius placed a hand on his son's shoulder. "I'm happy you came to visit."

Tullus stepped toward the edge of the tower and looked around the city. "Wow, you can see everything from up here. I can even see the inn!" He absorbed the scene for a few seconds, then stepped back next to his father and crossed his arms. "Any action today?"

Lucius rubbed his chin. "No, nothing significant to report. All is peaceful and under control."

Lucius turned his attention to Nona, who had stayed back while he greeted the children. She stepped forward. He held her hand and kissed her cheek. She blushed but didn't speak.

Decimus broke the silence. "Children, would you like to see more of the fortress?" Lucius nodded his appreciation to his perceptive friend.

"Absolutely," Tullus responded. Paulla reluctantly followed and the three disappeared down the stairwell.

Nona stepped to the edge of the tower, rested her hands on the wall, and gazed across the city. Lucius stood next to her but didn't speak. He hoped she would break the silence. After a few moments, she hadn't, so he did.

"You've been patient with me," he began. Nona remained stoic. He covered her hand with his. She let him, but remained still. "Over the years, I have not always treated you like I should."

"You took care of me," she said, defending him from his own accusation. "We always had a warm bed and food to eat."

"But you deserve better," he said quietly. "And so do our children."

She faced him, and searched his eyes for . . . well . . . he wasn't sure what she was searching for. "And what would 'better' look like?"

He broke their stare and turned toward the city. "I'm not sure." His eyes danced along the horizon. "I see how Benjamin loves Esther, and how Tobiah takes care of Deborah and little Abigail. Maybe I could learn something from them."

"You seem to be learning a lot from Benjamin and Tobiah these days."

Lucius lowered his eyes and smiled. This was the conversation that Nona hiked across the city to have.

"Are you sure it wasn't a trick?" she asked. "The magicians in Rome do some remarkable things."

"I know he was dead. I saw him breathe his last. And then, over the next few weeks, hundreds saw him alive."

"Did you?"

"No, I wish I had. But so many did." He recounted other things that had been circling his mind day and night. "I've been thinking about what Avitus experienced at the tomb—an angel, the stone moved, the earthquake. I saw the empty tomb myself. And the drastic change in his disciples. The prophecies. The pieces all fit together."

"But what about our gods? What about Rome?"

"I don't know." He paused. "But if Jesus is the Messiah of the Jews, and if he is, somehow at the same time, actually god, then I don't think there is room for any others. He is the only god."

Nona sighed.

Decimus returned with the children.

"Tullus, Paulla. Say goodbye to your father," Nona said.

The children hugged Lucius, then Decimus led them from the tower and out of the fortress. Decimus talked with Nona on the street. Lucius couldn't hear their voices, but she looked sullen. Decimus bid the trio goodbye, then they weaved through the streets of the upper city back toward the inn.

Decimus reappeared in the tower and stood beside Lucius. "She's worried about you."

Lucius remained silent. He wanted to reveal more of his thoughts about Jesus to his friend, but worried about the consequences.

"We've known each other for a long time. Been through a lot together. Always protected each other, covered for each other." Decimus cleared his throat. "But I can understand Nona's worry. The things you're saying these days, places you're going, people you're listening to. It's not you. It's not Roman." He faced Lucius. "This road where you're headed, I don't understand it. I don't care for it. But you're my comrade, my brother. I'll protect you as long as I can."

Decimus walked away.

Lucius's eyes welled with tears. He dropped to his knees. Raised his eyes and hands toward the heavens. "Yahweh, hear me. Guide me. Show me your way."

Lucius tried to sneak into the inn, but the door creaked and the setting sun cast his shadow across the wall. The dozen Jews who filled the dining room turned to see the centurion sliding onto a stool in the corner. A couple women gasped. The men sat up and stiffened. So much for being inconspicuous.

Tobiah glanced at Benjamin, alarmed. Benjamin gave Lucius a slight smile and a nod.

"He's safe," announced Benjamin. "He's my friend. His name is Lucius."

Those around the table exchanged glances but didn't speak. Lucius shifted on the stool, attempting to hide his sword behind his body. Next time he'll remember to leave it at Antonia. If there is a next time.

Benjamin's note had surprised him. The messenger arrived at Antonia with the parchment in hand. Lucius opened it to find the Jew's scrawled handwriting. "On the evening of the first day of the week, a few of us will gather at the inn for dinner. Peter will teach us. Please come if you are able and want to."

Lucius waited until they were done eating. He didn't know all the Jews' laws, but imagined some of them might not feel comfortable sharing a dish with a Roman.

He scanned the room without letting his eyes rest on any one person. Benjamin and Esther sat across from Tobiah and Deborah. Peter reclined near the center of the table, with others scattered around. Remnants of dinner remained.

Nona entered carrying a pitcher. She hesitated when she saw Lucius, then jutted her chin and refilled cups. Miriam followed a few steps behind Nona and pretended not to notice him. Neither lady offered him a cup.

Peter stood. His wavy, brown hair covered his ears. He stroked his beard, neatly trimmed, and smoothed over his faded woolen outer garment, which had once been blue. He raised his arms and his sleeves revealed the forearms of a man who knew hard work. His eyes filled with passion and his voice with zeal.

"We ate with Jesus the evening before he was crucified," he began. When Peter mentioned the crucifixion, no one looked at Lucius, but he could sense their animosity. "It was Passover." Peter's voice was gravelly. He'd likely been talking and preaching a great deal over the last few weeks.

He picked up a loaf. "Jesus took the bread and broke it. He thanked God for it. Then he passed it around and said, 'This is my body, given for you. Do this in remembrance of me.'" The disciple lifted the bread above his head and turned his eyes skyward. "Oh Lord our God, you have blessed us with this bounty. And you have blessed us with your son. We remember his body as we eat." He broke off a small piece, then passed the loaf around the table. Each person tore a piece and solemnly ate.

"Then Jesus lifted the cup of thanksgiving and said, 'This cup is the new covenant in my blood, which is poured out for you.'" The disciple lifted a cup from the table, prayed, and then pressed it to his lips. He passed it around and everyone drank.

Peter looked around at each person. His gaze rested on Lucius longer than it had on others. Lucius turned away. He had been mesmerized by the entire experience. He hoped the Jews hadn't mistaken his stare of awe for anger. Nona often told him that his face was impossible to read.

The disciple spoke quietly, "We didn't understand everything that night. It began making more sense over the following days. At Passover, we remember when God saved our forefathers in Egypt, when they smeared lamb's blood on their doorposts. Jesus became our lamb, our salvation. And Passover celebrates the covenant God gave through Moses. Now, God has established a new covenant through Jesus's blood."

Heads nodded around the table. The story of their god, their own story of desperation and hope, reached its pinnacle in Jesus. Some details remained hazy for Lucius, but enough of Yahweh's grand narrative had come into focus that he admired its beauty and he savored its hope.

Lucius rested his hands on his lap. He turned them over and studied his palms. This hope in Jesus, was it available to him, also? He wasn't a Jew. In fact, he spent years tormenting the Jews. And he drove the nails.

Peter closed his eyes and raised both hands. He began to sing. Lucius sat upright when he heard the first phrase, which Jesus had uttered on the cross:

My God, my God, why have you forsaken me?
 Why are you so far from saving me,
 so far from my cries of anguish?

Everyone except Lucius knew the words and joined their voices with Peter's. They sang solemnly, their heads bowed.

But I am a worm and not a man,
 scorned by everyone, despised by the people.
All who see me mock me;
 they hurl insults, shaking their heads.
"He trusts in the Lord," they say,
 "let the Lord rescue him.
Let him deliver him,
 since he delights in him."

Lucius's remembered the mockery Jesus endured.

I am poured out like water,

and all my bones are out of joint.
My heart has turned to wax;
  it has melted within me.
My mouth is dried up like a potsherd,
  and my tongue sticks to the roof of my mouth;
  you lay me in the dust of death.
Dogs surround me,
  a pack of villains encircles me;
  they pierce my hands and my feet.
All my bones are on display;
  people stare and gloat over me.
They divide my clothes among them
  and cast lots for my garment.
But you, Lord, do not be far from me.
  You are my strength; come quickly to help me.

Lucius closed his eyes and breathed deeply. The Jews continued singing, each of them raising their hands. Some let traces of smiles cross their lips.

For he has not despised or scorned
  the suffering of the afflicted one;
he has not hidden his face from him
  but has listened to his cry for help.
All the ends of the earth
  will remember and turn to the Lord,
and all the families of the nations
  will bow down before him,
for dominion belongs to the Lord
  and he rules over the nations.

The song reached its crescendo.

Posterity will serve him;

future generations will be told about the Lord.
They will proclaim his righteousness,
  declaring to a people yet unborn:
He has done it!

Peter stood, his arms raised and his eyes gazing heavenward. A few around the table took the same posture. Others sat motionless with their heads bowed and eyes closed. Many nodded slowly to the beat of the song, which lingered in the air. Some hummed its melody.

Lucius remained in the corner, still. His heartbeat throbbed in his ears. Colors and sounds mingled indistinctly. Emotions and memories ebbed and flowed.

An elbow struck his ribcage. He opened his eyes to find Nona standing next to him, her lips pursed and her arms crossed. Miriam sat next to Tobiah, who welcomed his sister with a hug.

"What is all this?" Nona whispered. Lucius knew better than to answer. Fortunately, someone else spoke before he had to.

"What was it like to be with him every day?" Esther asked.

The question brought Peter's attention back to the people in front of him. He smiled. "I don't know where to begin."

"When did you meet him?" she prodded.

"My brother, Andrew, met him first. He came to me, wide-eyed, and said 'We've found the Messiah!'" The disciple chuckled. "I thought he was dreaming. But just maybe . . . " He paused. "We'd been listening to a man preach, his name was John. He kept saying the kingdom was coming. He called people to repent and baptized them. So, our hopes were high. But still, the Messiah?"

The Jews leaned in as Peter continued. "He looked so normal. No purple robes. No sword. Not what we expected for the Messiah. He was like someone who might fish for a living, or build. Turned out he was a carpenter. His skin was weathered, his hands rugged." He tilted his head. "On that day when Andrew introduced us, Jesus spoke to me like no one else ever has. It's like he knew me before we'd even met."

Peter sighed. "Not long after that, Andrew and I were fishing on the Sea of Galilee. Just as we tossed our nets into the sea, we heard his voice. 'Come and follow me. I'll send you out to fish for people.' Andrew and I looked at each other, shrugged, and followed."

Those around the table smiled.

"It was an adventure! Jesus taught with such authority. He touched people. Even the sick, even lepers. And he healed people. Right there in front of us, the blind could see, and the lame could walk."

Lucius nodded.

"He cast out demons, walked on water. Even raised our friend Lazarus from the dead."

Nona scoffed.

"Sometimes he sent us out to preach. We told people that God's kingdom was at hand. And he gave us the power to cast out demons." Peter's voice quieted. "And then, we came to Jerusalem. A parade greeted us, but as the week unfolded, things changed, turned dark." He didn't need to continue. The people at the table witnessed it.

Lucius felt like every eye in the room turned toward him. He whispered a goodbye to Nona and slipped out as quietly as he could. He stepped into the market and found a place to hide in the shadows, where he could keep an eye on the inn's entrance.

Tobiah sat at the table, now cleared of its guests and dishes, the evening's events vivid in his mind. Remembering Jesus with the bread and cup. Peter's stories. The odd entrance and exit of the centurion.

Benjamin sat across from him. Both leaned forward, their hands wrapped around cups of water. Tobiah gazed into his cup, tilting it back and forth to make the water swirl.

Benjamin broke the silence. "It was generous of Peter to spend the evening with us."

Tobiah nodded. "There are dozens of groups meeting across the city. He was kind to come here." He leaned back. "Forgive me for being so quiet, my friend. I'm just . . . in awe, I guess."

"Me too." Benjamin smiled. He rested his chin on his hands.

"So now we continue to gather with others who believe in Jesus. We sing and pray. We learn from the apostles. We remember him with the bread and cup. We help the poor. And we tell people about Jesus."

"That sums it up."

"What about Sabbath? The feasts? Sacrifices?"

Benjamin responded carefully. "I get the feeling that the apostles are still working through these questions." He sipped his water. "We're still Jews, and we still worship Yahweh. But, it seems that Jesus has given our laws and ceremonies additional meaning."

"I'll never celebrate Passover in the same way again, that's for sure."

"Me neither." Benjamin drew out each syllable.

Tobiah felt conflicted. From the day he was circumcised, his life had been dedicated to Yahweh. He celebrated Sabbath, made pilgrimages to the temple for feasts, and meticulously followed the dietary laws. He revered Abraham and Moses, memorized psalms and prophecies. He's a Jew. One of the covenant people, yearning for the Messiah. Now the Messiah had come. Not in the way he'd anticipated, but he was sure now. Jesus was the one to whom the prophets pointed.

It was though he'd been hiking along a difficult, wooded trail. Carefully, obediently, religiously putting one foot in front of the other for his entire life. Now he'd stepped out of the dark forest into a radiant meadow, filled with bright, warm sunshine and all the scents and tastes of spring. The trail led him here. He appreciated the path he'd trudged. And part of him wanted to return to its security. But what lies ahead outshines what lies behind, a thousand times over.

"What do you think the priests and Jewish officials will do?" Benjamin asked.

The question brought Tobiah back to the present. "I can't imagine they're happy. I'm sure they'll resist any movement that says Jesus is the Messiah. I just don't know how forcefully they'll resist."

While they were throwing all the big questions onto the table, Tobiah decided to throw one more. "How do Gentiles fit into all this?" He stared into his water.

"Well, we Jews are God's chosen. He made his covenant with us. But I've been thinking about this very question. God told Abraham that all the peoples of the earth would be blessed through him. Not just his descendants, but all people. Our psalms say that all nations will worship him." Benjamin rubbed his chin. "And do you remember what Isaiah said about the Messiah? 'It is too small a thing for you to be my servant to restore the tribes of Jacob and bring back those of Israel I have kept. I will also make you a light for the Gentiles, that my salvation may reach to the ends of the earth.'"

Tobiah shifted in his seat. Miriam, who had entered the room and was wiping the table, frowned. Benjamin looked at Tobiah and nodded his head toward the door. Tobiah understood the signal. They picked up their cups and went to continue their conversation on the porch.

They gazed across the marketplace, lit by a partial moon and a few scattered fires.

Benjamin continued the conversation they began inside. "I need to ask one of the apostles to be sure, but I've heard that Jesus spent a fair amount of time with Gentiles. He showed compassion to a woman in Samaria, and healed a demoniac in the region of the Gerasenes. He cast another demon from a Canaanite girl." Benjamin cleared his throat. "And there was a Roman centurion up in Capernaum. Jesus healed his servant. From what I heard, Jesus said the centurion had even more faith than the people of Israel."

Tobiah smiled. His friend couldn't be more obvious. "A centurion, huh?" Benjamin nodded. Tobiah presumed this conversation was coming but had avoided thinking about it. Lucius Valerius Galeo. Tobiah knew that Benjamin had talked with the centurion, but didn't know how far those conversations had progressed. Tobiah was as surprised as anyone to see Lucius walk into the inn earlier that evening. When Benjamin said of the soldier, "He's my friend," Tobiah filled with a mix of emotions, too many to identify. Anger and betrayal, certainly, but also a tinge of hope that the grace of God and the story of Jesus could penetrate even the most calloused heart.

At that moment, Lucius appeared from the shadows. The centurion planted his feet before the two Jews. He stood tall and resolute, with determination in his eyes. Tobiah felt pangs in his ribs and leg. He swung his head toward Benjamin, who gave Tobiah a slight nod but whose face betrayed concern.

"Greetings, my friend," Benjamin said. Though it was the second time he'd heard Benjamin call the centurion his friend, the word still felt like a needle in Tobiah's ear. "We thought you'd left for the evening. How can we help to you?"

Lucius inhaled deeply, which caused his shoulders to grow even more broad. He raised his chin and rested his hand atop his sword. He looked as though he were issuing a command to his troops. He stared at Tobiah. "I need to speak with you." His tone then softened, but only slightly, "If you are willing."

Tobiah turned toward Benjamin, hoping for guidance, but Benjamin looked as perplexed as Tobiah felt.

"Of course," Tobiah responded carefully, "we would be glad to talk."

Lucius exhaled. His shoulders sank. He turned toward the marketplace. Tobiah turned that direction, also, allowing Lucius to take the lead in the conversation.

"I am allegiant to Rome," Lucius finally said. "Or at least, I have been allegiant to Rome." He shifted his weight from one foot to the other. "Out of that allegiance I sometimes did things that, now, I wish I never had."

Tobiah stole a glance at the centurion, hoping to read his expression. He saw moisture glistening in the corner of Lucius's eye.

"Tobiah, that day in Caesarea. At the hippodrome. During the games."

Tobiah froze. He didn't need reminded. He remembered every time he raised his arms or limped across a room.

Lucius continued, "Sometimes at night when I'm lying in bed, the scene goes through my mind. I try to reach out and stop my fists, but I can't stop them."

The centurion faced Tobiah. "I wish I could change what happened. I can't. But I hope that you can, somehow, someday, forgive me."

Tobiah felt compassion—grace, even—rush through his soul. He never imagined this conversation would happen. He rested his hand on Lucius's shoulder. The man standing before him was not the same man who beat him in the hippodrome.

"I thought I was dead," Tobiah choked out. "But Yahweh, and Deborah, saved me." He considered his next words carefully. "And now, I think, Yahweh is saving you."

Lucius and Tobiah clasped wrists. Benjamin beamed. The centurion released his grip and wiped moisture from his eyes.

"There's someone else I need to talk to," Lucius said.

Benjamin nodded. "I'll get her."

A few minutes later, Miriam stood before the centurion. Tobiah and Benjamin remained on the porch so that Miriam would feel safe, but took a step back to let the two talk.

Lucius turned back toward the marketplace rather than staring straight at Miriam. "I was out there on that day," he began.

"I know," Miriam responded.

"I didn't kill anyone. Or even hit anyone. I'd planned to. But when the time came and Pilate raised his arms, I couldn't. But I was there. And I did nothing to stop it."

Miriam let a tear fall from her cheek without wiping it away. Her jaw was set firm. She breathed quickly and loudly. She wouldn't look at the soldier. Tobiah almost stepped forward to protect his sister, but chose to remain in place. She would see it as an intrusion.

Finally, she spoke, matter-of-factly, "I loved Ephraim from the first time I saw him."

Lucius gulped.

"Ephraim was everything to me. He was a gift from Yahweh. He was kind. Courageous. Generous." Her tone softened but only slightly. "He was the best man I've ever known."

"Miriam—"

"I don't want to hear anything from you," she snapped.

Tobiah glanced at Benjamin. She was a courageous woman. A Jew speaking to a Roman soldier—a centurion, no less—in such a manner could expect a backhand and a bloody lip, in the least. But Lucius just hung his head.

"And now I have to run this inn without him." Miriam spoke forcefully. "A woman alone in this world has a difficult path." She pointed at the centurion. "And you put me on that path."

She paused, then whispered, "Every morning I wake up, I roll over to kiss him and to talk with him about the day ahead. And every morning I lose him again."

Tears streamed from her eyes and she clenched her jaw. Tobiah stepped forward and put his arm around his sister's shoulder. She leaned into him and continued weeping.

Lucius said nothing more.

Lucius watched Tobiah and Miriam disappear into the inn. He remained on the porch with Benjamin, watching the stars sparkle and eavesdropping on conversations that rose from the marketplace. Buying and selling ceased hours before, but the market provided an open space for people to gather in the evening, though often for less than honorable reasons.

"Tobiah showed me great grace tonight," Lucius said.

"He's a man of Yahweh. Of Jesus. It's been a struggle for him, but I knew he would eventually forgive."

"But Miriam—"

"It will be more difficult for her. She's grieving. Her anger has lessened, but it's still there."

Lucius nodded. The conversation with Miriam went about how he expected. He certainly didn't deserve her forgiveness. And she had been so kind to Nona and the children. He appreciated her and hoped that their relationship improved someday.

"She'll get there eventually," Benjamin offered. "It was courageous of you to have those conversations."

"Maybe. I hope it was the right decision."

"It was."

The men stood silently for a moment, then Benjamin asked, "What did you think about Peter and the things he taught tonight?"

Lucius appreciated the change of subject. "It helped put some pieces together for me. It's amazing how Jesus continued the story of your god. What he taught, his miracles." Lucius paused. "Even how he died. You can look back to your prophets, feasts, and things that happened centuries ago, and it all connects."

"Makes it hard not to believe, doesn't it?"

Lucius nodded. Benjamin obviously wanted him to believe. And he did believe, but he was still figuring out what that meant. "Every time I hear more, like tonight, it becomes obvious how much I don't know. You Jews have studied the Scriptures and heard the stories since you were children. It's all new to me. I feel like an outsider."

Benjamin thought before he responded. "I can understand why you feel that way. My friends weren't very welcoming to you tonight." Benjamin faced Lucius. "Our Jewishness is who we are. It's our identity. We are the people of Yahweh. His favored, blessed, covenant people."

Lucius nodded.

"There were times in our history when we've welcomed others into the community. But those times were the exception. We believed the Messiah was coming to save us, just us. He would restore us. And make us great again. He would defeat our enemies. Like Rome. Like you."

The last phrase felt like a dagger to Lucius.

"But," Benjamin continued in a more hopeful tone, "the Messiah that Yahweh sent was so different from the Messiah we anticipated. We're still figuring it out ourselves. For you, this is all new. For us, it's so different than we expected, we're having to reexamine everything we thought we understood. It's been frightening. And somehow exhilarating at the same time."

Benjamin looked Lucius in the eye. "I do know this, Jesus didn't want anyone to feel like an outsider. He spent so much of his time with the people that had been pushed to the edges, those who were shunned by the most righteous Jews. He ate with tax collectors and showed compassion to prostitutes. He healed people who were hurting, whether they were Jews or not. There's even a story," Benjamin said slowly, "about Jesus commending a Roman centurion for his great faith."

Lucius raised his eyebrows.

"It happened in Capernaum."

Lucius didn't speak for a couple minutes. Benjamin always knew just what to say. And he knew that Lucius could digest only so much from each conversation. Lucius struggled to express his emotions, but someday he needed to tell Benjamin how much he appreciated his patience and his concern. And his friendship.

"That day at the temple," the centurion said, "after Peter preached. You went down into the pools with the disciples, and they dipped you under water."

"There is a history behind that," Benjamin explained. "Our laws command priests to bathe themselves as a part of significant feasts and before making sacrifices. Also, we go through a similar cleansing after we have a skin disease or touch something unclean. More recently, some Jews have been baptizing themselves or each other to represent their desire for holiness."

"But this was something different."

"Peter called us to repent and be baptized in the name of Jesus. It wasn't about our laws anymore. It was about Jesus, following him. And Peter said we would be forgiven of our sins."

"But aren't your sacrifices for forgiveness?" Lucius asked. Benjamin smiled. The centurion thought for a moment, then said slowly, "But your prophets said that our sins would be laid on the Messiah. His life would be an offering for sins."

"You're getting it, my Roman friend." Benjamin's smile widened. "Everything has changed. But it's not a change so much as it's Yahweh's plan unfolding right before our eyes."

"One more question. When Peter was teaching on that day, he said something about a spirit."

"Yes, Peter said we'd be forgiven, and we would receive the gift of the Holy Spirit."

"What does that mean?"

"When Jesus was still here, he told his disciples that after he left he would send his Spirit to be a counselor and guide. And the Spirit would give his disciples power to tell the world about him."

Lucius didn't want to press the conversation any further. Benjamin had already given him a great deal to consider.

Yet, Benjamin had more to say. "Peter spoke of a promise of forgiveness and the Spirit. Do you remember who he said the promise applied to?"

Lucius shook his head.

"He said it's for us and our children. That part I expected. But, next, he said the promise is also 'for all who are far off, for all whom the Lord our God will call.'" Benjamin looked him in the eye. "That means you, Lucius. Jesus can save you."

Lucius sighed, then rested his chin in his hand. The men stood silently, staring into the sky. Lucius's mind raced.

"I know that following Jesus would have significant implications for you," Benjamin said.

"It scares me that I don't even know what those implications might be. My life as a soldier, my relationship with Nona. My entire future."

"A few hundred years ago, God told one of our great leaders— he was a soldier, incidentally—'Be strong and courageous. Do not be afraid, do not be discouraged, for Yahweh your God will be with you wherever you go.'"

A few minutes passed, then Lucius said quietly, "I need to get back to Antonia."

―――――――

The next evening, Lucius knocked on the door of the inn. Nona answered.

"You don't have to knock, you know."

Lucius smiled. Nona did too, briefly.

"You look ragged." She stepped onto the porch with him.

"I didn't sleep much last night," Lucius admitted, rubbing his eyes. "Then it was a full day. Decimus and I took our centuries for a hike and some training. I can't keep up with those young soldiers like I used to."

Nona brushed dust from his shoulder and then used a damp rag that was in her hand—who knows what all she had cleaned with it—to wipe his forehead and neck. "Did you come to see me or Benjamin?"

Lucius could sense some irritation behind the question. "You. Well, you first." He took a deep breath.

She waited.

"I believe, Nona," he began. "After what I've experienced. What I've seen and heard. I believe."

"You believe what?" she pressed.

"That Jesus is the Messiah of the Jews. He is the Son of God. He died. He resurrected."

"He's for the Jews?"

"He's for everybody."

Nona sighed and looked in his eyes. "What happens now?"

"I'm going to ask Benjamin and Tobiah to take me to the pools outside of the temple and baptize me."

"What does that mean?

"When someone decides to follow Jesus, they're dipped into the water. It's a way to accept what he promised and to say you want to live for him." Lucius knew this sounded like nonsense to Nona. He could understand. It would've sounded like nonsense to him, too, just a few weeks ago.

"I want you to come," Lucius continued. "And our children."

Her face showed her alarm.

"I'm not asking you to be baptized," Lucius added quickly, "but I want you there with me." This seemed to help.

Nona thought, then shifted into mothering mode. "I'll get some towels. You need to talk to Benjamin and Tobiah. Are you going to tell our children or do you want me to?"

"I want to tell them."

Nona disappeared into the inn. Lucius followed a few steps behind.

Moments later, he kneeled before his children, who sat on a bench in the dining room. Both leaned forward.

"You've probably heard your friends in the inn talking about Jesus," Lucius began.

Paulla tilted her head.

Lucius continued, "I've come to believe that what they're saying about Jesus is true."

"What exactly do you believe, Father?" Tullus leaned back and crossed his arms.

Lucius summarized what he had learned about the prophecies and Jesus's teaching. He also told them about the crucifixion, what Avitus experienced at the empty tomb, and the people who saw Jesus alive again. "I'm going to ask Benjamin and Tobiah to baptize me."

"Will you still be our father and take care of us?" Paulla asked.

Lucius hugged her and smiled. "Yes, of course."

Tullus was concerned, also, but for a different reason. "Will you still be a centurion?"

Lucius put his hand on Tullus's shoulder. "I think so, son. Being a soldier is all I know. I'll behave differently than I did before. And treat people differently." He paused. "I don't know what my superiors will think about that." The snarling face of Septimus flashed across his mind.

"So, you'll still be loyal to Rome?" Tullus asked with furrowed brow.

Lucius pressed his lips together, considering how to respond. "Yes, but maybe not in the same way. My perspective of loyalty has changed. I will do my job with honesty and in a way that is respectful, even helpful, to people. But if Rome asks me to do something that goes against what Jesus taught . . . well, I have a lot to figure out."

Tullus's eyes narrowed. Paulla hugged her father again.

Lucius sensed someone behind him. He turned to find Deborah standing in the doorway, her eyes full of tears and a hand covering her smile. She had heard. "I'll get Tobiah," she said.

A couple hours later, Lucius descended stairs into a pool on the south side of the temple. Tobiah and Benjamin stood to either side of him. Above them, encircling the pool, stood Nona, the children, Deborah, and Esther. Miriam remained at the inn.

Benjamin prayed. "Our Lord, you have opened a way through Jesus for us, all of us, to find grace in you. We thank you."

Lucius folded his arms across his chest. Tobiah and Benjamin placed their hands on his back and lowered the centurion into the water.

Lucius kept his eyes open. He watched the water enclose above him. The blurry figures of his family stood over him, against a blue sky. Fully submerged, he felt as if Jesus's grace and hope enveloped him. When his friends raised him, and as water gushed around his head and shoulders, he sensed release, freedom. Cleansed to his core.

Lucius inhaled and felt as though he breathed in the very breath of God.

Benjamin and Tobiah embraced Lucius. Nona stood at the top of the stairs with a towel. Deborah, her eyes closed, hummed a tune. Esther quietly sang along:

Wash away all my iniquity
and cleanse me from my sin.
Cleanse me with hyssop, and I will be clean;
wash me, and I will be whiter than snow.

Lucius ascended the stairs and hugged Nona. "It's a new day." He rested his head on her shoulder and wept. "I'm a new man."

EPILOGUE

AD 60

Lucius struggled to focus. Aging had compromised his vision, as did the flogging. He squinted as he looked down. His gaze roamed across his mangled, bloody body, which lay stretched on a cross.

Avitus wrapped a rope around his wrist and tied it. He wouldn't look Lucius in the eye. He appeared only slightly less boyish than when Lucius first met him. More sturdy, perhaps, and more confident. The crimson plume on his helmet suited him.

Lucius turned his head and watched Tullus tie his other arm to the crossbeam. "Son," Lucius uttered. Tullus looked his father in the eye, but only briefly. Lucius's heart filled with both pride and regret. His boy had grown into a man, a hardened and distinguished soldier. But he was ambivalent, sometimes antagonistic, toward the faith.

Septimus, fatter and grumpier than ever, peered over Tullus's shoulder. He shoved a hammer and a spike into Tullus's hand. "Drive the nail. That's an order."

Lucius's roving eyes found Decimus, standing at his feet. His friend had aged gracefully. He was even kind to Lucius when he arrested him.

Lucius's mind retraced the conversations that led to the arrest. "This faith of yours is raising a lot of questions," Decimus warned over the years. In recent weeks, he grew more intense.

"You don't really believe what they say, do you?" Decimus didn't like to admit that Lucius was one of the Christians, when, in fact, Lucius was a leader. "Well, at least keep quiet about it. I can't keep ignoring what I see."

"I do what my faith requires. Besides, you ask a lot of questions. Perhaps the seed has been planted in you?"

Decimus ignored his comrade's prodding, as he always did.

A few days later, Decimus and a half dozen legionaries burst into the church gathering that Lucius and Nona hosted in their home. Most of the Christians cowered, but Lucius stepped forward. Decimus approached and the old friends stood face-to-face.

"The charge?" Lucius asked.

"Desertion."

"I'm right here."

"Who is your lord, Lucius?" Decimus whispered. "Is it Caesar? Or Jesus?"

Lucius smiled as a man smiles when he resigns himself to the inevitable.

He felt a prick on his wrist and his mind returned to the present. Tullus positioned the spike. With three blows, he sent the spike through his father's wrist and into the crossbeam.

Avitus nailed his other wrist, and Decimus his feet. The two soldiers raised the cross and dropped it into a hole. Pain bolted through Lucius's body. He cried out.

Nona wailed. Lucius looked upon his wife. Her hair was white and her hands shook. Her curved spine left her hunched forward. Even so, fire still burned in her eyes. She fell at the foot of the cross.

Paulla sank to her knees next to her mother, whimpering. Lucius appreciated his daughter. She had grown into a graceful, determined woman. Just like Nona. She wrapped her arms around her mother. "We'll make it. We have to." She stroked Nona's back.

Lucius wanted to hold them. To tell them everything would be alright. "Be strong," he bid them through bloody teeth. "Stay faithful."

A few others stepped forward and kneeled, Christians from the church that met in their home. Some prayed, all wept.

Lucius groaned. His hands and feet grew numb, his breathing difficult. He barely had the strength to raise his head, but his eyes remained open. He inhaled as deeply as his fluid-filled lungs allowed.

His mind turned toward Miriam. Feeble from age, she still lived at the inn but had delegated the day-to-day management to Tobiah and his family. One evening, years before, she approached Lucius during a church gathering. "The body of Christ," she said, extending bread. "The blood of Christ," extending a cup. The two embraced and wept. Lucius could still taste the grace of that bread, that cup.

Decimus nudged Tullus forward. "You need to say goodbye."

Lucius looked down upon his son. His heart ached.

"Father—" Tullus choked on the word.

"Son. I love you." Lucius coughed up blood. "I forgive you."

Tullus stepped backward, tears streaming down his cheeks.

Decimus locked eyes with Lucius and nodded. He removed his sword from its sheath and held it out with both hands. Then he leaned it against the cross. He stood next to Tullus and put an arm around his shoulder. He pronounced, loudly enough for Lucius to hear, "This man, your father, is a son of God."

Lucius closed his eyes and rested his chin on his chest. He exhaled slowly. His thoughts came no longer in words, but in images. The massacre in the marketplace. Decimus. The empty tomb. Paulla. His baptism. Nona. The church in his home. Tullus.

Darkness.

Light.

Jesus.

"I have been crucified with Christ,
and I no longer live,
but Christ lives in me."
(Galatians 2:20)

ABOUT THE AUTHOR

Daniel Overdorf grew up in the mountains of eastern Tennessee and southern West Virginia, where he experienced the value of the blue-collar work ethic, the wonder of Appalachian storytelling, and the joy of being raised in the home of a preacher who loves the church with all his heart. These early influences continue to shape his perspectives of life and ministry.

He graduated from Johnson University, then spent the next ten years ministering with churches in Illinois and Georgia. In the meantime, he earned a master of divinity from Lincoln Christian Seminary and a doctor of ministry from Gordon-Conwell Theological Seminary.

Since 2005, he has taught at Johnson University in Knoxville, Tennessee, where his current position is professor of pastoral ministries and director of preaching programs. He has been married to his lovely and gifted wife, Carrie, for twenty-five years. They have two sons and a daughter. He enjoys watching college sports, playing golf, and, most of all, cheering for his kids at their softball and basketball games and choir performances.

In addition to *A Death Well Lived*, his books include:

- *One Year to Better Preaching: 52 Exercises to Hone Your Skills*
- *Rediscovering Community: What the Bible Says About the Church*
- *Applying the Sermon: How to Balance Biblical Integrity and Cultural Relevance*
- *Ministering to Your Minister*

Learn more at DanielOverdorf.com.

Printed in the United States
By Bookmasters